THOSE WHO
ARE WITH US
Dale Hoeppner

Publisher's Note: This novel is a work of fiction. Names, characters, places and incidents are either products of the author's imagination or used fictitiously. All characters are fictional and any similarity to people living or dead is purely coincidental.

Editing team: Tom Liebe, Heidi Blundell, Karen Hoeppner, Jacqui Higginbottom, Dora Hoeppner

Cover by Matej Balaz

ISBN 978-0-9921100-0-0

Published by Northlife Press

Printed and Bound in the United States of America

To Karen, my amazing wife:

Thanks for your encouragement,

your patience and your love!

To Nahum, Simon, Tiana and Alise:

You continue to make me proud!

To the Almighty God:

beyond my imagination,

but close to my heart!

A Note from the Author

My inspiration for *Those Who Are With Us* grew primarily from three sources. Firstly, I have always been fascinated by the accounts of angels in the Bible. We are given enough information in Scripture, nearly 300 passages, to gain a reasonable understanding of angels and the spiritual realm. Unfortunately, the portrayal of angels in modern culture is far from the Biblical perspective. My goal was to involve angels and demons in the story without contradicting the Bible. I have taken some liberties in what I have *added* to the Bible's description; this is fiction after all. As a framework, I used the angel hierarchy developed by Thomas Aquinas in the thirteenth century. Perfect? Not possible, but a place to begin.

Secondly, I gained inspiration from Louie Giglio's *Indescribable*. Our universe is immense! Our God is great and our understanding of God's creation is still in its infancy. I appreciate it when information, like what Louie shares about the universe, stretches my brain and helps me gain a deeper appreciation of God!

The third block in the foundation of the story comes from the work of Hungry For Life International. Those involved with HFL continue to make the world a better place. Thanks for all you do!

My hope and prayer is that some part of this story will stretch *your* brain and draw *you* closer to our Almighty Creator.

Dale Hoeppner

CHAPTER ONE

Those who are with us are more than those who are with them.

2 Kings 6:16

The presence of the enemy was heavy in the air, like campfire smoke filling human pores. Alea's fingers closed ever so slightly. Tension. Energy. With grace and absolute control, Alea drew her sword and moved around the corner to her left. In the dim rays of the streetlights, the demon named Barac stood motionless in the middle of the street.

The town of Corison Springs was quiet in late fall. Few locals were anywhere to be seen on a sunny day, much less a rainy evening in November. To the left was the large Corison Resort Hotel. Not new, but it stood with enough grandeur to say "expensive". Even in this slower time of year a valet was parking a shiny, new Mercedes beside a bright red Corvette. The winding promenade walkway began in front of the hotel and carried on like a meandering brook around the edge of the lake. Today, the lights of the hotel appeared dimmed and the promenade was barely visible beyond the slightly hunched over body of the enemy.

"Had it become this obvious that the battle was being lost?" Alea thought to herself. One demon, although a massive beast he was, alone on a mission! The enemy did not even fear being attacked anymore. Arrogance? Maybe it was a weakness in the enemy. At this point, unfortunately, some arrogance on their part was well deserved.

Not tonight. This night would not be one Satanael and his army of demons would enjoy.

The sound of Barac's breathing and the small waves lapping on the shores of the tourist town were soon overrun by the sound of an engine revving too high. Barac was not looking at the fancy cars by the hotel. His black eyes were fixed directly on the road to the right. Alea was close enough now to see a sneer on the demon's face as a silver sedan slid around a corner two blocks ahead. It was picking up speed as it raced toward the hotel and the hulking frame of Barac.

A wooden door opened only feet away from the sword in Alea's hand. The light caught the dark slits of the demon's eyes. His sneer fell at the recognition of his company. Alea's warm, golden eyes smiled back. Two figures left the quiet Bavarian-style restaurant through the open door. The couple in their mid-thirties paused only long enough to open an umbrella before quickly stepping across the street to the promenade. They ascended the few steps up the slight embankment before gently locking arms. The woman's head was resting on her husband's shoulder as they strolled back toward the Corison.

Neither had any awareness of the beings they had brushed moments before.

Nor did they realize they were about to start a war.

The silver car swerved across the center line before returning to its own lane. Barac adjusted his position as he walked along the bottom of the embankment behind the oblivious couple. Alea's slender, yet strong, frame sprung across the street. Within a fraction of a second she was even with the walking couple. A slight breeze lifted the woman's hair and she snuggled in closer to her husband. The drunk driver of the sedan swerved to avoid a parked minivan before correcting his car's path.

For the couple, this would be over in a breath or two. For middle ranked angels like Alea and her hidden ally Shamus, time meant little. An important event like this seemed to last an eternity.

A sickening howl left the car as a small, brutish demon twisted the steering wheel through the drunken driver's hands. The car caught the curb and started to turn over on its side along the embankment and toward the strolling couple.

Shamus, who had been waiting on the balcony of the Bavarian restaurant, leaped clear across the street above the unsuspecting Barac. At that exact moment, Alea plunged her blue, shimmering sword at the legs of the demon beast. As he sensed the presence of Shamus from above, Barac hesitated long enough to realize he was in trouble. He lowered his head to elude the red sword of Shamus just as Alea's sword caught the back of his leg. Barac staggered, but regained his balance and returned his focus to the approaching car. The eyes of Shamus and Alea met for a moment, and without spoken words, they turned opposite each other and thrust their swords at the enemy's feet. A shriek of pain echoed. The car continued to slide. Barac willed himself to remain in the path of the car, but the sudden pain in his feet was too much for the beast. He reached down.

It was enough. The car grazed the demon's back. Alea jolted the front of the car to adjust its trajectory. The sound of grinding metal bounced off the water as the car hit a streetlight pole along the promenade. Shamus stretched to grab the falling pole. His muscles pulsed as he slowed its fall.

Alea turned, sword ready, waiting for a reaction from the demon. None came. With a low growl he was gone into the mist. She did not pursue him.

Brenden Tavis and his wife Shawna turned to see the streetlight pole come down on them, the car bent around its base. Impact was solid. The couple lay on the ground in a heap.

Shamus directed the streetlight pole like a surgeon with a scalpel. The crack of a broken bone and the gasp of lungs being collapsed sent a shiver through the angel Alea.

Then all was still.

The waves lapped against the shore.

A victory.

CHAPTER TWO

The Lord looks down from heaven on the sons of men to see if there are any who understand, any who seek God.
Psalm 14:2

"That was quite an anniversary," remarked Shawna with a strong tone of sarcasm.

"One we won't quickly forget," replied her husband as he moved at a turtle's pace up the front steps of their North Alderwood home.

The overnight stay in emergency at the hospital had left them exhausted. It was a sore head for Shawna. For Brenden, the doctor diagnosed a fractured right radius, three broken ribs, and a concussion. The slow moving couple did not bother taking their luggage from the back of their Tahoe. A quick check of messages and email were accomplished before husband and wife slid into their king size bed for what they hoped would be a decent sleep. After several joyful "I love my bed" moans, Brenden broke the silence.

"That could have been a lot worse you know."

"Yah," was the reply.

"I mean, a lot worse. If that car had hit us instead of that pole. . ."

"Yah," was all he got again.

"You're still cute."

"What are you going to do about it?" Shawna said with a slight smile.

"Absolutely . . . nothing." Within minutes, both were asleep.

Alea and Shamus arrived at the North Realm, or Battle Realm, at about the same time as Brenden and Shawna arrived home in Alderwood. Travel through space by spiritual beings was known as cosmic travel. Alea was well aware that human comparisons did not exist. People had broken the sound barrier, but surpassing the speed of light was altogether different. It was relaxing, Alea realized, as long as nothing interrupted the flight. The North Realm was the closest realm to Earth, and it was also where Alea and Shamus needed to go to report on the success of their mission to the Dominion angel who had directed them.

The Dominion angels were head of operations and communications for most of the angelic world. They would ensure that the Almighty's commands were carried out in all corners of the universe. The Battle Realm was the headquarters, and lately, had been a constant bustle of activity. Today was no exception.

Alea and Shamus ascended directly to the center of the realm and the Hall of Red. The nearest stars to the North Realm cast a reddish glow on the region and the central meeting hall was given its name accordingly.

Doroniel was the Dominion in command of Alea and Shamus' mission on Earth. He was not massive in appearance, but he was massive in reputation. Doroniel was as faithful and diligent as any servant of the Almighty that Alea had ever seen. She was nervous around him, but only because she wanted to earn his respect.

Alea had only been a Virtue angel for a short while. Specific angel education was done in the West Realm, or Training Realm, and Alea had just spent three earth years learning the ins and outs of what it meant to be a Virtue.

Virtues brought God's blessings to people. Often this was in the form of miracles. Virtues were also involved in guiding men and women toward bravery and acts of heroism in the battle against Satanael and his demons of darkness. Today had been Alea's second mission since her acceptance into the angelic choir of the Virtues.

She paused to look around the lavish Hall of Red. The architecture and light were like nothing seen on a planet like Earth. Rounded columns molded into intricate designs were standing symmetrically throughout the structure. Each column gave off a light, an energy. Depending on the situation or need of the angels near each column, the light changed. The effect was breathtaking. A mix of power, mood, expression and beauty blended together when you looked around the expansive room. It released tension and could leave you spellbound for long periods of time.

Some areas of the hall were designed for just that purpose. These areas had plush chairs and artwork that bred peace and meditation. To the left of Alea was one of these sections, and on the wall was a massive painting simply called *Worship*. It had been created by the Seraph Nathanial before the planets had been formed. It was like looking into the eyes of God himself. A complete peace filled your being with just a glance. It was not uncommon to see angels of any rank staring into the picture, lost in the splendor of *Worship*.

On the opposite side of the hall, Doroniel stood alone. His brow was furrowed. As Alea and Shamus approached, he brightened in expression.

"It's good to see you so soon," he said in a sincere, but not surprised tone. "I assume you were successful?"

"We achieved what was asked of us," replied Shamus.

"Please, tell me what was accomplished. It's critical that we judge the situation accurately. Alea, why don't you begin?"

Alea felt honored to give the account. "The demon Barac was there as our Intel predicted," she began. "He was alone except for the demon of drunkenness who possessed the driver of the car. The evil ones did not anticipate our attack in this situation, and I believe they may still be unsure of our intentions as we'd hoped. We were able to stop Barac from blocking the car. Shamus and I directed a streetlight pole into Brenden and Shawna with enough impact, we believe, to shake them up. We discovered only short term injuries upon examination of their bodies."

As she was giving her account, a sturdy, rugged looking Dominion approached from across the hall. Alea had seen him before, but was unsure of his reason for joining them.

"This is Dominion Kana," spoke Doroniel. "He's spearheading a similar mission on Annaxis and would like to follow our progress to see how the enemy reacts."

The usual greeting of "Immanuel" was exchanged along with a noticeable bow. Alea had heard tidbits of information about Annaxis from her Virtue teacher Vrielle. It was the first of the seven planets with human life to be created. Earth was the fifth. Although creation of the human planets was not simultaneous, advancements in science and reasoning were similar among the seven planets. A few hundred years may separate the creation of life on the planets, but the comparisons in human development were astounding. Annaxis and Earth were experiencing strong information ages. More importantly, the strongest nations with the most wealth, and the most to give were falling for one of Satanael's most powerful weapons against good. It was called a number of things depending on whom you asked. Selfishness. Greed. Ego-centrism. Indifference. Materialism. They all played a part, but in the angelic world one simple word was used: apathy.

This whole battle revolved around it. Nations could fall because of it. Souls were lost because of it. Good things were not done because of it. Alea had been taught that when good things were not done, when there was no light shining bright, darkness filled the void. There was no middle ground. There was no in-between. Either there was light or there was darkness.

Apathy was the absence of activity. It was knowing but not doing. It was living so tightly within one's own small shell that nothing else was accomplished.

Apathy was Brenden Tavis.

Alea knew this, but so did Satanael and his demons. In fact, the enemy had not only encouraged apathy, they had perfected it. Barac was not in Corison Springs to injure Brenden and his wife. It was quite the opposite. Humans were predictable. If something happened that gave them a sense of security, they usually became more focused on themselves and more apathetic to the world around them.

The car was supposed to crash, but Barac was supposed to stop the vehicle just short of the couple that was strolling down the promenade. The couple would hear the noise and turn to see what had happened. They would be thrilled that they were not hit, and they would deduce that the swerving silver car was crashed by a hammered driver. They might call 911. They might stroll to the hotel and tell someone at the front desk what had happened. Either way, they would continue on with their perfect anniversary weekend. All the while, Brenden and Shawna would feel secure in the knowledge that they were *not* alcoholics. They were *not* bad people. *They* wouldn't crash. A deeper sense of security would be created within them, and even though they would be reminded that alcoholism existed, they would do nothing about it. This was apathy.

People like Brenden existed all over Earth and, apparently, on Annaxis as well.

"So, just to make sure I understand correctly, Virtue Alea, you interfered with the enemy's plans by allowing the two humans to be injured?" Kana brought Alea back to the present with the question.

"Yes, Dominion Kana," responded Alea. "By allowing some injury, the Tavis' are now forced to . . . think. They will, with all hope, seriously re-evaluate their day-to-day lives. It is the first step of the process. Moving a human from apathy to action will take time, but Brenden Tavis, we believe, will be a huge factor in the battle when, and if, he decides to take action."

"And you believe this accident was enough? There were no serious injuries if I heard you correctly?"

Alea had asked herself that same question many times in the planning and execution of the mission. You could never entirely predict human behavior, but she was confident in the Almighty's plan. She answered with a confident voice. "It is a beginning."

"Very well. Keep me updated on all activity." When Kana had disappeared through a side door of the hall Alea asked, "Do you have further orders from the Almighty, Doroniel?"

"Not yet. Giving a short time for Brenden to . . . think, as you put it, is probably the best course of action for now. I have sent angels to protect the Tavis' house from any demonic intrusion in your absence. There are a few people who continue to pray for Brenden and Shawna. When have you two last been to Center Realm?" Doroniel tilted his head and furrowed his brow again.

With excitement dripping from his face, Shamus responded. "It has been awhile, Dominion."

"Then you are free to go. Report back to me when you return. Immanuel."

"Immanuel," called Shamus and Alea in unison, the light of the pillar beside them flooding the room with a rainbow of color that reflected the mood.

CHAPTER THREE

There is a time for everything and a season for every activity under the heavens.
Ecclesiastes 3:1

It was the ringing of the phone that woke them four hours later. Brenden reacted out of habit and tried to grab the cordless phone on his bedside table. The initial twist of his torso sent bolts of pain through his body and paralyzed all his movements. The painkillers having worn off, each rib cried out and his head throbbed as though it had just been used in a high-speed squash match. Neither Brenden nor Shawna answered the ringing device, but the damage had been done. Sleep was over.

After a few minutes of thinking about sleep, curiosity about who had called inspired Brenden to peek at the call display on the phone. As he had expected, the name Bill and Helen Montgomery was revealed. It was his in-laws. The kids had been staying there over the weekend while the happily married couple went out to celebrate their eleventh anniversary. Shawna was positive that her mom would overreact if they called her about the accident the night before, so she had not let Brenden call. It probably was best in the long run, but right now he wished that they had made the call from the hospital. Shawna's mom would have, in all probability, volunteered to keep the kids for another night, and that would mean the phone would *not* have rudely rung when Brenden's body still longed to be asleep. His ribs were in need of time to heal and parenting six, four, and two year old children would not make that easy.

He decided to make an attempt at moving out of bed. The red digital numbers on the bedside clock shone 2:30pm. Shawna's parents, whom he just called mom and dad, would have had the kids at church in the morning and then spoiled them by taking them out for lunch. By now, Mom would be wondering if she would have to make dinner for them as well, or if Brenden and Shawna would be picking them up before that. Mom was predictable. She was kind. She was loving. She always put others first. She was what he thought an angel would be like, and he was thrilled to have become part of the Montgomery family eleven years earlier.

He and Shawna had met on a church youth trip to inner-city Los Angeles in grade 11. They had helped in soup kitchens, low income housing projects, and the food bank. It had truly been an eye-opener for the 17 year olds. Perspective. That was what his leaders had called it. It certainly was. To have met real, ordinary people who were homeless or living in extreme poverty, or both, had made them glad they could help. They were, however, even more glad that they lived in middle class America. The potatoes they ate at home were not the half rotten ones they had peeled and sliced pieces off of to serve the homeless. The clothes they wore were clean and smelled of laundry detergent or that "fresh off the rack" new clothes smell that Shawna loved. That had not been the case for the people they served in L.A. Now that he thought back to it, that week had created a sense of purpose and accomplishment that he had rarely felt since.

Group dating led to double-dating. Double-dating led to "finally it's just me and you" dating. "Finally it's just me and you" dating led to "will you marry me?", and that led to November 22, eleven years earlier. Tyler, Rachel and Amanda had entered the family along the way. They were great kids, but Brenden was ready to be done with highchairs, car seats and diapers. Shawna, on the other hand, was not sure if she was done with having kids. One of these days that bridge would have to be crossed. Not today. Not even practice would happen today.

At the present moment the only thing this man wanted to do was make a pot of coffee and take more drugs, but he was having trouble moving his arm off the bed much less anything else.

Brenden did succeed, eventually, and sat down on the chocolate suede sofa in the living room with an aromatic cup of Starbuck's Komodo Dragon Blend and his cell phone. It took a while to work up the willingness to call mom and fill her in on the details of their romantic anniversary night, but just as he was about to hold down the speed dial and make the call, Shawna emerged from the bedroom. Her long, dark hair was still wet from her shower and the familiar scent of her shampoo reached his brain. Shawna had always had the ability to make him freeze when she entered the room.

As if by instinct, he knew he should watch her, just for a few steps, just long enough to make eye contact. Many things were communicated between husband and wife in that quick connection of the eyes. Her eyes were dark brown, but that was not what he was looking at. Sometimes her eyes smiled. Sometimes they had too much worry in them. Sometimes Brenden knew from her eyes that she needed to talk about something that he probably did not want to talk about. And, sometimes, they had *the* look. A mischievous, perky, "I want you" look. That was definitely the best one. What came after a look like that varied. Sometimes, usually, there were kids around so nothing really happened. But he knew what she was feeling and that did matter. Sometimes, far less often, when kids weren't around, that look led to fun and intimacy. These were the moments that strengthened their marriage. They were spontaneous, they were fun, and these were the moments that told each other everything was okay.

Today, Shawna's eyes said something like, "Hi! I love you but I am really sleepy and have a headache." She, too, grabbed a coffee and two ibuprofen and plunked down on the recliner which matched the couch Brenden sat on. She put her feet on the ottoman and pulled a blanket over her legs.

"So, do you want to call your mom?" he asked without trying to sound like he was pleading.

"I could, but you seem to have a way with my mom. If you want to make sure the kids stay with their grandma and grandpa tonight, it would be safer if you called."

It was apparent to Brenden that the knock on the head Shawna had suffered had not altered her ability to manipulate him. "You are too beautiful to be that smart," he replied.

After a quick smile and a ten minute phone call, Brenden propped his feet up on the couch feeling relieved. The kids were taken care of until after lunch the next day. His body was starting to feel numbed again from the medicine. Everything was quiet, and between the caffeine and the sunlight coming in the living room windows, he felt awake and alert.

He spent a few minutes looking out at the distant coastal mountains. When the clouds did roll away, it was beautiful in the Northwest. The row of windows on the front of the house was put there for exactly that reason. When they had built the place three years earlier, the tall windows were one of the things he knew he wanted. The view was tranquil. The house rested on the edge of a steep hill, so there were no houses blocking the view. If you looked to the right, the furthest mountains in the distance reached toward the Canadian border. If you looked left you could see clear to the edge of the Pacific. The actual water was not visible from here, but one could get a sense of where the land ended and the endless waves began.

Even in November when the deciduous maples and alders had lost their leaves, the vast numbers of fir and cedar trees kept the land looking green. The lawn had not been cut for about six weeks and would not need cutting again until March, but it too, was green.

With the clouds of the day before having drifted away, it was cool and bright on this particular November 23rd. Brenden's injuries would heal. The kids were not around, but they were looked after. He was living in a gorgeous new home. He was happily married. He relaxed even deeper into the couch. He knew he should feel totally content with his life. And yet . . . inside . . . there was conflict? *He could have died yesterday. It could have been the end of the life of Brenden Tavis. Was his life all that it should be? What was he missing?*

Brenden Tavis spent many more motionless minutes trying to answer those questions as Shawna read on the chair beside him.

Looking back at Brenden through the row of tall windows, hovering over the edge of the slope, were two others, their black eyes focused on the injured man.

CHAPTER FOUR

All the angels were standing around the throne and around the elders and the four living creatures. They fell down on their faces before the throne and worshiped God,
Revelation 7:11

Even stretched out in the Hall of Red, Alea was feeling impatient. It was comfortable here, but her thoughts kept reaching to Brenden Tavis. It felt as though time was being wasted, even though she knew that each move in the mission was important and needed to be fully examined before being carried out. She was glad the Dominions were in discussion with the Thrones and Seraphim. She trusted their decisions. Their understanding of the greater picture and of all the heavens was far better than hers, and the angels with those ranks took every order directly from the Almighty.

There was something about this mission that created a sense of urgency. It was as though the ramifications of what was happening with Brenden and Shawna were even more important than she had anticipated. To have two Dominions, that she knew of, watching this closely? To be taking this much time in consultation? Alea knew…

no…she felt that she had been asked to be a part of something big. Waiting was hard.

Also on her mind was the possibility of going to Center Realm. Shamus would reveal the answer to that possibility as soon as he returned. Shamus resided in the North Realm where they now rested. All the angels ranked as Powers lived here. The Powers carried swords of red representing the realm in which they lived, and they *were* powerful, as their name implied. They were elite fighters. They were feared by even the strongest of demons. Shamus had gone to his personal quarters to eat some manna and check if there were any other tasks that he would need to respond to while they were here. If he could get away, they would go to Center Realm. If not, she would have to remain here. It was not safe traveling alone between Realms anymore. The enemy was becoming bold.

As if he could tell she was thinking about him, Shamus strode through the door and walked to where she was relaxing. His broad shoulders and thick muscles seemed to quiver as the light caught them, yet he still had a look of swiftness and agility about him. Alea was glad that Shamus was on her side. When his eyes were soft, as they were now, she felt perfectly at ease around him, but she had seen his eyes in the heat of battle and in those moments, they were something to be feared.

In one fluid, graceful motion, Alea's slender frame moved from prone to standing. Her long, golden hair was half covering her face, but through the unhindered eye, she stared at Shamus awaiting his news. She knew his answer before he spoke, however, as the bright, lively light of the pillar next to Shamus gave away his emotions.

"We may go," he said, a smile forming on his face.

"Then what are we waiting for?" Alea replied already moving to the hall's main doors.

"Have you eaten anything?" Shamus called after her.

"I nibbled while I waited. I'll be fine. Come on!" She raced out the doors into the courtyard. The main path curved to the right between rows of flowering trees. She raced along the path taking in the fruity fragrance of the flowers. Shamus caught up quickly.

"How long has it been since you have been to Center Realm?" Alea asked without slowing her pace.

"Three missions. About 41 days as our Earthly friends would measure it. Things have been hectic. Even now there was another mission seeking my help, but I know I will not be at my best unless I first visit Center Realm."

They ran a number of effortless strides further before Alea replied. "It has only been eighteen days for me, and yet I already feel weaker and less aware. I have never been away for even this long."

"Then let us hurry!" roared Shamus as he leaped off the path and, as though gravity no longer existed, continued rising from the red realm. Alea followed closely behind.

Center Realm was literally the center of the heavens. It was the home of the Almighty. It was the dwelling place of the Seraphim, the Cherubim, and the Thrones. These were the three highest choirs in all the angelic world and they took direction from the Almighty. The Seraphim, covered in eyes, had rarely left the presence of their Lord. They spent most of their time praising the Almighty, and knew Him better than all the other living beings in the universe combined. The Seraphim *were* worship.

The Cherubim were the ultimate guards of the universe. It was Cherubim that protected the "tree of life" in the beginning of humanity on the planets. Their bodies resembled a lion with majestic wings; their face was like the other angels, like the humans. They were serious. They were fierce. Any demon of darkness who ventured near

Center Realm was likely to be extinguished by the Cherubim before questions were asked or answered.

Then there were the Thrones or Elders. They were unlike all the other angels. They, like the Seraphim, were covered in eyes. They could not only see *around* themselves, but they could see deeply *into* other beings. There was nothing you could hide from the Thrones. They often left Center Realm to bring orders and direction to the Dominions when time was short and action was crucial. There were stories of the Thrones traveling to the seven human worlds to give help when battles were being lost. When a Throne issued a command, it was as though the voice of the Almighty himself echoed through your entire being.

As the two of them approached Center Realm, Alea half hoped to see Dominion Doroniel speaking with the Thrones about their mission. To be invited to speak directly with a Throne would be a great honor. She would keep an eye out for this possibility.

Unlike the other realms, the light in Center Realm did not come from the stars. Here the golden light emanated from the Almighty himself. It was not blocked out by walls. There were no shadows. Light permeated everything and everywhere. It created an unmatched clarity. You saw so clearly that your senses melded together. When you looked, you also smelled, tasted, heard and felt. It was one of the things Alea loved about being here. Everything was . . . real. Deception did not exist here.

The first sounds of singing sent a rush of emotion through Alea. All angels came here to be in the presence of the Almighty. As sleep was to humans, worship in the presence of the Almighty was to angels. It was refreshing. It breathed life into the core of who you were. It revived. It was craved. It was the reason Alea and Shamus were here.

A large throng of angels was approaching the captivating city at the same time as Alea and Shamus. Alea was so lost in her thoughts that she bumped one of them and had to apologize. The group of angels, which must have numbered over a thousand, looked equally excited to be entering the Realm. Deciphering small pieces of their conversations, she could assume they were coming from Annaxis. Among their excitement, Alea could sense some tension and confusion. She couldn't help but wonder how the battle was going on Annaxis. Was it really the same battle she was fighting on Earth? This, too, she was hoping to discover.

The multitude of angels flew through one of the many gates of the walled city. Although you could see into the city from above, you could only enter through the gates. Two mighty Cherubim stood guard, one on either side of the massive opening. One might have thought they were sculptures, except for their ever-watching eyes. The human-like head of the Cherub closest to Alea examined her as she moved by. She was not afraid. She knew the Cherub was her protector. Again, she found herself glad to be on the same side of the battle.

To her surprise, a strange warmness filled her and the Cherub head bowed. She *felt* it say her name. She was sure it had not been audible, but the sensation was unmistakable. This mighty creature knew her name: Alea the Virtue. She should not have been surprised. The angelic realm was not about superiority or inferiority. Whether a guardian on one of the seven worlds or a Seraph in the presence of the Almighty, all were important. All were one entity. Humility, however, in a majestic angel such as this Cherub could still catch you off guard.

"Immanuel," she said quietly, unsure of whether her greeting had been perceived. Before any response, the angels around her swept Alea through the gate and the city opened in all directions. Shamus was visible a few feet in front of her and within seconds the crowd dispersed and the two were left, for the most part, alone.

Center realm was like an enormous wheel. The main road, often referred to as the Golden Road, wound around the entire perimeter. Between the Golden Road and the temple in the center of the realm were many other roads, much like spokes on a wheel. Gathering halls and the private quarters of the angels who lived in Center Realm were built between the Golden Road and the wall on the outside edge of the city. In the open areas between the "spokes" were manicured gardens of unsurpassed splendor. Groups of angels could be seen sitting around fountains, relaxing on benches or leaning against the trunk of a millennium-old cedar tree. Flowers bloomed at all times here. Unlike on the planets, weather did not even exist. It was perfection.

Also between the spokes, mixed throughout the gardens, were the homes of the believers. It was mile upon mile of dwellings for the people that God had granted permission to enter into this heavenly place. Angels and humans in their spiritual state existed in perfect harmony.

For Alea, however, the thing that really distinguished this place from all others was the sound of it. Cities on Earth were noisy places with the sounds of engines running, sirens blaring, and airplanes overhead. Even at night there was commotion. Here there were no machines. There were no vehicles. There were no hospitals or schools or fire halls. There was only the sound of the temple of the Lord! Sometimes it was quiet and soothing. At other times, it blasted like thunder and forced one to listen. Singing. Praise. Worship. It was delightful and harmonious. Just listening brought vitality and joy. Participating in it brought LIFE! A sense of energy, purpose and significance not found in any other place in the universe. Alea and Shamus found themselves moving toward the temple. No words were necessary. It was time.

About halfway down the road leading to the temple, Alea's strong, melodic voice added to the sound of the city. Then something changed. Shamus was beside her. Something had come up behind them. Alea could feel its presence on the back of her silky, blonde head. Instinctively, she turned.

The Virtue's initial thought was to draw her sword, but it remained sheathed. Shamus had not only thought about reacting, but without hesitating now held his red-glowing weapon in front of him as he also spun to face whatever had approached them. The creature before them rose to its full height like a tower. Its head was level with the top of the gwualla tree beside the road whose fruit was heavily weighing down its branches. The face of an eagle peered down, unwavering, unconcerned. Curious was the word that came to Alea's mind. The eagle face turned toward Shamus, and Alea saw the second face. It was that of a lion, staring, waiting. Four faces in all. One set of wings covered its human-like body. The second set of wings was spread wider than the road they stood upon. Bright, dancing flames emanated from the angel and, although all angels shone with the glory of the Almighty, Alea found herself squinting at the bronze glow surrounding the Throne angel before her.

Before full comprehension came to Alea, a voice boomed forth.

"Why are you afraid in the city of our Lord? Is this not the safest place in all the universe?"

Shamus responded first. His sword now sheathed, he bowed.

"Immanuel, Great Throne Aziel. What you say is true. We should not have reacted so. It seems to take longer and longer to relax after we leave Earth."

"I am sorry to hear this. You are here to worship." It was a statement, not a question. Both Alea and Shamus stood straighter. With confidence they looked into the eyes of the eagle. The presence of the Lord covered the entire city like a thick, down duvet.

The golden eyes blinked slowly. "When you are refreshed, we request your presence in the Chamber of Thrones." Lightning flashed. The wings covering the Throne's body opened as wide as the already extended pair. The hundreds of eyes covering the body of the angel searched deeply in every direction. Then with a rush of wind, Aziel was gone.

Only one word came to Alea's mind. She spoke it aloud. "Unexpected."

"Exciting!" Shamus turned and flew off toward the temple.

I think I like being an angel of Virtue was the last thought through Alea's mind before she was overtaken by the sound and sight of worship.

The temple was all-consuming. Golden walls reflected the Glory of the Lord. Huge arches inlaid with diamonds and emeralds and sapphires opened all around the roofless structure. It was not an earthly temple. If anything, it resembled a spectacular stadium that might be home to a sports team on a human planet. But bigger. In fact, Alea had been told by Vrielle back in the Training Realm that at nearly any given point in time, half a million angels would be in the temple in worship of their Lord. Many believers were also there in worship. Half a million angels and all the people barely filled the closest circle around the throne. During celebrations of great victories, the stadium would hold ten times that number, with myriads of others worshiping from outside the walls.

Yet, it did not feel enormous. From any spot within the jeweled arches, the warmth and love of the Almighty existed as in the rest of Center Realm, but with more intensity. All senses merged into one sensation. The physical was overshadowed by the spiritual. All focus. *All* focus. *Everything* praised the Lord. The Almighty. The Creator. God.

As a song of praise hundreds of thousands strong grew out of those in the temple, Alea and Shamus gave themselves in worship. And they were filled.

If a human had looked with total focus, they may have seen two slightly darkened silhouettes against the backdrop of the sky. But humans rarely focused. One silhouette was taller than the other, both stood dignified and confident.

"Is there cause for concern?" the shorter one asked.

"If you think there is not cause for concern, you underestimate the power of the angels of light," the taller one responded harshly. "Are you confident it was a Virtue and a Power who ambushed Barac?"

"Yes. One sword shone blue, the other red. There is no doubt."

"Then we must take it seriously, and we must respond immediately."

"What do you ask of me?" questioned the shorter one.

"Distraction. Travel."

"Is it time to use the influence we have gained over Matt and Marci Hollingsworth?"

"You have learned well."

"Thank you, master. I will begin immediately. May I enter this house?" the demon asked while looking back at the tall windows and the two people watching TV.

"The prayers for this couple are too numerous. You may not see it from here, but I am sure it is protected. It would take more strength than you alone have to enter." The taller angel of darkness was gone while his words still lingered in the air.

The Seattle Seahawks were, remarkably, having a good season. At this particular moment, they were trouncing the Broncos and the Tavis' were watching with mild interest. Brenden's head ached and intense swelling around his broken bones made for general misery even with his team winning. The phone had not rung, which was unusual for a realtor on a sunny Sunday. Shawna had been up to put some laundry in the washer after retrieving their luggage from the truck. Otherwise, she had been in and out of sleep on the chair. Somehow she could sleep anywhere. It was still baffling after all these years. The car's engine could still be cold and Shawna could be fast asleep. Her head would hit the pillow on any given night and within two minutes, tops, she would be asleep. Brenden's mind did not allow him to be like that. It took longer to rev it up, but once it was running, it took a while to shut it down. Right now, his mind was racing and sleep was not an option.

It was one of those internal battles going on in his head. Being only thirty-four, it was not a mid-life crisis. At least he figured he was too young for that. It was more of a purpose thing. On one hand, the housing market had been consistent. Finances were stable and, if anything, improving. He was a good father and a good husband. Actually, he was a great father and a great husband! He attended the Alderwood Evangelical Church most Sundays. He believed in God. He believed he was going to heaven when he died. He was respected by most others. At least his perception was that others respected him. A person could never be sure about what others said in one's absence. His black Tahoe had nice rims and was spotless. To top it all off, he was watching the football game on a 60-inch flat screen. What more was there?

On the other hand, when all was said and done and people were eating potato salad at his funeral, what would Brenden Tavis be remembered for? Houses needed to be sold, but did it make a difference in the world if he did a good job of it? He was a good person. He was honest. He was trusted. But. There was the "but". Why was there always the "but"? There was a sentence he could not get out of his head. It was Pastor Phil from the Evangelical church who had said it a few years earlier. It wouldn't go away.

"To whom much is given, much is expected." Of course there had been a whole sermon that morning, but Brenden couldn't remember anything else, just that one simple sentence from the Bible.

He had been given much.

What was it exactly that was expected of him?

He turned to look at his wife. She sensed it, and looked up from the crossword puzzle she had begun. Brenden uttered the words, "What do you. . ." when the phone rang.

Call display.

Matt and Marci.

CHAPTER FIVE

But I am afraid that just as Eve was deceived by the serpent's cunning, your minds may somehow be led astray from your sincere and pure devotion to Christ.
2 Corinthians 11:3

"It just isn't right. You two get all busted up on your anniversary and then come home to an empty house. No romance, no fancy dinner, no cuddling. Well, be discouraged no more, my dear friends!" Matt was, as usual, boisterous and the life of the party. At the present moment, he was cooking up a storm in Brenden and Shawna's kitchen and proclaiming what a wonderful friend he was to them. The smell of sautéed onions and Caesar salad was drifting over the counters and filling the open, two-story great room where Brenden remained planted on the sofa.

"Just you wait. These are not ordinary burgers. These are gourmet anniversary burgers. You could fly to Texas and not find burgers this good. I mean *gourmet* burgers this good." The word gourmet was of course heavily accented in something like French with a hint of Japanese. "I belief ze parfait collection of 'erbs and spices on ze potatoes will also work as an aphrodisiac. Ze romance will soon follow me friends. Nutting but ze best for you! Master Matt vil take care of you!"

With that, he was out the side door to the patio and the barbeque. His talking turned to whistling and then to singing some crazy version of "Happy Anniversary to You" that now sounded strangely Russian.

Life had not been the same since "Master Matt" Hollingsworth had bought a house from Brenden a couple years earlier. Matt had met his wife Marci at a bar in Chicago. Marci had been visiting a high school friend and had gone for drinks when the never shy Matt had walked right on over and told her he was going to marry her. Most men would have returned to their sad conglomeration of single friends across the room with a slap on the face or, at the very least, a slightly wounded ego. Not Matt. Charm and charisma oozed from every cell in his body. When you were with Matt, common sense told you not to get sucked into his evil ways, but you did anyway. Marci got sucked in. Brenden got sucked in. Shawna got sucked in. The koi fish in the pond in front of the house got sucked in. Within four months, Matt had become tired of a long distance relationship and had moved from the Windy City to Alderwood to be with Marci, the love of his life.

Many laughs and countless memories later, the Master was serving up dinner and, apparently, romance for Brenden and Shawna. Marci and Shawna were lost in some scrapbooking magazine and gingerly sipping a bold, Washington State Syrah. Brenden had heard Shawna mutter something about strange chemical reactions between her wine and her ibuprofen, but otherwise she appeared to be enjoying herself. Shawna was certainly capable of hiding pain around company, but Matt and Marci were not considered company anymore.

The Seahawks had won. Brenden had napped, and then Matt and Marci had arrived only a few hours after calling to see how the anniversary celebration at Corison Springs had gone. In their hands when they arrived were the ingredients for dinner and the rest of the evening. Brenden's ribs didn't appreciate all the laughter, but he was glad they had come.

It wasn't until dinner was over and the gourmet, anniversary burgers were digesting in their rounded stomachs that the phone rang. Matt's cell. Matt had wandered onto the back deck so the others could not understand what was being said, but from the facial expressions and arm waving it was obvious that he was not talking to his mother. An initial expression of joy had melted into concern. Then frustration. Then calm. Then more excitement. Finally, there was resignation. Matt stood motionless, a silhouette against the darkened sky. The other three shrugged at each other, not quite sure what to make of the call.

After stifled giggling, Shawna whispered her best guess as the three of them stared out the window. "Black market babies!" Jabbing pain in the ribs nearly took Brenden's breath away as he burst out laughing.

With hardly a delay, Marci offered, "a new penile enlargement drug?"

This time, Brenden laughed so hard that tears, real tears, ran down his cheeks. It was a mix of joy and severe pain, and the only responses he was capable of were quiet, short bursts of, "Stop it! You're killing me." Matt peeked his head into the room to find the three stooges wiping the tears from their eyes. All three of them looked at Matt, back at each other, and then burst out in a new round of unadulterated laughter.

"Wine and ibuprofen. I am going to have to try that!" Matt said with a shake of his head that meant something like, you are all *seriously* messed up. "Nuthead wife of mine. Can I talk to you?" He went back out the door. Marci walked halfway through the room before she turned and said, "I don't know if I am more excited about us getting a baby or him getting the enlargement drugs." Cries of laughter followed her out the door.

It was not a conversation Brenden and Shawna would have had with anyone else. Most of their other friendships had started with a connection at church. They loved spending time with many of those friends, and the conversations rarely ventured to the crude, sexual or risqué side; conversations with Matt and Marci, however, did. It felt uncomfortable at times. Matt and Marci said what they thought. Period. They *had* filters. Brenden had seen both Matt and Marci use them around children and at work, but Matt and Marci only added them when they needed them. Most people Brenden and Shawna hung out with lived with filters and rarely removed them.

The nature of the phone call Matt had received was not a mystery for long, and it strangely had nothing to do with black market babies or penile enlargement drugs. In actuality, the phone call was far more exciting. Matt and Marci marched into the great room, sat down on the love seat across from the sofa, and smiled at Brenden and Shawna like little school kids. No words. Just silly smiles and a *"I know something you don't know"* twinkle in their eyes.

Shawna grew impatient and her response was more aggressive than usual, aggressive but effective. She started rifling throw cushions at the love seat as fast as she could find them.

"Ok. Ok. It's all fun and games until someone breaks their ribs!" Marci shouted with a direct glance at Brenden.

"We have something to ask you." Matt hesitated and then corrected himself. "No. *We* have something to tell you." Marci nodded in agreement, a silly smile still stretching across her face. Even looking goofy, like at this moment, Brenden could see why Matt had picked her out of a crowd. Marci was raw beauty: perfect complexion, eyes you could get lost in, and an athletic body that was thin where women wanted to be thin, and curved where it should be curved.

"When was the last time you two left the state? Real estate conferences don't count, big guy."

"We went to Vancouver Island on our honeymoon. That was overseas and even out of the country," Shawna answered with a weak tone of sarcasm.

"You can practically see Vancouver Island from your roof! That doesn't count."

"Then I guess . . . NEVER would be the correct answer."

"Well, it is time! That was my boss. Apparently I met my sales goals last month. No one usually meets sales goals, but I did. I'm not even sure how, to tell you the truth. Anyway, first I got a nifty bonus. Merry Christmas to me!" Matt proceeded to stand and do a twirly, ballerina dance before he sat down again on the edge of the love seat.

"Second, the company decided I deserved some time away. They are sending Marci and I on a Caribbean cruise, all expenses paid. Flights, hotels, meals. Everything."

"Awesome. That's . . .," Brenden began.

"Stop! I'm not finished!" Matt now stood and cleared his throat as if he were the President addressing his country. "The trip is over Christmas. Marci and I will be in Chicago for Christmas, and my mom will kill me if we don't come this year. We bailed on her last year and she still makes me feel guilty. Besides, we've been on a couple cruises before. We would like you to go," Matt's finger waggled back and forth between the sofa and recliner where Brenden and Shawna had now inherited dumbfounded smiles that stretched from ear to ear.

"Merry Christmas?" Marci whispered.

"But our . . ."

"Stop again! No buts. Don't even think about saying no because of your children. You and I both know that your mother-in-law is an angel, Brenden. The kids will be fine. It's only a week. She'll take the kids. I'll call your mom myself if I have to. I don't want to hear any noises come out of your sorry, broken up body Mr. Tavis. Just smile and nod. Smile and nod. And that goes for you too, Missy," Matt added as he stared menacingly down his finger at Shawna.

Brenden Tavis did what any scolded man who had just been given a spontaneous cruise would do. He smiled. And then he nodded. Twice.

A demon sat against the chimney on the house next to the Tavis'. Both the side patio and back deck of the Tavis house were within view of his vantage point. All was quiet on the patio now.

Earlier, a small, stringy looking angel of darkness named Hartan, had brought news to this demon that the owner of a tech company in Dallas had been *persuaded* to purchase a large contract from Matt Hollingsworth.

The demon on the rooftop had then made a trip to Matt's workplace, Vertigent Technologies. There had been no interruptions. The angels of light were nowhere to be seen at Vertigent. Nobody bothered to pray for businesses anymore. They were rarely protected, and it sure made things easier.

Matt's boss, a wealthy entrepreneur who kept a blanket and pillow in the closet beside his office couch, finished up paper work on Sunday afternoons when there were no employees to get in the way. He had been the only one in the building when the demon entered. An inaudible suggestion was made for the boss to check the weekly sales numbers. A second suggestion encouraged the young business owner to call Matt today after the realization that a late Friday sale had bumped Matt passed his usually unreachable sales goals.

Most people are easily convinced to do good things, the demon said to no one in particular.

The phone call to Matt from his boss in the office was timed to perfection.

"Give the trip to Brenden and Shawna," the demon had announced from his nifty rooftop location during Matt's phone discussion on the side deck. Matt would not have known where the suggestion had come from. He would not have heard the words. Matt would have thought he had come up with the brilliant idea all by himself.

Gifts around Christmas. They were justifiable. They reeked of love. The intentions were sincere. *It was so easy to distract humans from what was really important*, the dark demon thought to himself. He mouthed the words *"enjoy the trip,"* and then let out a guttural gurgle in an effort to laugh.

Long after Matt and Marci had gone home and Brenden and Shawna had lumbered their way back to their bed, the demon remained on his perch.

It was always a pleasure to interfere with angelic missions. Distractions, like going on a trip, could stall human decisions and activities for weeks before and after. Exactly why the angels were so interested in Brenden and Shawna Tavis was not clear to the demon, but one thing was. The Tavis' would be distracted and the angels of light would not like it.

CHAPTER SIX

"For I know the plans I have for you," declares the LORD, "plans to prosper you and not to harm you, plans to give you hope and a future."
Jeremiah 29:11

Jerry Moore watched a young boy throw a now slimy tennis ball. He had lost count somewhere around thirty-five throws. The chocolate lab that had been retrieving the ball had finally been distracted by a passing group of teenage girls who were throwing french fries at each other and leaving a trail that no dog in his right mind could ignore. The boy's mom pushed an even younger girl on the swings of the school playground outside the Starbuck's window that Jerry peered out of. It was a beautiful Sunday afternoon. It felt good to be home.

Mrs. Taylor, his grade seven teacher, had probably retired, but the classroom on the end of the back wing of Fitzsimmons Elementary still looked the same as when Jerry had attended the school. The ball diamond was the same. The tetherball poles hadn't moved. Starbuck's was new, however. Jerry downed the last of his Americano.

It had been two years since he had last stepped foot on his childhood stomping grounds here in Alderwood. Work kept him abroad. There were few, if any, school buddies that he missed in this city. Most he had lost touch with. No regrets.

Phil Janzen, however, was a different story. Phil had entered Jerry's life at a time when everyone else seemed to be leaving it. Phil's friendship meant everything.

Barb, Jerry's ex, had left with the kids, the dog, and whatever was left of Jerry's dignity. Phil and his wife Kathy had just accepted the job as senior pastor at the Evangelical church a block north of where Jerry now sat. Phil had not been able to bring Jerry's family back, but Phil had restored Jerry's dignity.

What path would my life have taken without the Janzens?

It was scary to even consider.

A thick hand grabbed his shoulder. The reverie evaporated as Pastor Phil solidified in the present.

"It is good to see you old man." The words were sincere and alive.

"You too, old man," Jerry mustered as he stood and wrapped his arms around his good friend. Phil and Jerry had both been born on May 12, 1962, all be it on opposite sides of the country. The "old man" greeting had begun when they were still in their mid-thirties and thought the reality of being old was further off than it turned out to be. Many things had changed in the fifteen years that had passed since then. Other things, like the pastor himself, had not. There was a slight touch of gray above the ears, and an extra belt size or two, but the real man inside was the same. One look into the warmth of Phil's eyes revealed a heart as big as a mountain and a soul that was right with the God he preached about each Sunday.

"Sit down, sit down," Jerry said as he pushed up a second chair to the table. "No amazing wife with you?"

"No. Kathy sends her deepest regards, but Allie needed someone to get her from a friend's house and take her to an extra voice lesson in Everett. Kathy would have much rather been here to meet you." Phil paused a moment as he looked more closely at Jerry. "You look good!"

"You know, I feel good. Some positive things are falling into place for me. I am actually making a difference, Phil! I am onto something that I really believe in! And this time it is not Budweiser."

Phil laughed, but his tone quickly turned serious as he questioned, "How long?"

"Not a drop in over four years."

Phil hated to ask the alcohol question, but drinking needed to remain a demon of the past for Jerry. It was dangerous to make assumptions when it came to drugs or alcohol, so whether it was uncomfortable or not, the question had to be asked.

Jerry knew the question would be asked. He also sensed the unease it caused Phil to ask him.

"Thank you for checking up on me. Really. I would have been worried if you hadn't asked me. That chapter of my life is gone. I don't want it. I don't need it. My soul is full and my cup runneth over!"

Phil didn't need to respond verbally to communicate. He was staring at Jerry, and smiling that big, ole Phil smile. They were silent another moment or two before the pastor excused himself to go get a latte. When he returned, the minutes rolled by as the two men shared stories of travel, work, and common friends that they had made at Alderwood Evangelical Church.

At the adjacent table, sat three others. They had listened. They had watched. They had not interfered. Zopheniel, an angel of light, was assigned to the pastor. Any congregation that was even *partially* effective in ministry could expect demonic attacks; the pastor was often the primary target. Alderwood had a strong contingent of praying believers, and this helped assure that Zopheniel, and other angels as well, would be close by to protect and encourage this pastor.

The angel Maspial fulfilled a similar role for the traveler, Jerry Moore. Like Brenden Tavis, about who the pastor and traveler were now discussing, Jerry was flagged by the dark angels as someone the angels of light had big plans for. Attacks on Jerry had become frequent. After this meeting today with the pastor, things were sure to get worse instead of better. The third angel, Ramuel, adjusted his amber-hued sword which signified his role as a Principality.

The three angels listened intently as the conversation regarding Brenden Tavis, the realtor, deepened.

"Brenden and Shawna have so much potential. They just lack focus. They need someone to help them to see it. They have great people skills. They're both excellent public speakers. People look up to them."

Phil nodded in agreement and then reported, "They were in an accident yesterday."

Concern spread across Jerry's face. "Are they alright?"

"A drunk driver hit a streetlight pole that fell on them at Corison Springs. Brenden has a few broken bones, and Shawna smacked her head pretty hard, but I think they'll be alright. We just found out. I am hoping to go see them tomorrow."

The conversation was cut short by the arrival of another of Phil's acquaintances who entered the coffee shop. This older lady was the fourth person who knew Pastor Phil to have entered during the meeting. Just like the others, she came and talked with the pastor as though he was her closest friend. Phil had that effect on people. A few minutes later, she was out the door with a hot drink in her hand. Jerry decided it was time to get down to business.

"Look Phil. As much as I love spending time with you, and as good as it feels to be home, I needed to meet with you for a more specific reason."

Phil looked as if he were about to reply with some witty comment, but he refrained. "Fire away!"

"I had an idea," Jerry began, but instead of continuing Jerry paused. A new thought had just entered his mind and he spoke it audibly. "Actually, as crazy as this may seem, I think I was given an idea. I can't believe I didn't realize it until this very moment, but everything came to me so clearly, so quickly before. It couldn't have just been *my* idea." Jerry was nodding in agreement to his own voice now. He noticed the perplexed look on Phil's face. "I think *God* has a plan for me, Phil."

"You're welcome!" interjected the angel Maspial who had just spoken the words, "It is God's plan," to Jerry.

"Of course He has a plan for you." Phil finished his second latte and placed the empty cup on the table while he waited for Jerry to gain clarity.

With some trepidation, Jerry began again. "This is it. Once I tell someone else, I am committed." Jerry was still trying to put his thoughts together even though he had gone through this talk with Phil many times in his head prior to this meeting. "I want to start something. Correction. *God* wants to start something. It's big . . . and . . . it involves you . . . and Brenden."

"People continue to amaze me." The third angel, Ramuel, spoke with a tone that was sincere, emotional. "At times it is hard to believe humans think about anyone but themselves. At other times, like now, you realize they do see the whole picture. They do want to follow the Almighty. They do know we exist. At least there is hope." Ramuel's fingers continued to fiddle with his sword.

"Jerry is gaining wisdom, Ramuel. His trials earlier in his life have made him stronger. He is not easily deceived," commented Maspial.

"He will need strength on the coming journey. I must return to Washington. I will return, when time allows, tohear how the pastor responds to the vision." With those words, Ramuel, the angel of Principalities assigned to President Mullen, was gone on wings that would carry him back to the White House.

A slight breeze sent a chill through Jerry as he divulged the details of the vision to Phil. He folded his arms for added warmth.

Three beings remained. One, the pastor, Jerry could see. The two angels remained hidden behind the curtain of the spiritual realm. All three listened to Jerry with great interest.

CHAPTER SEVEN

Then the angel showed me the river of the water of life, as clear as crystal, flowing from the throne of God and of the Lamb . . .
Revelation 22:1

The Chamber of Thrones was located beside the grandest entrance into Center Realm. The massive arch was called Eden's Gate, and anyone entering from the cosmic universe outside could see why as soon as they entered. A river ran out of each side of the enormous gate and remained on a straight path toward the temple in the middle of the Realm. About half a mile from the gate, the two rivers merged and crossed in a place called the Pool of Life. It was from this pool that the Almighty drew water for the creation of the human worlds. Ultimately, the Gardens of Eden, one on each of the seven human worlds, were given life from this pool. The Pool of Life remained like glass on the surface, and even appeared to give off its own light. Whether it really did give off light or whether it just reflected the light of the glory of the Lord, Alea was not totally sure. Either way, the pool was serene and awesome.

The crossing rivers continued on after the pool encircling the entire realm. They eventually wound back to the the temple of the Almighty. Golden bridges with walkways of diamond crossed the rivers at many places. Angels, being angels, did not really need bridges to cross the rivers, but many used them anyway because of their incredible craftsmanship. Each bridge was unique in some breathtaking way, and to explore the bridges and find each one's true majesty was quite enjoyable.

The oldest of all trees grew beside these rivers. The oaks and cedars and maples whose roots drank from these waters grew taller and wider than any trees Alea had ever seen on Earth: perfect light, perfect temperatures, perfect conditions, perfect trees.

The doors to the Chamber of Thrones were about halfway up the front of the wall, about level with the top of the thick oaks that stood at the building's base. A large deck stood out from the building in front of the massive granite doors, and Shamus and Alea rose to this platform. Alea had never before landed on this deck. She turned. The entire realm was spread before her. It was breathtaking. One never quite got used to perfection.

Tearing herself away from the view, she noticed Shamus had also turned. Shamus, however, was intently watching Alea, not the heavenly world beyond.

"I do not believe it is possible to stand in a better place unless we found ourselves directly in the presence of the Almighty! It is quite allowable to enjoy the moment, Alea." Shamus smiled and crossed his perfectly toned arms as if to say, *I am not leaving until you take one more look.*

For a moment, Alea considered marching right past Shamus into the Chamber, but inwardly she knew she would regret that decision later. She turned. She followed the paths of the rivers with her gaze. Purity. The word came to mind as she cross-referenced memories of rivers on Earth with the ones here. These remained totally pure. That was the difference. Another large contingent of angels led by Gabriel the Archangel entered through Eden's Gate. She watched as they were drawn directly to the temple to worship. Although definitely revived and revitalized, Alea already looked forward to her next time of worship in the temple.

"How many missions until we return again?" she asked without turning.

Expecting Shamus' voice in reply, Alea jumped slightly when the voice of Throne Aziel boomed behind her. "A question even I cannot answer. Why is it that you jump each time I approach, Virtue Alea?" The question had been asked by the human face of the Throne angel, and Alea was nearly certain a small smile had accompanied the question.

"Apparently you have a way of keeping me on my wings."

"Well, at least you did not consider drawing your sword this time," Aziel responded. The smile had definitely now returned to his human face, and Aziel laughed deeply enough to shake the entire structure they stood upon. "It is good to laugh, my dear Alea." One more deep rumble shook the deck as Aziel turned his body, but not his head. The human face still looked down upon the two visitors, but the face of the lion now became the front of the angel. Aziel began to move inside the chamber.

"Come now. We have much to discuss, and not everything we discuss will bring us joy." Aziel disappeared into the building. Alea and Shamus followed without a word.

The doorway seemed large from the exterior of the building, but as soon as Alea passed through it, all perspective changed. The Chamber's interior was enormous and made the doors, in comparison, seem insignificant. The three of them had entered from the middle of the building's height into a room that reminded Alea of a grand, earthly library. The main difference was that in this room, the décor was suited to the Thrones who were triple the size of her. A large, formal table lined the far side of the room. The side from which they had entered had lounging areas to the right and left of the main entrance that reminded Alea of the Hall of Red. The walls on the two sides of the room were filled with shelves of books and scrolls from floor to ceiling. Well, at least to the *beginning* of the ceiling.

The ceiling began about forty feet from the floor, but it was domed to a pinnacle that was at least double that height. The entire dome was a complex depiction of the universe. The Battle Realm was situated above the table at the far end of the room. It was probably three hundred feet from where Alea and Shamus stood to that point on the dome, yet it was totally clear. Above their heads was the Training Realm. The Eastern and Western Realms were off to the right and left respectively. Many of the universe's galaxies shone brightly and the three-dimensional effect of the visual masterpiece left Alea somewhat disoriented. She focused closely on the planet Earth to regain clarity before picking out each of the seven human planets scattered across the ceiling. The human planets had obviously been enlarged in a scene like this; the planet Bylar, not far from the Southern Training Realm, was nearly half the size of the entire galaxy that sat next to it. The dome was art after all. She had heard mention of it somewhere in her training. Both Alea and Shamus found it hard to look away.

At the pinnacle, right where Center Realm should have been, the dome opened. Alea could not tell what lay beyond.

"Come." The word filled the Chamber. The two visitors followed Aziel to the table. There were only two chairs designed for angels of Alea and Shamus's stature left at the table, so once Aziel had taken his spot, Alea and Shamus sat as well. A quick glance revealed fourteen others. Greetings of "Immanuel" were shared quickly, but names were not given. It was clear that Aziel intended to get right to the matter at hand.

Alea offered a quick smile to Doroniel who sat directly opposite her. A meeting like this meant decisions were going to be made that could have enormous consequences for humanity. It was an honor to be a part of it. Doroniel nodded back, but his face was serious as Aziel began to speak.

"Let me summarize the reason for this meeting. At this table are representatives from five human planets. We have reached a new age in human communications on Annaxis and Earth. People are able to connect anywhere on the planets within seconds. Information is being spread faster than ever before. The word of our Lord should be reaching more people. It is not. The enemy has hidden the power of our Lord in the minds of many. The nations with the most to give and share with their worlds are lost in themselves. Good things are being done daily, but great things are hardly even dreamed of! Fear. Passiveness. Apathy. Satanael has not relented, nor will he until the day of final judgment. The enemy has grown strong in both worlds. The demons are daring and bold. They are arrogant."

The final three words Aziel declared with a smirk. The change in inflection in his voice caught Alea's complete focus. She was sure that Aziel had paused for exactly that reason.

"I spoke directly with the Almighty just before my arrival here. Our Lord has been waiting for the moment when the enemy's arrogance could become our advantage. That time has arrived. We have been preparing for this moment for some time, but only a few understand the scope of what we are going to accomplish."

Again, Aziel paused. The eyes on Aziel's body were wide open and alive. Alea could see that at least a few eyes gazed directly at her. She found it difficult to know where to focus her own vision, but eventually found it easiest to peer into the eyes of the human face that was speaking to the silent table of angels.

"Those of you who are working on Cortu, Gazzal and Diyana were invited here because we believe your planets will be facing this same situation within a short while. Our success or failure on Earth and Annaxis will guide your future actions. Listen attentively." A number of heads nodded around the table. Alea assumed they were the representatives from Cortu, Gazzal and Diyana.

In all her studies, Alea could not remember hearing of a meeting of this magnitude in the last thousand Earth years.

Five planets.

Millions of angels.

One plan.

It was also becoming logical that there were three representatives from each of the five planets involved. And Aziel. That made sixteen. The part that was humbling and yet energizing in all this, was that if there were only three representatives from Earth at this meeting then Shamus, Doroniel and Alea were it. They were about to be let in on something huge. The same realization must have been going on for Shamus because he turned just enough to make eye contact with Alea. She could see the look of excitement.

"Do they not realize this is only my second mission?" Alea thought to herself.

"Each of you at this table have been chosen carefully," continued Aziel. Alea looked up to see nearly every eye on Aziel's body focused right at her. She had not needed to ask the question of her lack of experience audibly. It was true. You could not hide anything from a Throne.

"What I share next needs to remain unspoken after you leave this chamber. The ears of the enemy reach far. Furthermore, you will only be given the information and directives applicable to your planet in small chunks. Many small directives carried out diligently will lead to the final goal." Nods of agreement were given from all at the table.

The face of the lion took over from the human one. The lion's voice was even deeper and filled the entire chamber. "It is time to unite the believers!"

The next couple of hours were filled with questions, detailed plans, speculation on how the enemy would respond, and speculation on when the enemy would figure out what was being attempted. It became evident that the situation on Earth was further advanced then on Annaxis. The answers to many of their questions would unfold on Earth.

One thing was clear. The success or failure of the mission rested heavily on the wings of Doroniel, Alea and Shamus! There were others involved, but little else mattered if Brenden Tavis didn't come through. Brenden was their assignment!

It wasn't until later, after the visitors had left the Chamber of Thrones, that the scope of this mission sank in. For thousands of years, people on Earth had traveled to uncharted lands to find something better or to conquer more. Every mile of separation bred change. Different languages, different skin color, different food, different lives, different people. Belief in the Almighty God, the creator of the universe, however, lay deeply seeded wherever people lived.

The problem had always been communication. Stories traveled by word of mouth. Oral traditions were useful, but the further one got from the source of the tradition, the less power it held. Fights over beliefs were common. Churches split and divided in ever-increasing numbers. The people who believed in God focused more on what was different than what was the same. The result had always been fragmentation and limited success. While one group of people was making the world better and positively changing lives, another group was starting a fight and causing damage.

In a world where there was enough food for everyone, thousands were starving to death every day. In a world with the resources to create energy at will, widows were freezing to death because there was no heat. In a world with so much beauty and hope, people were committing suicide because they felt they had nothing to live for. The nations with plenty focused solely on keeping what they had or getting more. The nations where many people lacked the basic necessities of life continued to drown in poverty.

All of these things still existed, but one thing had now changed. Communication was rapidly becoming a help instead of a hindrance. The world was becoming smaller instead of larger for the first time! The internet, as the people on Earth called it, was leveling the playing field of knowledge. With a few key strokes, nearly anything could be learned nearly anywhere. Cell phones allowed people to connect at any time of day even if they lived in a different hemisphere. The vision of any given individual could be shared with millions even if it was not the vision of the government. The ramifications of these technological advances were peeling off like the layers of an onion.

Sometimes one layer had to be discovered and torn off before the next layer became visible.

One of the awesome powers of the Almighty was that He could see the heart of the onion even with the other layers in place. It was the job of the angels to help people to see what God could see, and then to give them the courage to act on that knowledge.

Throne Aziel had made it clear. God could envision believers around the Earth working together! Many incredible things had been done by individuals or small groups of people who were focused on a common goal, but the potential of what could be accomplished if millions were working together was mind staggering! What if millions prayed for the same thing? Few humans understood the true power of God and his legions of angels. People rarely asked, and consequently, they rarely received.

If they could be united.

If someone could unite them.

Brenden Tavis.

So this was the big picture. Alea now understood that what she and Shamus had begun in Corison Springs was the beginning of a larger plan. She knew Brenden was important. What she had not foreseen, was that Brenden was the one the Almighty had chosen for a task that could change thousands, if not millions, of lives on Earth. Alea and Shamus had been chosen to help carry out the Almighty's wishes in regards to Brenden. It was always fulfilling to carry out a mission. Angels offered guidance to people. They delivered messages from God to people in a variety of ways. They fought Satanael and his demons, and they protected and defended people on a regular basis. Once in many missions, however, an angel might be fortunate enough to help with something big, something vital, something world-changing. Alea was getting her chance!

After eating some fruit beside the Pool of Life, Alea found herself spinning with joy at the realization of what she had just heard. She could barely contain her enthusiasm. Shamus and Doroniel were going to be ready to leave after a few other tasks had been taken care of. This meant Alea could spend a little more time at the temple. With all the speed she could find, she flew along the river just high enough to keep from touching the surface. She went over some bridges and under others until she met the main road into the temple. She banked hard to the left and through the golden archway into the temple. The Almighty was not physically in the temple at the moment, but the Son was. There were more worshipers than Alea had seen in many visits. Excitement pulsed through each smiling face. Not many angels, Archangels, Principalities, Virtues, Dominions, Powers, Seraphim, Thrones, or Cherubim knew the details that Alea knew about the coming missions, but the atmosphere in the temple suggested that many angels knew something awesome was on the horizon. Alea joined the chant. A rush of energy filled her.

The Dominion Doroniel led the Power Shamus and the Virtue Alea out of Eden's Gate and a short while later the three were back in the Battle Realm. A sword fighting practice and a short meeting with Doroniel were soon completed. Once again Alea and Shamus headed back to Earth and the next phase of the mission. It felt like ages since the incident with Barac at Corison, but in actual Earth time, it had only been two days. Brenden and Shawna would have got home Sunday morning and done little as they recovered from the accident. It would be around noon on Monday when Shamus and Alea returned.

Shamus had said little since the meeting with Aziel, but Shamus was normally quiet, and he was not one for chatter and small talk. Alea, on the other hand, was still bubbling with excitement at the possibilities of what was to come. She just wanted to talk about it, to share her excitement.

"This is exciting," she offered in hope of a reply.

"Why?" Only one word was given in response.

"We were chosen to be a part of a mission that could be remembered for many generations of humans. You and me! How could that not be exciting?"

"How would you describe the enemy, Alea?"

"Powerful on Earth, but too confident. Our Lord is stronger."

"True . . . but not a complete description. The enemy is confident because they have controlled so many people. They might be lazy now, but how long do you think it will take before Satanael realizes what we are trying to accomplish?"

"It will take a while if we are careful."

"Yes, but he will find out! When he does, when Satanael realizes the potential damage our mission could have for him, he will unleash all the fury of the Hell he is destined for. The enemy will not remain lazy!" Shamus paused to regain his composure.

"Alea, that fury will be unleashed on you and me." Shamus lowered his head and moved far enough ahead to communicate the fact that he was done talking.

So that was why he had not shared Alea's excitement! Shamus had encountered the enemy in battle many times and had seen the ferocity of true evil. Alea had heard enough stories about Shamus and from Shamus to know that much. Before becoming a Virtue, Alea's missions as an angel rarely brought her into outright battle.

Alea knew she should be worried. She should be more concerned. But she wasn't. She was still excited.

"Bring it on, Satanael," she thought to herself. *"The Almighty is stronger and we shall win!"*

She allowed Shamus to stay ahead and allowed herself a slight smile.

The rest of the travel to Earth was uneventful.

Until they neared Alderwood.

CHAPTER EIGHT

For we do not wrestle against flesh and blood, but against the rulers, against the authorities, against the cosmic powers over this present darkness, against the spiritual forces of evil in the heavenly places.
Ephesians 6:12

Entering Earth's atmosphere sent a tingling sensation through Alea, a feeling she quite enjoyed. They had descended north of Alderwood where the snowy, mountainous Canadian landscape brought a beauty of its own. The Creator certainly knew how to mold awe-inspiring formations that left no doubt of His existence.

Something jolted her to attention. At first it was just a feeling.

She glanced at Shamus. His eyes showed that he concurred with what she felt. They hung in the air tense, alert. A deep, golden glow emanated from within. They stopped. Their blue and red swords were ready to strike. Even in the bright sun above the snow-capped Rockies the two angels gave off a light that would have been visible if anyone had been watching.

Someone was.

The darkness rose from below the two angels. As the darkness ascended, Alea began to make out the size of the attacking force. She guessed seven or eight demons. Shamus, whose experience and training made him a perfect weapon in situations like this, had already moved back-to-back with Alea and calmly gave instructions.

"There are eight. One appears to be an Archdemon. Stay close. Let them reveal their intentions before you strike."

The dark streak of demons did not slow, but continued to accelerate as they came closer. The enemy formed a wedge with their bodies and drove straight at Alea and Shamus. A glistening, black sword of the lead Archdemon approached like a spike on the tip of a bullet train.

"Move," shouted Shamus, as the two flung themselves out of the way. It took only moments for the eight black fighters to slow and turn. Alea tried to return to the side of Shamus, but she was quickly cut off. Six demon fighters attacked Shamus. Hideous shrieks echoed off the mountains below. Alea could see him pierce the first one after a rapid sequence of swordplay. Before she could see anything else, the other two were upon her. They attacked from both sides simultaneously. Alea blocked one dark sword with a quick reaction. The fighting went back and forth with little injury to either party.

Alea was beginning to gain confidence when she got the feeling she was missing something. She could glance every so often at Shamus to see how he was faring. At least two more demons had been pierced and sent back to the abyss. They would emerge again. But not for a while. Not till long after this battle had been decided. Her own opponents were not attacking with the ferocity she would have expected. It was like they were playing with her like a piece of food they were not sure they liked. Another few parries. A half-hearted attempt to strike at her. Then she knew.

But she was too slow.

More demons came.

A darkness fell over her. She could no longer see what she was slashing at. Alea was reasonably sure one swing had damaged one of the demons as she felt the penetration of her blade and a piercing shriek. Then she was moving. The demons were not here to pierce her and send her back to the Almighty. This was worse. The worst. They were trying to take her.

Seconds went by. Uncertainty. Fighting did not seem to have any effect on her adversaries anymore. Alea was securely shrouded in darkness and incapable of escape.

More seconds. Hope faded.

Then movement stopped. A swirl of red light flashed past her and the darkness dissolved for a moment.

Shamus.

Shrieks. Howls. Flashes of light mixed with the suffocating darkness. The hardest part was not being able to do anything even as the battle surrounded her on all sides. At any moment, Shamus might be pierced and it would be over.

That moment never came. In a flash that resembled lightning, the darkness was instantly gone. A glowing Shamus hovered with wings spread wide, his red sword still glimmering in his outstretched hand. His eyes remained alert. Nothing would surprise the strong Power now. Any further attack would be anticipated. Alea thought it might have to be a whole legion of the highest ranking demons to defeat her ally. He truly was a mighty angel. The thought again occurred to her. "I am glad he is on my side."

She moved to his side and not a word was spoken. The angel of Virtue and the angel of Power watched and waited for what might be another attack. None came this time, and eventually the two resumed their travel to Alderwood. They still did not speak until they were sitting within the Alderwood Evangelical Church. No one else was there on a Monday. Even Pastor Phil had Monday as a day off.

"Were you injured?" Shamus was the one to begin.

"No."

"I am glad."

"Thank you, Shamus."

"You are welcome, and fortunate. Had it taken even moments longer for me to dispose of the six demons, I would have lost sight of where they had taken you, Alea."

The thought of enemy capture and being brought into the presence of Satanael was not something Alea had sincerely thought about before. If the truth be told, she did not even know what that would be like. She knew angels of light had been captured before, but it was not something openly discussed. All she knew for certain was that it would be torturous and something she never wanted to encounter.

"How many more came?"

"Three more large demons. One was a Dominion. He fled when the others had been eliminated."

"Thank you again."

"Why, Alea?"

"Because you saved me!"

"No," Shamus replied with a slight shake of his head. "Not why did you say thank you, but why did they attack? This was a pre-planned assault aimed at capturing you, Alea. Why would they take that risk? They lost ten demons today. This was too strong an attack to be a response to our little incident in Corison. Why? What do they know, Alea?"

"Maybe they just suspect something important is happening?"

"Maybe." Shamus got up and paced in front of the church stage. Some sheet music was on the floor from Sunday's service. Pastor Phil's notes from his previous sermon remained on the pulpit. "We will have to talk to Doroniel. I do not want to fall into another trap."

"We need to be there when the pastor, the traveler, and the realtor meet."

"What if the enemy knows about that meeting, Alea? What we just fought through may have only been a small portion of the attack that is planned by the dark angels! I think we should have the meeting postponed. We can meet Maspial and Zopheniel beforehand and cause a delay. Also, we should think about bringing in a strong contingent of angels for Brenden and Shawna's protection."

"What if the enemy does not know about the meeting, Shamus? We can further the mission as was planned and then decide if we need more protection."

"I don't . . ."

"Wait!" Alea cut him off and stood to face Shamus beside the baby grand piano. "What if the enemy was just testing us? They really did not try to hurt me in that battle. I know you fought valiantly. The Almighty will be proud of you. But what if they wanted us to escape. This would not be the first time Satanael has sacrificed his demons for the bigger picture."

"Go on."

Alea was the one who began to pace now. "You said the demon Dominion fled. They tried to separate us and then they gave us a good battle, but not a great one. What if they are watching us now to see how we respond? If they do not know about the meeting, if the enemy only suspects that something big is happening, they may be looking for clues. If we send a strong protection force for Brenden, we are telling them exactly how important Brenden is to our mission. Maybe the enemy is not as lazy as we thought." With that, Alea turned and stared straight into the golden eyes of Shamus waiting for his response.

"It is possible, but what if you are wrong? The consequence could be detrimental to the entire mission. Are you willing to risk that?"

"My instinct tells me that they do not know about the meeting. I think we should move forward as though the attack never occurred. The enemy will not learn anything we did not expect them to learn."

Shamus turned to look at the cross on the front wall. He was silent for a few moments. "My instincts agree with you. Let us go." With that, Shamus leapt up and was out of sight. Alea took one last look at the cross before following Shamus to the meeting that was about to occur between the traveler, the pastor and the realtor.

CHAPTER NINE

Religion that God our Father accepts as pure and faultless is this: to look after orphans and widows in their distress and to keep oneself from being polluted by the world.
James 1:27

Amazingly the sun was still shining on Monday as Brenden and Shawna sat looking out the high windows from the dining room table. Shawna took a bite of her cinnamon/raisin bagel smothered with strawberry cream cheese and was feeling pretty much normal. One spot on the back of her head was still tender to touch, but she hadn't even needed painkillers this morning. Brenden was not faring so well. The real aches and pains from getting hit by the streetlight pole were evident as every movement he had done this morning had been slow and painful. Pastor Phil had called to say he would be by around one o'clock to see how the Tavis family was doing. He had mentioned he was bringing an old friend along.

Brenden had made some attempts to guess who it might be, but with little to go on, they figured they would find out soon enough. The kids would be getting dropped off sometime in the mid-afternoon. Brenden had called the office to cancel any appointments for the day, and then had put a message on his cell phone telling any potential home buyers or sellers that he would be unavailable for the day due to his injuries. Brenden worked closely with Alyssa Gladstone at Coastal Realty and they directed clients to each other on a regular basis. This made it much easier to take a day off now and then without the risk of losing deals. Alyssa had proven herself to be trustworthy, and they were both good at the job. A win-win deal they often called it. House sales were not usually strong in late November or December, either.

December. Holidays. The memories of the night before with Matt and Marci came rushing back to Brenden. In four weeks they would be leaving on a cruise! For years, Shawna had dreamed of spending Christmas somewhere warm. Hawaii. Mexico. The Caribbean. Those had been the reasonable options. The trip with small children in tow, however, had lost some of its appeal. Now that the kids were getting older, they were much easier to leave with their grandparents! Secretly, Shawna had been considering a trip sometime in the next year, and had even looked up some prices online.

The gift from Matt and Marci was perfect! Christmas. Free. Soon! All were words neither Brenden nor Shawna could argue with. They would miss the kids' Christmas program. Tyler was a shepherd. Rachel and Amanda were angels singing in the choir. They would also have to make sure Mom and Dad could take the kids. As far as Shawna could tell, though, those were the only real difficulties to deal with. She hadn't paid attention when Matt had described where they would actually be making port stops, but she didn't care. It would be warm. She would be with her husband. They wouldn't be worried about how much they were spending!

The doorbell rang. A quick glance at the clock on the microwave revealed that it was 12:56 PM. The pastor and his friend had arrived. Brenden laboriously stood up, and Shawna threw the few remaining dishes in the dishwasher before she went to greet their guests.

Pastor Phil came in with Jerry Moore. Jerry and Brenden had become good friends, but it had been a number of years since they had seen each other. After hugs all the way around, Brenden, Shawna, Phil and Jerry poured coffee and caught up on each other's lives while standing in the kitchen.

The angels Shamus, Alea, Maspial and Zopheniel were already in the living room discussing their hopes for the meeting that was about to occur. Shamus had relayed all the pertinent information from the meeting with Throne Aziel and their unexpected attack above the mountains with Maspial and Zopheniel.

"The plan is to unite thousands of believers around the globe?" Maspial repeated with joyful hope.

"It is about time!" Zopheniel yelled out at the news. "Satanael has had too much control. Far too many people suffer needlessly on Earth. The possibilities of what *could* be done are exciting!"

"Does Jerry buy into this fully?" asked Shamus.

"I think so. He doesn't see how big this could be yet, but he believes it is worth beginning. He can be very persuasive when he wants something. That is one of the reasons he was chosen for this," answered Maspial. "I have been assigned to Jerry for three years. He has become a man of his word, and his faith is strong."

"And Phil?" Shamus now addressed Zopheniel.

"He knows Jerry is excited, and the pastor won't stand in the way of any plan that could make the world better and help people. I was assigned to Phil about three years ago as well. I wonder if the Almighty had this in mind back then." Zopheniel looked at each of the other three angels waiting for a response.

"Of that, there is no doubt," came the reply from a voice behind Alea. As seemed to be happening often lately, Alea jumped. The Principality Angel, Ramuel, had entered imperceptibly. "The Almighty has had many things in motion previous to your meeting with Throne Aziel yesterday. Maspial and Zopheniel, you were specifically chosen three years ago to watch over Jerry and Phil. Brenden was chosen more recently. That is why you, Alea and Shamus, were only added to the mission now. The faith and actions of many men and women have been evaluated to see who will be ready to help when the time comes for specific parts of the mission to be accomplished."

Ramuel glanced over at the three men and one woman laughing around the table. "Perhaps you should know that there is a dark Dominion and a demon angel sitting next door. They are watching, but they do not dare come close enough to hear what is being said. I think Shamus' sword would scare off a legion of them."

"Do you know of the attack on Alea and Shamus?" Zopheniel asked.

"When? Recently?"

"Less than an hour ago," responded Alea who had been taking in as much of the conversation as she could. "If not for Shamus' sword, I would be in the hands of the enemy at this very moment."

"Alea believes they were testing us to see how we would respond. There is a chance that they wanted us to escape, but they did not want it to look that way. I pierced ten demons in the battle. Only a dark Dominion escaped."

"Considering what I saw outside, you may have been correct, Alea. Am I right in assuming you have already discussed what happened in detail with Zopheniel and Maspial?"

"Yes."

"And how do you propose we respond?"

Alea waited a moment to see if one of the others would respond before answering Ramuel herself. "We agreed that any major response in the way of extra protection for Brenden and Shawna would give the enemy the clue they may be looking for. We believe that they suspect something big is happening with Brenden, but that they do not yet understand how to attack. Our intervention in Corison was not that unusual, but it will have put the enemy on alert. At the moment, if we ignore the attack and continue with the mission as planned, it will add confusion to what we are doing."

"I would concur, Virtue Alea. Your intuition serves you well. It is possible that they already know more. If they do, Brenden and his family could be in serious danger of attack. But, if that were the case, why did they attack the two of you instead of going straight after Brenden? I think you have deduced correctly and I stand by your decision. Now, let's get this meeting moving. I have to be back with the President before he leaves the White House for a dinner engagement."

The five angels turned their attention to the people in the room. Maspial moved close behind Jerry and voiced the words, "It is time, Jerry."

Pastor Phil was finishing a story about a time when he had dragged Jerry out of a bar on one of his drinking binges. He had asked a large muscled, heavily tattooed

Harley rider to help him get Jerry to the minivan. When the Harley guy had hesitated, Phil had looked him straight in the eyes and said, "I am a pastor of the local church. If you don't help me now, I can't guarantee what God's judgment might be, but I wouldn't want to be you!" Nobody argued with Pastor Phil. Not even a Harley rider. When the laughter subsided, Jerry felt the urge to talk about the real reason he was along for this visit.

"Hey, there's something else I would like to ask you two about."

"You are moving back to Alderwood for a while and need to buy a house?" questioned Brenden with a mixed tone of hope and sarcasm.

"Ahh, probably not. But I do need your help."

"Well, now I am curious."

"Me too," Shawna added.

"Are you too sore to move to the living room?" Jerry added looking at Brenden.

"I think I can handle it as long as you guys stop making me laugh."

After a few coffee refills, the meeting moved to the living room. Jerry wasn't sure why he wanted to have this discussion in the living room. Somehow it felt like this was really important and he didn't want anyone to take what he was about to ask lightly. Everyone fell into a chair. It became strangely quiet. All eyes went back to Jerry.

"Good," he began. "I wanted to make sure that you understand what I am asking you. I have already shared some of this idea with Phil." Phil nodded in agreement, but his expression didn't change. He, too, seemed to be waiting to hear what would come next.

"As I have traveled extensively across this globe in the last years, I have become keenly aware of some things.

They are things I had heard of before, but sometimes "seeing is believing". I met a young girl in India named Mandi. She was a cheerful, bright, young girl with a joy for life. Her parents were not her real parents, not her biological parents. They had found her. Mandi had been buried to her head in the sand behind the market where they sold their goods. She was only days old. Her parents-to-be had not heard her; she had already lost the energy to cry. They simply stumbled across her on their way home. She had been left to die because she was a girl. When there isn't enough money in a family to take care of many children, it is common for parents to abandon little girls. In their culture, a boy is far more valuable. He will be able to make money easier. He will carry on the family name. This little girl was given a second chance because the right people found her at exactly the right time. If they had not come, she would have withered in the hot, Indian sun like a plant without water. She would have died in only a few hours."

"Why would the parents have buried her only to her head if they wished her to die?" asked Shawna with solemnity.

"Imagine your own child, Shawna. Would you have the heart to throw the sand that would ultimately complete the murder? Somehow, it is easier to leave the child with a slim hope that they might survive. The nightmares must be less gruesome. In this case, it did save the child's life, but few people in India would have taken the child even if they had found her alive." Jerry paused as his eyes clouded over, the memories clear and real in his mind. That girl had taught him what it truly meant to live. What he could teach her seemed to be of little importance in comparison.

"I met many widowed ladies in Eastern Europe who have no family to take care of them and there is no social service network of any kind to provide for them. Many of these ladies cannot pay for heat in the cold winters. They sit at home trying not to freeze to death, trying not to starve to death. They are alone. Only a few dollars a month could pay for heat and allow them to eat properly. So many men died in the wars in Eastern Europe! What are these women to do?"

"Orphanages are closing down because they are overrun with children and there is no funding from governments in many third world countries." Jerry paused, lost in thought. Images of helpless children were flashing through his memories. Images he could not forget. Images he was choosing to do something about.

"27000 children died today. In Africa, a child dies every 30 seconds because of malaria which is easily preventable and treatable. Kids like Tyler, Rachel and Amanda." Jerry pointed at the family photo on the fireplace mantle. "Do you believe your children are more special to you than many of those children were to their parents?"

Brenden and Shawna shook their heads slowly as Jerry went on.

"Half of all the hospital beds in the world are filled with people because of water-borne diseases! Fresh, clean water could empty half the hospital beds on the planet and the water is there to do it with the right resources!"

"We won the lottery, guys! That is it. We are not more special. We are not more loved by God. We were born into a wealthy country. The 27000 who died today of starvation weren't."

"On the other hand, the world produces more than enough food for the entire population of the Earth. The cost of providing the basics of life for everyone . . . everyone on Earth who doesn't have it . . . is estimated to be about $40 billion a year. I know that number is a few years old, but it can't have changed much. It would give them a chance."

"In North America, we spend double that on dog food, and could meet the bill with the money we spend on dieting programs. That's not even mentioning what we spend on the military or golf or ice cream or perfume or cosmetics. Europe spends more than enough to pay for it on cigarettes! God has given the planet the means to provide for everyone, and paying for it would hardly affect the lifestyles of the wealthy, developed nations!" No one else spoke. Solemn nods of agreement were offered now and then. Men and angels waited to hear what would come next.

"I know you have heard some of these things before." More nods. "And there are some organizations out there that are changing lives and helping people." Jerry took a moment to gaze into the eyes of each person. First Phil. Then Shawna. Then Brenden. "I would like us to do something about this."

"Like starting an organization of some sort?" Brenden asked.

"Well, yes. And no."

"That makes it clear," interjected Shawna with a smile.

"I believe God wants us to start a movement! It will need a name. It will have to be organized. But, I want it to be simple enough, that with a little coordination and help, it can grow way beyond anything the world has ever seen."

"What if we could start something where people, churches, communities, and clubs in the developed nations partner up with people or churches or communities in countries where people are dying needlessly? Not just once, but on an ongoing basis. In North America alone, there are hundreds of thousands of churches. Can you imagine what could happen if each church just took on one project. Our church in Alderwood could help with a community of widows. The church around the corner from us could take on an orphanage in Africa as a partner. Hundreds of thousands of groups. If each church helped only 10 people with the basics of life this project could change the lives of millions! Millions! I haven't even included communities that get together, or other wealthy nations in Europe and Asia and around the world. It could be done. . . Brenden, Shawna, Phil. We could change the world!"

"Wow." Brenden uttered the word only to erase the silence.

"I thought at first you were going to ask us about something big," Shawna added with heavy sarcasm. "You know, an investment in some company, or maybe traveling with you somewhere. But all you want to do is change the world! That's a huge relief!"

It was Phil's turn to comment. "My first reaction was similar, Shawna. The whole idea is pretty far-fetched. It seems idealistic, not realistic. It seems too big, too huge, to even begin. I figured someone must have tried this before. And failed. But. But. I am sure the disciples thought it was impossible to feed the 5000 with a few loaves of bread and some fish. I am sure the Israelite army in the Old Testament thought it was impossible to break through the walls of Jericho. I am sure they believed it would be impossible for David to beat Goliath. These things were all impossible except for one important factor. God. With God all things are possible. Jerry feels confident that God has called him to begin this. I can't answer for you guys, but as for me? Who am I to stand against the Almighty?"

"Well spoken," answered Zopheniel after listening to the pastor. "And I see what you mean about Jerry being persuasive, Maspial. How could the Tavis' turn this down?"

"I agree, but men are unpredictable. We shall soon see."

"Wow." Brenden again wasn't sure how to respond. "So, what is it that you are asking us, Jerry? Why is this discussion happening here on my couch?"

"I have spent many hours thinking, praying, doubting and then believing in this idea, Brenden. In order for this to be successful, I believe we need a foundation that will not crack. I believe God will bless this. That is the most important. I also believe we need key leadership in a couple of areas. I believe my strength in this is my network of friends and associates around the globe. I have met political leaders. I have met church leaders. I have worked around red tape. I have experienced many cultures. It will take a great many partners to exhaust the need I already have connections to."

"Pastor Phil. I know you asked me that same question yesterday, and I asked you to wait until today to hear the answer. You are a respected man, Phil. You are a Godly man. I am asking you to be the spiritual leader on this team. The one to keep us focused on what is important. The one to keep us humble. The one to connect us to other churches. The one to be a mentor for those who join our team as it grows. I know of no one else I would rather have fulfill that role." Jerry didn't wait for a response before turning his attention to the Tavis'.

"An international correspondent." Jerry pointed at his chest. "A mentor and local correspondent." A nod at Phil. "And, a leader to rally behind. The face of the team. The inspirational speaker. Someone with great people skills. Someone with great presentation skills. Someone we trust. You, Brenden. I believe God wants that to be you."

It wasn't really a question. It was a statement that Jerry let hang in the air. All eyes were on Brenden now.

The angels were standing in the back. "It is God's will." Ramuel's words reverberated around the room.

"Wow!" Brenden looked at Shawna with questioning eyes, hoping for insight. He had a deep desire to yell, "Yes. I'll do it!" His heart told him that it should be an easy decision. Who am I to stand against the Almighty? Those were the words Phil had used. His brain took over, however.

"I have so many questions. When? How much time will this take? What about my job? Will I have to travel?" Brenden's brain rolled through obstacle after obstacle.

"I was hoping to sleep soundly tonight," Shawna began. "So much for that! You have given us lots to think about."

Jerry leaned forward and looked closely at Shawna. Her eyes met his. She held his gaze. "Do you believe God can do it?" Jerry asked.

"I have no doubt of that, Jerry. It is not God that I doubt. It is myself. You are asking us to change many things. You are asking us to give up our security. I don't know if we can do it."

"Just say you will try. Trust God for the rest. Are you willing to say yes? Shawna? Brenden? Just say yes."

A battle was raging inside of Brenden. He had just spent two nights thinking about what was really important. He had nearly been killed less than 48 hours earlier. Life was short. Life was fleeting. He could feel that this was right. It was as if God was right there asking him to do it.

He glanced at Shawna. Her face was serious. Could he do this to his family without thinking it through? He would be changing careers. Where would the money come from?

Brenden gave the easy-way-out answer. "We will have to think about it. We will have to pray about it." Shawna nodded in agreement with him.

"As much as I would like to hear you commit now, I guess I could wait until tomorrow."

"Tomorrow? That is not much time, Jerry. Why the rush?" Shawna did not like to make important decisions quickly. The last time they had rushed a decision, they had bought a vacation timeshare. It had taken only hours to regret the decision. It had taken months and the loss of several thousand dollars to get out of it. Surely this was more important than a timeshare.

"Look, Jerry. We will discuss it. We will pray about it. We have only three weeks until we leave on a cruise over Christmas. We have a bunch of things to do between now and then. We haven't even started Christmas shopping! The trip will give us a full week to be alone as a couple and come to a decision. What do you think, Brenden? Can we have a decision by the New Year?"

"What trip is she talking about?" Ramuel asked the other angels.

"I don't know? We have been watching Brenden and Shawna for weeks. There has been no mention of a trip," Alea replied.

"I thought we were free of distractions," Shamus added. "The enemy has not been allowed near them. I don't know what she is talking about! The angels who stood guard here over the past two days left quickly when we returned and we did not debrief. It is possible this development happened while we were in Center Realm."

"I didn't know you were going on a cruise," responded the pastor. "Where are you going?"

"It will be in the Caribbean. I actually can't remember the ports, can you Brenden?"

"I think Cozumel, Grand Cayman and the Bahamas. We were just given the trip as a gift yesterday. Can you believe that? Quite a Christmas present!"

"Now it is my turn to say it," replied Jerry. "Wow! Who gives cruises as Christmas presents? Santa Claus?"

"It's from our friends Matt and Marci. Matt earned the cruise as a bonus at work, but they are going to Chicago to visit Matt's family and couldn't use it. I guess we looked pathetic and needy after the accident. They had pity on us or something."

"That's exciting . . . but . . . I really feel strongly that we should get the ball rolling before the New Year." Jerry stood and was pacing now. "Can we at least agree to meet in the next couple weeks and begin discussing details of how this might work? It might help you make your decision."

"That sounds fair, doesn't it Shawna? We meet a few times to get a better idea of what this will look like before we commit fully. Then we go on the trip and make our final decision."

Shawna nodded in agreement.

"Christmas is a busy time of year," remarked Phil. "If we can get through all the Christmas programs and dinners, maybe we will be in a better frame of mind in the New Year anyway."

"The irony gets me every year." Zopheniel was pacing now as well. "The biggest distraction the enemy has put in place is Christmas! Celebrating Christ's birth is important, but when the celebrating takes all the energy for the month, nothing else of importance gets done. Once again, good things will happen, but great things are put on hold."

"Satanael is wise and cunning," agreed Ramuel. "In fact, I believe he has interfered in our absence. What do we know about Matt and Marci?"

"They have been friends with the Tavis' for a number of years. They get together occasionally. Matt and Marci do not yet believe in the Almighty. We have had little to do with them. They do stretch the moral boundaries of Brenden and Shawna." Shamus looked at Alea as if to ask, "Is there anything else?"

Alea shook her head but added, "I have not seen immediate demonic activity around Matt and Marci. I was not all that concerned about them. I believe Brenden and Shawna have influenced Matt and Marci enough that they have at least begun to consider that the Almighty exists."

"Do you recognize the smaller demon outside, Shamus or Alea?" questioned Ramuel.

Alea and Shamus disappeared outside for a moment. They returned within seconds. "We have not seen him before now. Either he is newly assigned to interfere here, or he has been extremely careful to avoid detection," reported Shamus.

"The timing of the trip as a gift," continued Alea, "is too perfect. I would guess that the enemy has been ready to use Matt and Marci as a distraction for some time. I should have recognized that potential!"

All five angels stood silent now. The meeting in the living room was done. The traveler and the pastor were leaving. The next meeting had been set for Thursday morning.

"What now?" Alea asked the question almost apologetically.

Maspial drew himself up to his full height and spread his wings wide. Maspial's silver sword started to glow as he pulled it from his side. "I say we pay our two demon neighbors a visit."

Maspial was already leaving when the voice of Shamus stopped him. "No. Not now, Maspial. We agreed not to react strongly. I still do not believe that the enemy knows the nature of our mission. They knew we had a meeting. They know we were all present here. By now they may have even spotted Ramuel. We must not give them any other clues as to the importance of this mission. Although I would love to interrogate them and turn them into vapor, I do not think it would be wise."

Maspial descended and folded back his silvery wings. "I do not like it, but you are right, Shamus. I will accompany the traveler home. Immanuel." With that, Maspial was gone. Zopheniel quickly followed the pastor. Ramuel left for his presidential dinner engagement.

Alea and Shamus remained alone in the living room. They said nothing. Doroniel would be visiting by the end of the day. Until then, no demon would trespass without detection. With folded arms, the angel sentries waited and watched.

CHAPTER TEN

Be alert and of sober mind. Your enemy the devil prowls around like a roaring lion looking for someone to devour.
1 Peter 5:8

Only minutes after sitting on the Tavis' neighbor's roof, the dark Dominion demon reported back to his superiors as he had been ordered to do. It was night. A wisp of a moon appeared between passing clouds as the gathering of demonic leaders debriefed. They were high in the Himalayas. Places like this were far from the paths of passing angels.

"What is there to report?" asked a large, high-ranking angel of darkness. The words demanded an answer with substance.

The dark Dominion named Ygal stepped forward. "We ambushed the Virtue and the Power as planned. The rest of my team was destroyed."

"They were not important."

It was a simple statement, but when next Ygal spoke, there was a hint of nervousness in his usually deep voice. "We followed the angels to a nearby church. Soon after, they met with three other angels at the house of Brenden Tavis. A pastor and the traveler, Jerry Moore, were also at the house. Harpan and I waited and watched. When the meeting was over, the pastor left with his angel, the traveler left with his angel, and the Power and Virtue angels remained to guard the house. When the activity was over and it was clear nothing more would be happening soon, I left Harpan alone and came straight here."

"No other reinforcements were sent?"

"None, Master Kilael."

"Did you recognize the fifth angel?"

"We did not see him arrive, and it was only because of our careful surveillance that we caught a glimpse of him leaving. We were not close enough to identify him. I believe that was his intention."

"Were the angels aware of your presence, Ygal?"

"Yes."

Kilael looked skyward. His lips stuck out and his eyes narrowed as he considered the information. "No reinforcements. They did not attack you, even though they were aware of your presence. They will now be aware that we interfered with Brenden and Shawna's Christmas plans. Yet . . . no reaction." Again, the giant demon's lips tightened and he looked up. "What do you believe this means?" This time the question was directed at all those in attendance. The demons shifted nervously, glancing around to see who would dare answer.

The demon Barac stood directly across from the one in charge. "They are planning something, but they are weak." His words were rough, slurred. "We should attack the Power and the Virtue quickly. With them removed, the threat will be reduced."

Kilael moved a step closer to Barac. Their eyes met. Barac could not will himself to look away. "They are weak, you say? Have you forgotten that the blonde Virtue gave you that limp before you scurried away like a coward?"

"No, Master."

"Perhaps it is revenge you are after, then?" Barac gave no response. "Perhaps you would like to lead that assault, Barac?" Kilael was now only inches from Barac, their dark eyes locked on each other.

Barac issued no reply. Kilael stepped back and looked at the rest of the dark angels. The Dominion Ygal stepped forward again. "Either the Tavis couple is less important than we anticipated, or the angels are trying to hide something from us. We should continue to watch their activity before determining our course of action, Master."

Kilael relaxed slightly. "Have Harpan continue to monitor the Tavis couple, but we will watch the pastor and the traveler even closer. We need to hear what they are planning. Make sure the Tavis' go on that vacation. I will talk to Lord Satanael. Barac, do not disappoint me again." After sneering at the grotesque demon, Kilael, second in command only to Satanael himself, was gone.

Wednesday afternoon, an eighteen-year-old girl walked into the Starbucks in Alderwood. She sat down with her caramel Frappuccino and spent the next hour watching music videos in the dark, back corner near the restrooms. Years of abuse and a train of foster homes had left her empty. She felt unwanted, worthless.

The demon that possessed her was careful not to draw attention in her direction. The young girl would easily be aroused and amused by the Internet for the better part of an hour. The scraggly, feminine demon could listen without distraction.

Pastor Phil downed two lattes as he and Jerry talked at the next table. They had plenty to talk about in regards to Jerry's idea and decided to meet one more time before the Thursday meeting with Brenden and Shawna. Three other demons were causing a disturbance in the parking lot. The angels Zopheniel and Maspial were taking care of it.

The scraggly demon heard every word of the conversation between Pastor Phil and the traveler Jerry and then reported back to Ygal with more than enough detail to determine the importance of Brenden and Shawna Tavis to the angels.

Three weeks passed quickly for Brenden, Shawna, Tyler, Rachel and Amanda. Christmas presents were purchased. The Christmas play was prepared for at church. Amazingly, three real estate deals were closed.

An early Christmas celebration was held at Shawna's parent's house. Turkey, mashed potatoes, and about a thousand other dishes were devoured at rapid rates. The table was cleared and the dishes were done while the children waited for what seemed like days. The opening of presents eventually followed, as did chocolate and lemon meringue pie. This year, for the first time, the kids went to bed at Grandpa and Grandma's once the excitement of the gifts had subsided.

Brenden and Shawna returned home alone, finished packing and went to bed for a few hours. They had to be at Sea-Tac Airport by 6:30 AM to make their flight to Miami. Nothing unusual happened outside of the usual line-ups and delays all the way across the continent, and Brenden and Shawna found themselves lying spread-eagle on the fluffy, soft, white blankets in their cruise ship cabin before they really slowed down. It was hot and sunny outside. The kids were thousands of miles away. There was nothing that had to be done for at least seven days.

When the cabin steward knocked on the door to deliver their luggage, Brenden and Shawna had to ask him to come back later. The cabin steward was quite accustomed to this request, even if Brenden and Shawna felt a little embarrassed by it.

It didn't take many seconds to forget about the interruption.

It took most of day one to explore the massive ship. Brenden and Shawna booked side-by-side massages in the spa for the day two. They had talked about doing this many times before, but could never justify spending the money. With the trip costing them nothing except what they spent on extras, they decided this was the perfect opportunity. Brenden's injuries were healed enough that he was fairly confident it would be enjoyable and not painful.

They had had so many drinks and snacks by the time their assigned dinner seating came, Shawna almost convinced Brenden to skip the formal dinner. When it came down to the final decision, however, they were both excited to see what it would be like. Everyone they knew who had ever been on a cruise came back bragging about the food, as much as you could eat, with a great selection, and excellent service. How could you pass that up even if you weren't hungry?

After changing into more formal attire, the happy couple arrived at the dining room just as the doors were opening. Brenden had brought his newest suit. It was black with a lavender shirt and he had even bought a new tie.

Shawna had bought a long, navy blue gown for a fundraising banquet before babies had had the audacity to change her body shape. This was the first time she had been able to wear it again. Even Shawna had to admit it looked great on her. Something about the fancy clothes gave them both a sense of confidence, and Shawna loved having heels that clicked. Brenden noticed a few turned heads of guests checking out the babe in the blue dress. He didn't mind.

They were escorted to their round table on the left edge of the dining room right up against the windows. Seeing as they were the first guests to arrive at this table, they chose seats that gave them the best view of the Caribbean Sea.

A middle-aged couple with their two teenage daughters joined the table a few minutes later. The conversation flowed easily, and by the time anyone had opened a menu Brenden and Shawna had made new friends. The Argyris family was from San Diego, and they owned a jewelry shop. The girls were in grade 10 and grade 12. They spoke English, Greek, French and Spanish, and they were on their seventh cruise.

Brenden was having an internal debate about whether to order the steak or the prime rib when he was interrupted by a voice over his shoulder.

"I hear the fried sea urchin is the best!"

Brenden swung around so fast he nearly knocked over his water glass. "Matt? Marci? What. . ."

"Are we doing here?" Matt finished the sentence. "Going on a cruise, of course! Now let us sit down already!" Matt and Marci sat at the last two spots at the table, and introductions were exchanged with the Argyris family.

"So when did this happen?" asked Shawna. "How long have you known about this? Did you plan this from the beginning?"

"I wish we had," answered Marci, "because this is going to be fun, but we actually only booked ourselves onto this cruise two days ago. We were supposed to go to Chicago to be with Matt's family, but his Mom's mom, Grandma, had a stroke. So, his parents are going to Boston to stay with Grandma in the hospital. At this point they didn't know how long they would be there, or whether Grandma would make it through this. The whole family discussed it on a conference call, and we decided to postpone our get-together until we knew how Granny was doing." She flitted her eyelashes. "Surprise?"

"Yes, but that means you had to pay for your own trip, while we are using your free one."

"Stop!" Matt jumped back into the conversation. "We knew that would come up, and after this conversation, I do not want to hear you mention it again. My parents felt so bad about bailing on Christmas that they gave each of their kids a hefty cash Christmas present. In fact, it was hefty enough, that it more than covered the cost of our trip. So, Merry Christmas to all of us." Matt raised his water glass and everyone joined in tinkling his or her glasses. Even the Argyris family joined the toast.

"I suppose you just *happened* to end up at our table, too?" Brenden asked skeptically.

"Well, Matt worked some magic by flirting with the hostess, and we lucked out. The couple that was supposed to sit here happened to ask where this table was as we were talking to the hostess. Matt gave them a tear-inspiring speech about surprising our best friends that we hadn't seen in such a long time. They couldn't say no. They are sitting on the opposite side of the dining room where we were supposed to be. Sometimes things work out perfectly."

"I think it is time to order a bottle of wine. Then we can toast for real," added Shawna.

The table server happened to be bringing out the first salads and heard Shawna's request. "What kind of wine are you thinking of, my lady?" he said with a slight bow.

"Something red, yummy and expensive."

"Oh, I have just the wine for you. I shall be right back." Marcel, the server, was quickly gone and quickly back.

He fulfilled the same request a few more times before dinner was over.

CHAPTER ELEVEN

So, because you are lukewarm—neither hot nor cold—I am about to spit you out of my mouth.
Revelation 3:16

"Do you think they will say yes when this is all over?" asked Shamus as he leaned over the railing of the cruise ship. Brenden was reading a fantasy novel on the tanning deck wearing nothing but his blue swim trunks. Shawna had barely moved in an hour as she was taking in the Caribbean sun on the chair beside him.

Alea waited a bit before answering. People were still unpredictable. "I think so. They both seemed excited about it at their last meeting with Jerry and Phil. The cruise will be distracting, but I think they know it is the right thing to do. I am glad we will know soon. If Brenden rejects the proposal, the entire project will be greatly delayed. The timing is right. Now. Not in another year."

Neither one spoke for several minutes. Matt and Marci strolled up. Each had a slushy, fruity drink with a plastic umbrella sticking out of it. Matt was polishing off a pastry. They pulled up two more chairs, removed any unnecessary articles of clothing, and joined Brenden and Shawna in the task of sun tanning.

Alea spoke first this time. "Are these two a threat?"

"As long as we keep the enemy away, I do not think they are a threat. There have been no attacks since that night above the mountains. Only that one demon watches from the neighbor's rooftop. I think the enemy has lost interest at this point. I wanted to destroy the dark Dominion and the watching demon that night, but you were right. No reaction appears to have been the correct response. Doroniel, Ramuel, Zopheniel, and Maspial all agree. There has been nothing to give cause for concern."

"Although I still believe that we made the right choice, I wish there were more angels with us here. I know you could fight off a legion on your own, Shamus, but what if Satanael sends two legions. I would be more confident if we had seen a little *more* interest from the enemy over the last few weeks. The enemy has been too quiet." Alea flew inches above the sun-tanners. She locked her eyes on Brenden. "Make the choice. Do something great. Trust the Almighty, Brenden Tavis." The words were not spoken loudly. Alea had spoken them clearly. She longed for Brenden to see what God could see. He would have so much more drive. And faith. Faith would bring about enough courage to at least begin the task. Faith would bring the courage to say 'yes'.

Brenden put his book down and stared out over the deck at the gently rolling sea. This was definitely the best trip he had ever been on. He had dreamed of doing something like this for years. Sunscreen and December were two terms that didn't go together in the Northwest, but as the ship neared Cozumel, the two words were as common together as peanut butter and jelly.

One thing could have been better.

When Shawna had suggested leaving the decision about Jerry and Phil's venture until after the cruise, it had felt like the right call. What Brenden didn't anticipate was the fact that he would be thinking about one of the biggest decisions in his life during the cruise. At this moment, it was hard to fully relax because the final decision had not yet been made. Brenden could leave work behind. He wouldn't even lose a minute of vacation thinking about work. He would miss the kids, but even they would not take up much of his thought. But until he and Shawna had fully committed to join Jerry and Phil, which he was leaning toward at this moment, Brenden knew he wouldn't fully relax.

It would make the most sense to just make the decision. Do it now and enjoy the rest of the trip. Right? There was not much point in dragging it out. He glanced at the motionless Shawna beside him. She wasn't losing any sleep over it! It was only an hour until their massage appointments. Brenden decided to bring it up with Shawna after the massages. Maybe they could even discuss it on the way to the massages. Why not make a great massage into a fantastic massage! Brenden got up and stretched his arms to the cloudless sky.

"Nice stripes buddy!" Matt was pointing at Brenden's back. The white lounge chair had left a perfect pattern on Brenden's skin. Brenden looked a bit like a dog trying to get his own tail as he spun around trying to get a better look at his backside.

"Don't you worry. In about an hour, some beautiful, Swedish babe is going to massage all those lines right out of my back. I figured they would make her job more interesting. All those non-striped backs must get pretty boring after a while."

Matt stood up and turned his back to Brenden. "When your back is rippling muscle after rippling muscle like mine, it never gets boring, Mr. Stripes. I can make zose Swedish girls say "ya, I like you" by just flexing." Matt's Swedish woman accent was surprisingly good.

"That's just pity in their eyes, Mr. No-stripes. They just look at your plain, boring skin and wish they could see my stripes again." Brenden followed up his banter with a mocking flex of his own muscles, and then kissed his bicep for good measure.

"If you two don't stop your pathetic proclamations, I know at least two American chicks who are going to throw you over that railing and enjoy those massages on your behalf. Shawna, would you be opposed to woman-only massages?" There was a hint of playfulness, but also a hint of seriousness in Marci's threat.

Shawna, who had been listening to at least portions of the previous conversation, responded without opening her eyes. "It doesn't really matter to me. If there is a blonde, Swedish masseuse, I am taking her. She isn't touching my man. I like stripes!"

"You're pathetic, too," was all Marci could manage.

"Thank you, Mrs. My-Man-Has-No-Stripes."

Without hesitation, Marci was up off her chair. "That's it, woman. Never insult my stripeless man." This was followed by a steady stream of suntan lotion that quickly created white stripes all over Shawna. Shawna didn't move. She just waited . . . and waited . . . until more air was coming out of the suntan lotion container than lotion.

Both husbands, and anyone close to them on the deck, merely stood back and watched. There were many smiles, but no one spoke. Anticipation of Shawna's reaction kept them glued to the scene.

Shawna looked around, slowly. Then she stood up. She took her towel off the chair. Shawna surveyed her surroundings, and then stuck her nose in the air. "I am the white-striped wife of my back-striped husband and we are too good for these unstriped peasants. Let us return to our quarters before we catch their plainness disease." Brenden paused only a moment before raising his nose a little higher and walking beside his coconut-smelling wife. He spoke the only words that were appropriate.

"Yes, dear."

The two paraded down the center of the deck. Their noses were high, and each step was deliberate. It resembled a runway walk at a fashion show.

The Tavis' disappeared through some glass doors to the sound of laughter and applause.

By the time Shawna had finished her shower to remove the excess globs of sunscreen, there were barely enough minutes for the two of them to make their way to the spa. They were ushered into a room with two massage tables, soothing Caribbean music, soft light and the smell of relaxation. Husband and wife took off what needed taking off and climbed under the warm blankets on their respective massage tables. They had time to smile at each other briefly before the two therapists came in: both females, American, not Swedish. They were pleasant to look at, but not the stereotypical drop-dead gorgeous blondes that Matt and Brenden had been fantasizing about.

Brenden was somewhat concerned that he had not had a chance to talk to Shawna about "the decision" before the massages. His concern, however, was unfounded. With the music and sheer delight of the firm, yet soft hands massaging his body, "the decision" never crossed his mind for the next sixty minutes. Or during dinner that night. Or during the show after dinner. Even when Brenden's head hit his pillow on the extremely comfortable bed in their room, the slight rocking of the boat mixed with the few drinks in his system threw his mind into deep sleep before any other concerns could enter his mind.

He thought about it a couple times the next day, and the next two days after that. But there were so many excursions to experience, foods to try, shows to see, shops to check out and stripe inflicting chairs to lounge on, that it never felt like the right time to discuss "the decision" with Shawna. Maybe she had been right in the first place. Take the trip. Go home. Make the final decision when real life was about to set back in. Move on.

They would be on their way back home in two days.

If he wanted to join Jerry and Phil in changing the world, surely Shawna wouldn't stand in the way.

After all this time, what difference would two more days make?

CHAPTER TWELVE

In later times some will abandon the faith and follow deceiving spirits and things taught by demons.
1 Timothy 4:1

The demons had moved onto the ship while it was in port in the Grand Caymans. They had come up from below the depths into the lower levels of the ship. A large, battle-ready group waited for the signal from their Dominion Captain, Ygal.

"How long until we attack?" mumbled a strong, dark demon who was obviously tired of waiting.

"Ygal said it would be near the end of the day before all the pieces were in place. That could be soon. Now quit grumbling," responded Barac who was assigned to lead the attack.

Barac was proven correct as Ygal entered the bottom of the ship ninety seconds later. The group of forty dark angels rose. Many had their swords drawn. The flat, blackness of the blades sucked away what little light there was in the room. Ygal stared blankly at the demons before addressing them.

"I only want to say this once. It is imperative that we are unified in this mission. Any mistake could have you turned to vapor. Or worse. *Your* mistake could get *me* turned to vapor. Do you understand?" His dark eyes scanned the anxious looking force in front of him. Nods of approval were barely visible in the dark. Confirming grunts echoed on the steel around them.

"I think we have found a way to separate the couples. The angels have not yet noticed us. Only the Power named Shamus and the Virtue named Alea are watching the Tavis couple. They still believe that we are ignorant. They still believe that they can fool us by pretending. They are wrong! Tonight we will attack the trust in Brenden and Shawna's relationship. When that has been accomplished, we will attack everything else important to Brenden and Shawna Tavis. They will not join the traveler and the preacher. They will do nothing!" Ygal spoke the words slowly and carefully.

"We will break their dreams. We will destroy their visions. The Earth belongs to us! This is our domain! We will win enough souls, and gain enough power to fight off God himself! Hail Lord Satanael! Hail Lord Satanael!" By now the forty dark soldiers were chanting with their Dominion leader. They continued until he raised his hand to silence them.

"You will wait for my command. We will be unified. We must not be seen until the last moment. We only have to contain the enemy for a few minutes, but they must be the right few minutes. You know your jobs." Ygal turned his ear upward as though listening for a signal. He held the pose while the army before him held its collective breath. Then Ygal's head straightened and he whispered, "It is time."

The black force oozed through the ceiling without a sound.

Shamus and Alea had observed a number of demons aboard the cruise ship. Most were controlling the will of someone. Drunkenness. Adultery. Gambling. Depression. Any vice that could break the will and confidence of people. Once a person was without hope, they were no longer a threat to Satanael and his legions. People who felt worthless rarely did anything great. Self-centered, mired in their own troubles, and apathetic to the world around them. This was the evil one's greatest strength in the wealthy nations. Keep people focused on themselves.

Alternatively, there were some men and women of faith on board as well. Alea and Shamus had met with various angels of the Almighty who were on missions of their own. Shamus had alerted them to the possibility of a large-scale attack, albeit only a slight possibility. All of their allies had agreed to watch diligently. Most offered to fight if needed.

Shamus remained tense. His focus rarely left Brenden and Shawna.

Alea was becoming anxious. Angels were far better than humans at controlling their emotions, but Alea could not relax. Although the enemy had given no indications in the past month that they were interested in the Tavis couple, they had also given no indication of anything. First they attack Shamus and Alea and nearly drag her into captivity. Then they watch the Tavis' home night after night. Then they do nothing? If not for the delay with the cruise, Brenden and Shawna would have made their decision already. The whole mission could have been well underway by this time. The inactivity of the enemy was what was most discomforting.

Only two more days of delay. It was obvious that Brenden and Shawna would not make a decision until the distraction of the cruise was over.

Brenden, Shawna, Matt and Marci were currently trying on jewelry in one of the shops on the Promenade Deck. They had finished dinner and, as usual, had gorged themselves. The current plan was to walk for a while through the shops to help digest the fabulous Tiramisu, which had been the night's feature dessert. Then it was still being discussed as to whether they would go listen to the comedian in the main theater, or take it easy in one of the hot tubs.

Alea sensed the demon before she heard it. It had entered the store alongside a well-dressed young man whose diamonds in his Rolex flashed in the spotlights of the jewelry store. The presence of the demon was not alarming. It was the words spoken to Marci Hollingsworth that moved Shamus and Alea faster than the sparkling light of the gems.

Dark angels generally maintained their missions without interfering in the lives of the other people around them. Once in a while, words would be said, objects would be moved, or cars would be stopped. Little diversions in life. Sometimes they were just to create confusion. Sometimes they were to create frustration. Sometimes they were spontaneous.

But not usually.

The demon had specifically addressed Marci. The words had been spoken too quickly to decipher, but were no doubt meant to cause trouble. The demon tried to take possession of the young man. Once inside a person's body, the angels could not harm the demon. God could cast out the demon, but angels could not without direct power from the Almighty.

The demon was not fast enough. Alea's blue blade shot through his core and a murky vapor dissipated into the air. The demon would not speak again until Satanael released him from the void. Alea looked forward to the day when the void would be sealed with Satanael and all his legions inside.

The effect of the words was evident in less than thirty seconds. Shamus, wings spread, red sword glowing, light emanating from every part of his being, remained on guard behind Brenden. Alea's similar form was glued to the side of Shawna. The wealthy, young man left the store as soon as the argument began.

"How does this look?" Marci asked as she thrust out her arm. On her wrist was a white gold and diamond bracelet. It was delicate and sexy.

"Gorgeous!" replied Shawna who took Marci's hand to study the piece more closely. "It looks fantastic on you!"

"Well, I agree," Marci concurred. "What do you think Matt?"

It was a loaded question. "It does look good. How much is it?"

"Less than Mom and Dad gave us."

Matt came in for a closer look. It was a stunning piece of jewelry. Matt had been married long enough to know that if Marci asked for his opinion, she had already decided she wanted whatever it was that she was looking at. His response was standard. A joke.

"Good thing you're so beautiful that you don't need jewelry!"

Marci knew that she was prone to spontaneous purchases. Matt had freaked out more than once when he opened credit card bills and found numbers far greater than he had been expecting. There was something about this bracelet, though. It was exactly what she had been looking for. She did spend money unnecessarily sometimes, but it was usually on things for the house or the yard. Rarely did she splurge on something like this. Something for her. It was Christmas. She deserved this.

"I really want it Matt." Marci looked up with determined eyes.

"That money is going toward the car loan. I already told you that. We can't afford to spend $800 on a bracelet." Matt still managed a bit of a laugh as he spoke.

"So you can spend thousands of extra dollars on navigation systems, bigger rims and leather seats in the car, but I can't spend a few hundred bucks on something I like." Marci wasn't quite sure why she was so irritated by his response. She decided this must have been something brewing in the back of her mind for a while. Matt thinking about Matt. As usual. She wanted the bracelet. They were on holidays. It was Christmas. What was Matt making such a big deal about this for?

Matt's tone got more serious this time. "No, Marci."

"You are so self-centered sometimes! I am buying it." The salesman behind the counter had backed away and pretended to organize another display case.

"At least sleep on it. It will still be here tomorrow." Matt tried to salvage the moment, but he wasn't backing down.

"Whatever, Matt! I'm going to the hot tub." Marci tore off the bracelet, turned and left the store. Brenden, Shawna and Matt watched her go, and then followed out onto the promenade deck.

"I'm not sure where that came from." Matt broke the awkward silence. He was obviously upset.

They walked a few more paces toward the glass elevators. They had to wait for a group of Asian passengers to vacate the elevator before they got on. "I guess we're going hot tubbing," was all Brenden dared to reply.

"I don't really want to hot tub," answered Matt. "Besides, I think my wife would shove my head under water and hold it there."

"I am burnt in a number of interesting places. I can't say I am looking forward to hot water either," said Shawna as they turned toward their room. "I was looking forward to that comedian."

Not another word was spoken until the three of them reached Brenden and Shawna's room. Matt and Marci's room was down one level and further to the back of the huge ship. "I don't mind going for a soak," Brenden said as he swiped his keycard. "If you two want to go see the comedian, go for it."

"Are you sure?" questioned Matt.

"Yup."

"Ok. We'll be back in a couple hours." Shawna gave Brenden a quick peck on the cheek, and then she and Matt headed off to the theater.

Brenden sent Marci a text to confirm which hot tub they would meet at. Within a few minutes, she had responded and the two of them found themselves neck deep in bubbling water, staring out over the Caribbean.

The conversation flowed easily. The view was spectacular. Marci didn't mention the bracelet or appear to be angry any more. It was another moment Brenden figured would stay in his memory for many years.

Neither Brenden nor Marci noticed which towel the teenage girl took as she left the hot tub room.

Shamus did.

He did not interfere.

Subtle. Hard to perceive. It was the way of the enemy. Shamus had stayed with Brenden after the jewelry shop exchange. Alea accompanied Shawna to the theater. This was not a great time to separate. The possibility of attack had increased. Alea was convinced the demon's comment in the jewelry shop was pre-meditated. Shamus was not sure. It was not uncommon activity. Arguments about money between spouses were as common as swearing on a construction site. Even the fact that the demon's comment instigated the disagreement, and that the argument had been the cause of the separation wasn't any evidence that formal attack was imminent.

The teenage girl took Brenden's towel. His room keycard had been in that towel. Was it just a girl who had forgotten her own towel and took his? Was the enemy at the root of this too? Shamus took a quick look in the rooms close by on this deck and the decks that were above and below. He peaked into an office that backed up against the hot tub room. A flash. A demon leaving the scene. The disappearing towel was no accident.

When he returned, the slender body of Marci stood facing the windows. She was wearing a yellow bikini, and had just picked up her own towel and had begun to dry off. Brenden watched her for a moment before getting out of the tub as well. He wandered over to the chair on which he had left his towel. He checked other chairs. It didn't take him long to realize his towel was gone.

"I think my towel is gone," he called over to Marci.

"Are you sure you brought one?"

"I know I did. My keycard was in it. I always tuck my keycard into my towel at places like this."

Marci glanced around as she finished drying off in hope that the towel would magically appear. It didn't. "Here," she called as she chucked her own towel at him. "You may as well use this for now."

Brenden toweled off. The towel smelled like a mixture of chlorine and Marci. Brenden found it calming, appealing. He took a deep breath as he dried his face and neck.

"I guess I'll have to go ask for another key."

"Any idea what time it is?" asked Marci as the two began the walk back to the elevators.

"It must be about ten. Why?"

"The show should be done in about an hour. We may as well wait for Shawna. I'm sure she has her key. You can get a new one tomorrow when we are fully clothed. You can hang out in our room until they get back."

"That'll work," responded Brenden. "Maybe there is a movie on or something."

Shamus watched, listened and followed. *"Is this a concern?"* he thought to himself as Marci opened the door to her room. People could be unpredictable. Lust was very predictable. Shamus flew to the theater and appeared beside Alea before the door to Marci's room had even closed. He outlined what had happened with the towel and the current situation with Brenden and Marci alone in the room.

Nothing unusual had occurred in the theater that would suggest any dark angel attack. The two angels, a slight glow emanating from their seamless garments, were looking down at the balding head of the performer from the top of the curtain at the back of the stage. Cruise ship travelers were laughing, drinking and, occasionally, heckling the comedian.

Alea was trained to predict people's actions and to help them have the courage to do what was right in the eyes of the Almighty. Her intuition was excellent. Vrielle, who had instructed many Virtues over the years, had told Alea she was one of the best she had seen. It was why she had been chosen for this mission. Deep down, she knew that. Now may be one of those situations where her involvement could be crucial, so Shamus agreed to stay in the theater until the show was done, and Alea left the giggling gaggle of people to return to the Hollingsworth room.

She never made it.

CHAPTER THIRTEEN

From the roof he saw a woman bathing.
The woman was very beautiful,
2 Samuel 11:2

The heavy door slammed closed behind Marci. The king-sized bed, small couch and dresser took up the majority of the floor space. Marci opened the door to the bathroom and grabbed another towel. Brenden dried his thighs where his swimsuit had been dripping onto his skin, and then wrapped the towel around his waist. He was about to sit on the couch when Marci stopped him.

"We could be here an hour. Why don't you throw on a pair of Matt's shorts?" It was a statement, not a question. She fumbled through the dresser without much success, so Marci opened the closet in the hall and took out one of the white robes. "Close enough," she said as she tossed it at Brenden. She then fumbled through some other drawers to find her own clothes. With a pair of pink lace panties and a long white shirt in hand, she disappeared into the bathroom to get herself changed.

Going "commando" was not a normal experience for Brenden, but without much option, he stripped off his wet shorts, dried off anything that was still wet, and proceeded to put on the robe. He was still tying the belt when the bathroom door opened and Marci came out.

She was still wearing the yellow bikini. Her hair was thrown over her right shoulder and she was struggling with the clip on the back of the bikini top.

"This clip is broken or something. I can't seem to get it open." She turned her back to Brenden and dropped her arms at her sides.

Brenden hesitated a moment. Marci's tanned back had a few drops of water on it from her hair. Her skin was tight and smooth. Brenden gingerly picked the strap off her skin and began to work at undoing the troublesome clip. It didn't take long to see that part of the strap had been looped around in such a way as to create a knot around the clip. Brenden pulled and fiddled with it before coming to the realization that it would be easier to just pull the clip apart under the knot than to try and undue the knot.

"I think that will work," he said as he held the strap in his fingers waiting for Marci to take hold of it.

"Are you going to let go, then?"

Brenden let go. The bikini top swung loose, and Marci slid it off her arms in one fluent motion. "Thanks," was all she said as she stepped forward.

Brenden had dated, seriously dated, only one person in his life. Shawna. He had married young. He had never physically been with any other woman, and had in fact, never even been in the presence of another naked woman. He watched as Marci started off toward the bathroom. Marci was nearly around the corner of the door when she flipped around and came back to the dresser. Brenden instinctively spun around and sat on the couch. He reached for the remote. His mind was not thinking about television, but he knew it would not have been right to stand and stare at Marci. The TV clicked on.

Marci was combing through her hair. "Did you just spin away so you couldn't see me?" The question was asked softly, gently.

"Uh . . . maybe."

"I thought men liked breasts." Brenden couldn't tell from Marci's tone whether she was serious or sarcastic.

"One of God's greatest creations," Brenden replied, determined to sound confident yet calm. Marci continued to work at straightening her hair.

"I am really making you uncomfortable right now, aren't I?" This time there was a definite tone of pleasure in her voice.

"Yup."

Again no one spoke. Brenden finally focused on the TV screen. It was a 'kids at college' movie. With ironic humor, two peeping Toms happened to be succeeding in their attempt to get a view into the girls' showers. Two beautiful blondes were lathering their bodies, backs turned to their admirers. Predictably, they turned to the camera and the giddy teenage boys. The four perfect breasts filled most of the screen. Brenden considered changing the channel, but couldn't make himself do it. Instead he just began to laugh.

"You can't hide from them now, Brenden. It must be your lucky day!"

Shaking his head in disbelief, he answered, "I guess so."

"Have you ever seen another woman naked? I mean in real. Movies don't count." Marci was still enjoying the fact that she was making Brenden noticeably awkward.

"I don't think so."

"In other words, no."

"Shawna was the first person I ever seriously dated. Oh, and I don't usually hang around the girls' showers."

"So in your whole life you will only be with one woman. Don't you ever wonder what you're missing? Don't get me wrong, Shawna is great, but aren't you curious?"

"I love Shawna. There is something amazing about being with someone that has never been with another man. She is totally mine. I know she feels the same way about me. It is how God meant it to be."

"I guess," responded Marci. She had stopped combing her hair. "You must still be curious, though. Other women must still be attractive to you. You are a man."

"Yup."

"I get it that you don't want to cheat on Shawna. That is why you get married, right? You are pledging to be faithful to each other. I feel the same way about Matt. But, why did you turn away from me like I was hideous or something? It is not like we were about to have sex. They're just boobs." Marci walked up beside Brenden. He was still absently watching the movie. "Don't you find me attractive?"

Brenden hit the power button and the TV went off with a click. He turned toward Marci and made sure to look directly into her eyes. "You are absolutely beautiful, Marci. That's why I didn't look. How could I look at you without getting . . .?" He left the sentence hanging.

"So you didn't want to look at me because I am beautiful and it might turn you on? You don't make much sense. Do you really think Shawna would care if you looked at my breasts? You could see most of them when I was wearing the bikini anyway. What's the difference? I don't think Matt would even care. Although I probably wouldn't see any reason to tell him," she added with a laugh.

Marci moved around to face Brenden. Her dark, brown eyes looked into his. "See." She cupped her breasts with her hands. "I have always liked my breasts."

Brenden did look. "They are very nice." He looked back into her eyes.

"That's it? You're done? You have only been with one woman in your whole life and all you take is one little peek. You can touch. . ." Marci stopped as the room phone rang. She looked at the phone and then back at Brenden. "Who would that be?" Marci walked over and answered.

A conversation regarding a change to Matt and Marci's flights the next day took a few minutes. Snowstorms in the Midwest were causing delays and flight changes. Matt and Marci would be leaving an hour later than expected out of Miami. The cruise ship had flight information for their disembarking passengers and did what they could to inform people of flight changes.

By the time the call was done, Brenden was watching sports highlights. Marci finished changing into her nighttime attire and sat on the bed. They found the last half of *Avatar* playing on a different channel, and were still watching when Matt and Shawna came back.

With minor delays, the two couples returned to Seattle the next day.

Brenden agreed with Marci about one thing. There wasn't much reason to tell their spouses about the troublesome bikini clip.

Besides, within hours, Brenden didn't have time to think about Marci's smooth, bikiniless body.

CHAPTER FOURTEEN

For the eyes of the Lord are on the righteous
and his ears are attentive to their prayer,
1 Peter 3:12

The black barrier of dark angels solidified into an impenetrable wall right before Alea's eyes. She instinctively turned in hope of reuniting with Shamus, but a second wall had formed behind her. As she analyzed the enemy, it became evident that this was a well-orchestrated maneuver. Her escape, without help, was improbable. Alea recognized the dark Dominion who stood before her. She had fought sword to sword above the mountains with him.

"Make sure the girl needs help getting changed. Go! Now!" The dark Dominion had directed the order at a stoic looking demon at the end of the wall nearest Matt and Marci's room.

"Yes, Dominion Ygal," came the reply. Alea watched the demon disappear behind the wall of blackness. She did not move. Was there any way to escape? Was there any way to alert Shamus?

The Dominion answered the questions for her. "You are alone, Virtue. Escape is not possible. We are glad it was you returning to the side of the man Brenden Tavis. Your partner would have been foolish enough to try and fight his way out of this. He would have been destroyed. You, I believe, are sensible enough to realize you only have two options. You can wait until we let you go. We may even decide not to pierce you. Or you can feel free to join us. One simple pledge of allegiance to Lord Satanael and this becomes really easy." The other demons grunted and laughed.

"What will it be, beautiful one? We have so few feminine angels around here. Most of these ones are quite hideous in comparison to you." Ygal pointed at a number of surrounding demons and laughed. "You would be a pleasant addition."

Alea recognized one of the demons as Barac. As their eyes met, he narrowed his bumpy brow and sneered. "I say we just finish her off now," Barac grumbled under his breath.

"Maybe for a little sport we should see how you fare alone against our guest, Barac. That is if your foot isn't too sore." Another round of grunts and laughter were aimed at Barac this time. "Be patient, Barac. In a short while this angel will be of little consequence to us anyway."

The demon that had left at Ygal's command reappeared. "Mission accomplished, Commander," he spoke with a slight slur.

"I guess it is my turn to make sure Marci causes sufficient damage to our poor, innocent Mr. Tavis. I am sure it is very difficult to be faithful in the presence of such a beautiful woman." Ygal smiled at Alea. As he turned away, the smile quickly disappeared. "If she tries to escape, destroy her." With those words, he was gone to manipulate the unbelieving Marci.

Alea knew now that the argument in the jewelry shop had been part of the plan. Anger and selfishness were great precursors to further sin. With the sour taste of the argument in her mind, Marci would be easily convinced to blur the lines of faithfulness in her marriage. Brenden was strong, but without any of the Almighty's legions to offer strength and protection, Alea was not confident this would turn out well. Whatever the enemy had in mind, Brenden would be tempted to the extreme limits. Obviously the stolen room key was also by design.

Shamus would not know what was transpiring. He had said he would come see how things were going, but surely that would not be for a while yet. Alea knew she could make a break for it and try to alert Shamus, but she also knew that it would most likely result in her destruction. She was not afraid to be pierced. The Almighty would bring her back, but that process did not follow with human years. It would be many human years before Alea was involved in missions like this. She knew that her part in this mission would be over.

Still, she would do it. If she thought it would make a significant difference for Brenden and Shawna Tavis, she would do it. Alea, however, could not see the benefit. Even if Shamus made the call for help, by the time this army of dark angels would be defeated, the damage would already be done.

Barring some other intervention, Brenden Tavis was indeed going to be alone against the full strength of the enemy.

Alea, with little option, decided to turn her attention to the distraction of her guards. "Barac," she called with a playful voice. "Could you fetch me some water. I think I still have some of your foot residue on my sword." A third round of laughter was cut short as a number of demons had to restrain the bulking Barac. The real hatred in his black eyes was hard for her to look at. Such a mistake these angels had made to follow the Evil One instead of the Almighty.

She was about to make a comment about how he looked particularly good in blue, especially when it was sticking out of his foot, when Alea sensed the slight change in the surrounding spirit on the ship. The light had come.

In their living room in Alderwood, thousands of miles from the Caribbean Sea, Shawna's parents, Bill and Helen Montgomery, and their grandchildren Tyler, Rachel and Amanda held hands. Mom and Dad would be coming home tomorrow, but Mrs. Montgomery had become restless. It was one of those feelings that was simple to ignore, even when you knew you shouldn't ignore it. Brenden and Shawna, her kids, had clearly entered her thoughts. They needed prayer. She had no idea why, and it might just be her imagination, but one thought kept reformulating in her mind.

Pray. Pray. Pray.

In her younger years, she would have dismissed something like this and gone on with the next task of the day. Not now. Helen had interrupted the grandkids' bedtime snack and brought everyone into the living room. Rachel was still crunching on a piece of apple. Amanda sat on her Grandpa Montgomery's lap.

It was at least a few hours ahead in the Caribbean, she knew, so it must be getting late over there. What would Brenden and Shawna be doing late in the evening on a cruise ship? It was hard to say. All she knew was that it was time to pray for their protection.

It was Tyler who offered to go first. "Dear God, please keep Mom and Dad safe on their trip . . ."

The Spirit of God enveloped the house as this group of believers prayed.

Many warriors of the Almighty answered the prayers and descended on the Caribbean cruise ship.

CHAPTER FIFTEEN

May they be like chaff before the wind, with the angel of the LORD driving them away;
Psalm 35:5

What had been still and calm now resembled a beehive that had been tossed down the stairs. Demons scattered. The sound of blade upon blade echoed from places visible and places Alea could not see. She found herself essentially alone in the midst of turmoil.

As she was not sure where to fight, Alea hurried to check on Brenden and Marci. The chaos of the battle behind her, Alea flew into a totally different predicament. Marci stood beside Brenden wearing nothing but her bikini bottoms. Brenden wore only a white robe. For a split second, Alea feared that she was too late, but the uneasy tone in Brenden's voice and mannerisms gave her hope. Alea considered saying something, but the time for words had, for the moment, passed. A distraction was needed. Now.

The phone rang. Marci, who had just moved directly in front of Brenden, looked at the phone, looked back at the man standing before her, and then wandered over to answer it.

It was a perfect distraction. The strange part about it was that Alea had not made it happen.

"You might want to suggest to Brenden that he watch sports highlights or something." The angel who had spoken the words descended onto the bed.

Alea took the advice and then turned to ask the only sensible question she could come up with. "How did you know?"

"I am Naya. I was sent with a great many others in response to prayer. It looks like we arrived just in time. I was the first to get around the enemy's defenses. I had to wait until the dark Dominion commander was drawn away from this room before I could intervene." Naya looked over at Marci who had just hung up and walked to the bathroom. "The phone diversion had the desired effect, I see."

"It did. Thank you, Naya." Although not knowing what was transpiring in the battle on the rest of the ship was difficult, Alea knew her role was to protect Brenden. She stood beside Naya, blue sword ready for battle, wondering how Shamus was doing.

Marci came out of the bathroom. She was still seductively dressed, but it was clear that the danger, at least for the present, was over. Marci sat on the bed, but neither angel moved.

"Shall I stay with you for a while, Virtue . . ." Naya hesitated as she waited for Alea to give her name.

"Alea. My name is Alea. I would appreciate you staying. At least until my partner on this mission returns."

The two angels remained still and alert. When Matt and Shawna returned from the theater, both couples went to bed in their respective rooms. Alea accompanied the Tavis' to their room, and was soon joined again by Naya who had checked in with her mission leader. A number of angels had been lost in the battle. Others were returning to Center Realm and some were remaining behind to protect the area from another attack. Naya was asked to remain with Alea.

Two things still bothered Alea.

One. Shamus had not returned.

Two. If the enemy had attacked with this kind of force, they knew much more about Brenden and Shawna Tavis than the angels expected. Attacking the marriage was only minimally successful due to the prayers of believers, but this was just the beginning. Who or what would be attacked next?

CHAPTER SIXTEEN

The heavens declare the glory of God;
the skies proclaim the work of his hands.
Psalm 19:1

There was a fresh layer of snow in Alderwood that was thick enough to turn the landscape white. It was good snow for snowballs and deep enough for making Frosty with the kids. The sky was still gray and threatening to drop more. With the temperature rising, it would probably be more rain than snow. One thing about living in the Northwest was that you couldn't put off playing in the snow. Any procrastination usually meant the snow was gone, melting or it had been rained on and refrozen which rendered it useless for anything fun.

Rachel was already putting on mittens and boots even though her bowl of Fruit Loops was still half full on the table. Tyler had slept the longest, but he was running around the house looking out every window to try and get a better view of the white stuff. He was wearing only his Seahawk pajama bottoms.

Amanda was sitting in her booster seat and sucking on some Cheerios. Snow was not something she had any clue about, but she was excited to have Mom and Dad back. There had only been a few moments where Amanda had not been telling stories about Grandma and Grandpa's house or singing or mumbling or giggling or laughing. Some of it was decipherable.

Coming home from holidays in the Caribbean was easier to stomach when everyone was still on holidays when you got home. So, even though Brenden was still wearing his white robe that he had brought back from the cruise ship, it was clearly evident that he was going to be out in the snow with his kids before he had finished his second cup of coffee. The neat part was that he was just fine with that. There was nowhere to rush to. He would check in with Alyssa regarding any activity with house deals, but it was doubtful much would be happening until the holidays were over.

Christmas holidays, a wonderful family, snow, and a tan from the Caribbean sun all at the same time. What a great start to the day!

Within a half hour, Brenden and Rachel had finished a mini-snowman. It ended up that Fruit Loops made great eyes and a mouth for the snowman until Dad decided he was a snowman monster and took a bite out of the snowman's head. Frozen Fruit Loops, Dad found out, were way better than soggy ones. Soon Dad and daughter were picking cereal off the slowly disappearing snowman and having a second breakfast in the snow.

"I get the puple eye," Rachel excitedly said. Her mittens were too big and constantly falling off making it troublesome to pick out the eyeloop so Rachel resorted to being a snowman monster and bit it right off without hands. Brenden threw her down in the snow and the two giggled for a while before Brenden remembered something else fun to do in the snow.

He picked up the bundled four-year old and carried her to an untouched part of the yard. He carefully laid

Rachel on the snow and then lay down beside her. He slowly dragged and flapped his arms and legs. Rachel figured it out quickly.

Brenden could not remember the last time he had made a snow angel. There was something special about lying there, half buried in the snow. The bustling world around disappeared and everything went still. The sky was mesmerizing as a few flakes drifted down from the heavens and landed gently on the earth. *"What an amazing world,"* Brenden thought to himself.

He remained still as long as he thought his daughter beside him could handle it and then got up carefully so as not to destroy the pattern in the snow. He lifted Rachel to see what they had just done.

"Do you see the angels, cutie?"

"Oh yeah! A daddy angel and a baby angel."

"Maybe they can watch over the house today," Brenden offered.

"Let's make the Mommy angel and a baby angel for Amanda and a baby angel for Tyler," Rachel added. Brenden wasn't sure Rachel had even heard his previous comment.

They managed a few more flaps in the snow and soon the whole angel family was lying in a row. Rachel explained three times which one was Mommy and which one was Daddy and Amanda and Tyler and her because Mom came out carrying Amanda and then, shortly after, Tyler came out. Of course Tyler insisted on making his own angel so he lay right on top of the one that was supposed to be him and made a slightly larger version.

Soon the whole family was standing and admiring their angelic replicas.

"Mommy," Rachel began again. "We can go in now. The angels are going to watch over us today. Dad said so." With that, she turned and trudged back toward the house.

Her hat was barely hanging on and she held both hands up so her gloves wouldn't fall off again.

Brenden made eye contact with his wife and then looked back at their independent second child. "How can you argue with that?" he said.

"I don't think you do."

"Why don't I go in with Amanda and our fearless leader, and you and Tyler can stay out for a while?"

Totally aware of what was transpiring, Amanda began squirming to get down. Walking back inside was not what she had in mind. Shawna wasn't dressed to be out, so before long, Brenden was making snowman number two with child one and child three. It still amazed him sometimes how much joy children could bring.

Unfortunately, the snowman was only two balls high when Brenden heard Shawna call him.

The tears in Shawna's eyes when she had called his name were not something Brenden had often seen in their eleven years of marriage.

CHAPTER SEVENTEEN

Do not be anxious about anything, but in every situation, by prayer and petition, with thanksgiving, present your requests to God. [7] And the peace of God, which transcends all understanding, will guard your hearts and your minds in Christ Jesus.
Philippians 4:6-7

Preparations for the launch of the Unification, as Doroniel had called it, were happening across the globe. That was the quick summary of what Alea learned back at the Battle Realm. Doroniel had given a few details to her, but nothing more was important for Alea's part of the mission at this time. She, however, had returned for a number of reasons. An update from Doroniel was only one of them.

No one had seen Shamus. A few angels had seen him sending demons to the abyss during the fight on the cruise ship, but nobody saw him get pierced and nobody saw him leave. One warrior had counted not less than ten shrieks as angels of darkness dissolved into grayish vapor at the hands of the Power Shamus and his lightning fast sword. The last account of his whereabouts had Shamus trading blows with Ygal, the dark Dominion.

All indications were that he had not returned to the Battle Realm as his quarters appeared unused in the past number of days. Alea picked up a piece of manna that lay half-eaten on Shamus' iridescent living room table. She ate the rest somewhat absently. Shamus had not checked in with Doroniel, either.

Alea had wanted to go straight to Alderwood as a further attack was nearly certain, but the fact that the enemy was aware of at least some of the plans for Brenden had changed things. The element of surprise had quickly transferred to Satanael and his legions. The attacks that would come next would be premeditated and meticulously orchestrated.

It would take more than suggestion or the encouraging words of a fellow believer to guide Brenden to accept his role. Unless Alea was entirely overestimating the enemies' knowledge, Brenden would find himself in the midst of a flurry of events all aimed at keeping his focus on himself. They may be seen as positive things. They may be seen as negative things. Either way, the enemy would stop at nothing except the full separation of Brenden and the plans of Jerry Moore.

The Almighty was aware of events. In most cases, even what appeared to be setbacks were planned for by God. It would be at some later date that the reasoning would become clear and it would be shown that the Almighty had been in control all along. Alea was well aware of these things, and they always gave her reassurance.

On the other wing, people had been given the power to choose. Satanael had been given dominion over the planets. Not everything that was in the best interests of mankind occurred. Until the final Day of Judgment and the ultimate end of darkness, there would be battles. Angels would be given direction by the Almighty as He answered the prayers of the people.

If only more people understood how much power their words to God held. They wouldn't whisper their prayers at night. They wouldn't look around to see who was watching while they prayed in public. They wouldn't worry about saying exactly the right things. Men and women would shout their prayers to God without ceasing! The strength of ten thousand times ten thousand angels would be ready to respond at the command of the Almighty! The enemy and his followers would be outnumbered at every turn. Men would stand strong in the knowledge of God!

But most men and women did not understand this.

Alea decided to ask permission for something that was not often done. Doroniel would not be able to grant this permission. Even Throne Aziel could not grant this request. Alea had to wait in the North Realm until Doroniel returned with God's answer.

She did not have to wait long for the Dominion's return.

"Permission has been granted, but only when you have exhausted all other means, Alea. Many are involved in this mission. Many prayers have yet to be spoken. Many decisions are uncertain. You were chosen for this. You will choose correctly."

Doroniel stared at Alea as though the conversation was to continue, but she was at a loss as to how to respond. They were in the Hall of Red. The light of the pillar beside Alea brightened as her excitement rose. Doroniel's eyes adjusted slightly. He had noticed the change.

"Few angels have been granted permission to do as you ask," Doroniel said clearly looking for explanation.

"I am aware of that, Dominion. My spirit flies although I do not move. I feel as though it will be necessary, but who can fathom all the ways of the Lord?"

"His response is proof of that, Virtue Alea. I did not expect this answer. Your intuition is exceedingly accurate. Now, return to where you are needed." Doroniel turned to go, but hesitated and turned back to look at the slender figure of Alea.

"May you succeed in the building of Brenden's courage. Immanuel." This time there was no hesitation, no look back. The Dominion was gone. Alea was certain that the light in the pillars had fluttered as Doroniel had spoken his last words proving that even Doroniel was excited. The only other time Alea had seen Doroniel show enough emotion to change the lighting in the hall was when he had told Alea that she was going to be trained as a Virtue.

Excitement poured through her. Every pillar around Alea in the Hall of Red brightened; golden light danced in the room! A group of angels across the huge hall turned to see why the light had changed, so Alea twirled around with joy to clearly show that it was her causing the change. When she was sure every angel in the hall had taken notice, she yelled, "Praise the Almighty!" and flew out the open front doors to a chorus of cheers from the angels who remained behind.

It took only moments to find a group of angels leaving for Earth that Alea could join in cosmic travel. Still reeling with excitement, the journey felt faster than usual.

The two-story house overlooking the valley and much of the city of Alderwood looked the same, but little else remained the same. Encircling the house and yard, fifteen feet off the ground, was a wall of light. A quick count revealed 144 angel warriors. Each angel held a sword with both hands. The swords rose vertically from waist level and they symmetrically bisected the right and left sides of the angels. The silver glow from the swords stood in contrast to the white brilliance of the angels themselves.

The display was meant to be impressive and intimidating. It was. The protective force was sent as soon as the battle on the cruise ship had ended. The problem was that the enemy would be at least two steps ahead. Whatever was in store for Brenden and his family had already been put in motion. The hope now was to anticipate the attacks and soften the harmful effects.

The real battle was just beginning. Even if Brenden got through the next events unscathed and accepted leadership, Satanael would be fighting every move the organization made. There would be no more hiding. This was a battle for change. If successful, more lives could be changed for the better than at any other time in recent history.

Alea saw Zopheniel, Maspial, and a Power angel that she did not recognize, within the perimeter of the angelic barricade. She joined them. The Power had fine features. Her eyes were narrow and her nose was small even for her thin face. Long, dark hair was braided perfectly behind her. Beneath the delicate face, however, was a strong, muscular frame. As with any Power, it would be a mistake to underestimate her abilities. As the humans often said, "Do not judge the book by its cover," Alea thought to herself.

With this defensive angel force in position, it was not likely that the next attack would be here. She wanted to hear the other angels' conclusions on how next to approach the situation.

Before she could ask about it, the feminine Power addressed her. "You are Alea the Virtue?"

"I am."

"I am Brand. Do you have any directives from Doroniel? I understand you have just arrived from the North Realm?"

"Immanuel, Brand," Alea tipped her head slightly. "There have been no direct orders from Doroniel or the Almighty. I am to assess the situation here and respond accordingly." Alea made eye contact with Zopheniel and Maspial to convey greetings. "I doubt the next attack will be here. What do you see as the possible targets?" Alea's question was directed to all of them.

Hierarchy within the angelic realm was not always clear. Angels, Archangels and Principalities were the three most common choirs. Clearly angels, who greatly outnumbered all other choirs, reported to Archangels and Principalities. Archangels and Principalities worked together on equal terms in most missions.

The second sphere was similar. Virtues and Powers clearly reported to Dominions, but Virtues and Powers generally worked as equals in responsibility and decision making.

All choirs took direction from the Thrones, Cherabim and Seraphim as they took their orders directly from the Almighty. Any decision in question among the third sphere angels was answered directly from God, so hierarchy was inconsequential.

At this moment, Brand had immediately asked questions as though she was in charge, but as far as Alea could tell, Brand had not previously been involved with this mission. Alea knew the Tavis family better than any angel except for Shamus. Although it was always comforting to have a Power around to fight, decision-making was clearly the responsibility of Alea in this case. Her tone and line of questioning revealed this logic. It was clear that Brand noticed. The Power had moved back slightly and looked at Zopheniel and Maspial to see if they were going to respond.

"General targets would be family, finances, faith, occupation, reputation and health," responded Zopheniel succinctly, but with his usual enthusiasm.

"Or all of the above," added Maspial. "What exactly do those categories represent in this situation, Alea?" Maspial had clearly given control back to Alea.

"Finances are stable. It would take a hefty financial burden to cripple the family, but it may take much less to distract them. Faith is solid and has been built with a firm foundation over many years. A breakdown of faith would not happen quickly. His real estate business comes and goes, but that is normal and hard to damage with a quick strike. He works with a lady named Alyssa Gladstone, but most other work associates are acquaintances as opposed to friends. Brenden's character is nearly as clean as the water in the Pool of Eden, but false accusations are definitely a possibility. Health is always a target, but it is not likely the enemy will get near enough to Brenden in the immediate future for us to consider that. Family. This is a large target. The children, Tyler, Rachel and Amanda, need to be fully guarded at all times. Shawna's parents are the next closest to them and live in the area, but both Brenden and Shawna come from close, solid families. An attack on siblings or parents would be the most probable."

"We can't forget the Hollingsworth family. They were already used in this situation. Further sexual advances by Marci are likely, and we can't rule out a reversal. Matt is charming. Shawna is also beautiful." Brand now waited for Alea to respond.

Alea's response was another question. "Have you been involved first-wing in this mission, or has someone given you the details of the situation?"

"I was sent to accompany the legion that saved you in the Caribbean, Alea. The prayers of the believers in Shawna's parents' house were strong and faithful. Many of us were sent. I remained in protection of the ship as you remained in protection of Brenden and Shawna on the vessel. I have met the humans we are discussing, and have been given further details from Zopheniel and Maspial. I am part of the greater unification mission in ways I cannot discuss at this time. "

Although Alea was not fond of the way Brand said the words "saved you in the Caribbean," it was clear that she understood the basics of what was going on. Alea decided it was no longer important to establish hierarchy. Decisions had to be made.

"Although we have not been given direct orders from Doroniel, we have many legions at our call. We must anticipate attacks in all areas. Have there been any signs of attack on Jerry or Phil? The enemy must know that they have a role in this. Are they safe?"

"You could say that," Zopheniel said with a slight smile. "Look around! Similar walls of protection surround Alderwood church, the pastor's house and the hotel where Jerry happens to be staying tonight. The enemy will not get close without massive losses and delays. Within minutes of the battle in the Caribbean the Almighty had these put in place. That is why we had the luxury to be away from Phil and Jerry for a few minutes."

"Excellent. Then all we have to concentrate on are the secondary targets. A watch needs to be put on Matt and Marci. We do not need any more surprises. Secondly, I would like to see some serious protection around Shawna's parents. If they are the prayer warriors, we cannot afford to lose that strength and power." Alea paused to allow input from the others.

"Is this Alyssa that Brenden works with a believer?" Brand asked. "Do . . . never mind," Brand stopped mid-sentence. "I have been called." Brand was gone before the sound of her words had reached the other angels. Alea turned just in time to see the angel who had called Brand away vanish.

"Alyssa is not a believer," continued Alea without hesitation. Quick departures were not uncommon or unexpected. "Should we put a watch on her as well? Any recommendations?"

"What do we have to lose? This mission is high priority. Mistakes could cost time and, ultimately, lives. Let's set up a watch." Maspial was clear and decisive. Alea liked that about him. *He might make a reliable Principality someday*, Alea thought to herself.

"Do you have time to set up the watches, Zopheniel?

"I do."

"Maspial, could you . . ."

"Get word to Doroniel that we need a perimeter around the Montgomery house?" Maspial finished the sentence.

"Exactly. Immanuel." All three angels had begun to move when Alea called, "Wait!" Maspial and Zopheniel were back and attentively waiting further instruction.

"Have either of you seen Shamus?" The usually confident voice of the Virtue was soft, almost pleading.

"No," Zopheniel whispered. Maspial shook his head.

"I had meant to ask Brand . . ." Alea's voice trailed off as she thought of her partner in this mission.

"I am sure many demons perished before Shamus would have been pierced. He is a valiant warrior."

"I know, Zopheniel, but I am not as strong on my own. Shamus gives me strength by his very presence. What if they have taken Shamus as they tried to take me?"

"If Shamus has been pierced or taken, you can be sure the Almighty is aware and is already responding. If he is on another mission, I am sure he will soon return. In any case, Alea, your job is to get a commitment from Brenden so we can get this unification underway."

"I know you are correct, Zopheniel. Thank you."

The three angels vanished.

Alea drifted over the snow-covered house. She was about to enter when she saw the shapes in the snow. Snow angels. Few people had any real understanding of the angelic world, although most people in this part of the world believed in the existence of angels. Most images were inaccurate representations: little cupid figurines shooting arrows, soft-looking female angels with puffy dresses on the top of Christmas trees. Occasionally, an artist or sculptor would get close.

It didn't really make sense. The Bible contained over 200 references to angels. Warriors, protectors, messengers of God, strong, powerful. Angels were clearly defined in many ways yet people bought into chubby little cupids!

Snow angels she liked, however. They were white. They were mysterious. The form was there, but the details weren't. Alea lay down in the largest impression, although she was taller than Brenden. It was strangely peaceful. She had seen kids make them before. It was usually a quick flapping of appendages followed by a laborious attempt to stand in a bunch of bulky clothing. Children looked, turned away and were gone.

Adults were different, though. When you caught a grown-up making an angel, it was usually slow and methodical. There would be a few arm and leg movements, and then, unlike the kids, there would be that moment of stillness. Alea had seen a faraway, dreamy, peaceful look in the eyes of men and women alike as they stared into the heavens. Perhaps it was the effect of snowflakes falling that brought this stillness, but that is not what Alea believed. She believed that at moments like this, when people slowed down and let the full expanse of the universe come over them, that they came a little closer to seeing the spiritual world. They got a little closer to seeing the angels. They moved a little closer to God. The child snow angels were nice, but the adult snow angels were better because each one represented a person who had come a little closer to the Almighty. It was a warm feeling.

Here, now, Alea felt the opposite effect. She felt closer to people than usual. She assumed Brenden had made this snow angel. Right now, it was almost like she could see through his eyes. It was a nearness to Brenden she had not experienced before. Alea found herself not wanting to move.

She couldn't help but wonder one thing. If Brenden were here at this moment looking up, would he be able to sense the presence and protection of the many angel warriors only a few arm lengths above him?

CHAPTER EIGTHEEN

How beautiful you are and how pleasing,
my love, with your delights!
Song of Solomon 7:6

Inside the two-story home, things were not so peaceful. Shawna and Brenden were packing up the kids. Dad Montgomery had called with the news that Mom was in the hospital. All early signs were pointing to a stroke, a serious stroke. Serious enough that even the optimistic, even-keel Mr. Montgomery conveyed urgency.

The family was in the Tahoe in the garage ready to leave when Alea urged Shawna to lead the family in prayer. When that didn't seem to be working, Alea whispered similar words into Tyler's ear. Following the lead of Grandma Montgomery, Tyler not only suggested that the family pray, he demanded it. It was Brenden who put the vehicle back in park, took the hand of his wife, and asked God to look after his mother-in-law.

Alea felt the rush of the Spirit of God carry the words away.

How would God respond? One could only speculate.

Would God respond? He always did.

The angelic guard encircled the truck as it drove through the unmarked snow on the driveway and turned onto the road. It was relayed by a messenger angel that things were indeed urgent at the hospital. Alea sent the angel who had brought the information to tell Zopheniel. Within seconds, Zopheniel spoke the words, "Brenden and Shawna, pray for Brenden and Shawna," to the Pastor who had just returned home from an eggs benedict breakfast at Denny's. Pastor Phil, as was usually the case, stopped everything and prayed.

"Dear God, I don't know why I should be praying for the Tavis family right now, but I ask that you be with them. Protect them, give them strength, and give them what they need in their current situation. You are faithful. You are loving, and I know you hear my prayer. Thank you, God. Amen."

Pastor Phil did not accomplish much for the rest of the morning. His mind kept returning to Brenden, Shawna and their kids. Many times that morning, words were spoken to the Almighty God on their behalf.

The power of the prayer sent more help. Lights were kept green, cars changed lanes, and a lady taking her dog for a walk, that was about to cross the street in front of the Tavis' Tahoe, suddenly had to go to the bathroom. She turned to go the other way before Brenden ever saw her. A wisp of wind moved the bell decoration on the top of a light pole as the angel responsible moved past it. A trip that would normally take eighteen to twenty minutes took twelve.

Brenden had taken notice of the "good luck" in driving and had mentioned it a few times along the way. The "luck" continued as a parking spot right next to the entrance at Alderwood Memorial Hospital sat open for the Tahoe to fill. An eighty-year-old believer had just driven past it. He parked a fair distance away and was never quite sure why he didn't park in the spot by the door. Four other angel sentries still sat on the hood of the old man's car, their eyes watching to see that the Tahoe parked in the spot next to the door.

Alea nodded in their direction as the family made its way through the automatic doors into the lobby. She sensed the presence of demons. The angels on the hood of the old man's Camry must have also noticed the danger as they were quickly at Alea's side. The posse was soon in Grandma's room. The smell of dark angels lingered, but none remained in the room now. Alea knew the wall of angels that had formed the fortress above the Tavis' house had now formed something similar above the hospital. She hoped some angels had arrived in time to intercept and destroy the enemy that had inarguably been present.

The four angels took position against each of the four hospital room walls while Alea assessed Grandma Montgomery.

Shawna stepped back from her dad after a long hug and asked, "How is she?"

His response was slow, labored. It was clear he was fighting off tears. "The doctor says it is unlikely she will make it through the day." He reached again for her hand and gently held it in his own. "She was in such good health, Shawna. I don't understand why. . ." His voice faded and he never completed the sentence, but Brenden and Shawna understood exactly what he was inferring. They had used nearly the same words at home when they first heard of the stroke.

"I am glad you are here," he added as he nodded in approval. "It feels . . . warmer somehow. Everything just feels better."

The kids had been watching without much movement. They seemed to understand something was wrong. Tyler, being six, spoke the simple truth the adults had been thinking. "Is Grandma going to go to heaven soon?"

Trying to stay emotionless for the children, Brenden was the one to respond. "We don't know, Tyler, but she is pretty sick."

"Can we ask her?" Tyler asked with a tilt of his head. He looked expectantly at Brenden, but Brenden turned toward Grandpa without an answer. Grandpa managed a small smile and said, "You can try, but she has been sleeping for quite a while and isn't waking up. Why don't you take her other hand and ask her?"

Tyler started to move, but Amanda took up the invitation even faster. She shuffled over beside her Grandma and took hold of her pinky finger that was lying near the edge of the hospital bed. With a look of pride, she raised her head to look at the adults in the room. Tyler and Rachel soon held on to part of Grandma's arm, and then Tyler worked at gaining her attention. "Grandma." He looked expectantly at her motionless face. "Grandma," he said a little louder the second time. He glanced back at Grandpa looking for direction, but Rachel decided to try.

"Wake up, Gwamma. We want to talk to you." Rachel leaned right up to her Grandma's face looking for a response. Again there was no response. The slight rise and fall of Grandma's chest was the only movement detectable.

Shawna's eyes filled and a tear rolled down her cheek until it stopped just above her lip. She put her head on Brenden's shoulder and the tear smudged onto his black jacket. She looked out the window to attempt to stay in control of the pent-up heaviness within her. Brenden gently kissed the top of her head before resting his cheek on her dark, smooth hair.

A nurse entered, did her tests and checks, and left without a word. No one said much for a few minutes.

Alea had done her own tests and checks, in about a second, and knew the reality of the situation. She moved beside Brenden and spoke into his ear.

"Pray." It was simple.

Brenden responded.

"How about we pray for God to watch out for Grandma, okay?" Brenden felt a little guilty for not thinking of prayer earlier.

Shawna retrieved Amanda from the bathroom she had gone to explore and returned to the main room. Brenden led in prayer.

"Dear God, please be with Grandma right now. We don't know exactly what is wrong, but we know you can heal her. Make her better, God."

Grandpa's voice was deep and strong as he continued. "Thank you for Helen. I would love it if you would heal her and bring her back to me." He paused a bit before continuing, "But if it is time for her to go home to be with you, please take her painlessly and give us the courage to live without her."

Shawna wanted to pray out loud, but she had to say the words inside so she could get them out without crying. It was little Amanda that spoke next. Amanda's voice was strong like Grandpa's. "Gamma." It was a single word, but unmistakable.

It was with that word, that the full Spirit of God filled the room. Those bowing in prayer felt it. It was relief mixed with a slight dizziness. Shawna felt some of the heaviness leave. Alea took direction from the Spirit and acted accordingly. She touched the mind of Helen Montgomery.

"Amen," said Brenden. There was nothing more to say.

The family opened their eyes. All of them including Grandma. She blinked slowly at first, but she was unmistakably conscious. All three children reached for her hand again, as did Shawna.

"Hey, Mom." Her mom slowly blinked again. She squeezed Shawna's hand lightly. Tyler, Rachel and Amanda all said hi at once, and their Grandma's head tilted slightly in their direction. She managed a perceptible smile.

Then it was Grandpa's turn. He gently brushed her cheek. "It is good to see you again, Beautiful." Brenden loved how his father-in-law still called his wife "Beautiful". The first time Brenden had met his girlfriend's parents was at a dinner at the Montgomery house. When the meatloaf was gone and the dessert plates had been scraped clean, Mr. Montgomery had looked at Mrs. Montgomery and lovingly said, "Thanks for the dinner, Beautiful." It had stuck with him clearly. Brenden had heard it many times since. He couldn't think of anything more fitting for the moment.

The smile on Grandma's face was short-lived as a wheezing, choppy breath took her attention. After a few moments, Grandma once again focused on the family surrounding her. Her face changed to serious. Her voice was a whisper, but as clear as day.

"I love you all. Thank you for being here with me." She took a few labored breaths before continuing. "I have experienced so much joy . . . in my life. No matter what happens, I have been blessed." She methodically made eye contact with each person in the room. When she looked at her oldest granddaughter, Rachel leaned in again and whispered, "I love you too, Grandma."

Grandma closed her eyes again for a moment. When she reopened them, Rachel kissed her on the cheek. Another smile.

"Take it easy, Helen. Get better. There is no hurry." Grandma looked deep into her husband's eyes. She was smiling, but there was something more in her eyes. Her husband saw it, and then he knew. He put a hand on her face and cupped it carefully. He leaned over and kissed her on the lips.

A nurse poked her head in the room. Upon recognition of the patient's consciousness, she asked how long Grandma had been awake. She informed them she would be right back with the doctor. Everyone turned to the door except Grandpa. His eyes never left his wife.

He was the only one who saw the life leave her body.

He was the only one in the family who saw the curtain waver.

Alea watched the two Powers enter the room. They took the woman from her human body and began guiding her toward Center Realm. The curtains did waver as the three spirits passed by.

Helen Montgomery smiled back at her loved ones until the hospital disappeared out of sight.

A single tear rolled down Bill Montgomery's cheek. "Bye, Beautiful," he whispered. "I love you."

CHAPTER NINETEEN

Therefore do not be foolish, but understand what the Lord's will is.
Ephesians 5:17

"Do we know that it was the enemy?" Alea asked Doroniel. The Dominion had come to Alderwood this time. The gathering of angels took place on the back deck of Brenden and Shawna's house with the wall of angelic protection hovering back in the same position Alea had first seen it. Zopheniel, Maspial, Alea, Brand and Ramuel all looked at Doroniel awaiting his reply. The half-dozen angels of light stood in a perfect circle.

"We are sure. One of the angels assigned to Helen Montgomery escaped the attack with minor wounds. Not less than forty angels of darkness descended upon the Montgomery house without warning. By the time we had pieced together what had happened on the cruise ship, the damage was already done here. The attack on Brenden's faithfulness using the Hollingsworth girl on the ship and the attack on Brenden's praying mother-in-law were planned in tandem. The Spirit of the Almighty had been upon the Montgomery house, according to our surviving angel. It was only minutes after the full presence of the Holy Spirit moved away that the dark angels moved in.

Ramuel's eyes narrowed like a cat ready to attack. "Are you telling us that the attack on Helen Montgomery was three days ago, but she only suffered the stroke today?"

"Yes."

"How can that be, Dominion Doroniel?"

"We were aware of the attack on the Montgomery house, but the contingent of angels sent to check the damage . . . could not find any."

"What are you telling us, Doroniel?" Ramuel persisted.

"The enemy has devised a weapon that has a delay. The damage done to Mrs. Montgomery's brain manifested itself several days after the attack. This kind of weapon has been used before, but we have always figured out how to detect and destroy it." Doroniel looked confidently at the others. Alea was always impressed with Doroniel's poise. "We could not detect it this time, but we will figure it out. Soon. A team has already been assigned to that task."

All were silent a moment, contemplating the news. Doroniel continued. "The damage from the stroke could, of course, have been reversed if the Almighty had chosen to heal Helen Montgomery."

"But he never gave that directive," Alea pointed out.

"No, He did not. We never know the mind of our God fully. I am sure there is a reason he allowed the passing of Mrs. Montgomery."

"I am having trouble seeing the reasoning, but that wouldn't be the first time," added Zopheniel. "She was the most consistent prayer warrior for Brenden and

Shawna. The help on the cruise ship would not have arrived when it did if it weren't for the prayers of Helen."

"Perhaps others will step in to pray when, and if, Brenden ever decides to be a part of the unification." Maspial had stepped back from the circle and was looking up at the angel warriors above as he spoke.

"What are your thoughts about that, Alea?" Doroniel asked. The words were direct, but not critical.

"The process of mourning a loved one along with the planning and time put in to the funeral often supersede other events and activities in people's lives. Concurrently, however, it forces introspection for the people who have just watched a mortal life end. Brenden was already contemplating joining the unification before. I am confident he can be persuaded to make that decision now, even if he doesn't put action behind the decision until after the funeral is over."

Doroniel tipped his head in agreement. "Well said, Virtue. Let us see to it that the funeral is not delayed. I will send a team of angels to make sure that all plans for booking the funeral home, catering and church go smoothly. Power Brand, could you check in with the angels watching the Hollingsworth couple. The enemy will not wait long to use the influence of Matt and Marci on Brenden and Shawna. If there is any sign of demonic activity, report it immediately." Brand nodded and was gone.

"Zopheniel, encourage the Pastor. He, if anyone, will understand that the death of Shawna's mother was an attack by the enemy. He does not know about the attempt to seduce Brenden, so this will be his first sign that the enemy is fighting back."

"I am sure the same encouragement will be necessary for the traveler, Maspial. He must remain strong a little longer. Do not let the vision diminish."

Both Zopheniel and Maspial disappeared. Doroniel, Alea and Ramuel stood alone on the deck. All three turned toward the window of the house where the figure of Shawna was clearly seen staring out at the lights of the city. A tear rolled down her cheek. She stood without wavering until Brenden appeared behind her. He gently put his arm around her. Her head leaned against his shoulder, and for a moment, nothing changed.

Without warning, her face fell. Shawna turned into her husband and let all the pent-up emotion come out. She sobbed in Brenden's protective arms until the shoulder of his grey hoodie was damp with tears. Brenden stood, resolute, allowing his wife to mourn although inside he was holding back similar feelings.

Alea moved to the outside of the window and reached her hand through the pane of glass. She placed it on Shawna's back and immediately, Shawna's body relaxed.

"I know you loved her, Shawna," Alea whispered, "but the Almighty God loves her, too. You will see her again in paradise." The sobbing softened. Shawna simply stood, enveloped in comforting arms. "Don't waste the time you are given on this Earth, Brenden and Shawna Tavis. Be a part of something great!"

Alea took back her hand. She turned to see Doroniel and Ramuel watching her intently. There was a softness in Doroniel's eyes that she had not witnessed before. Alea gracefully moved across the deck to join her companion angels.

"People are so distraught at the loss of a loved one. They are incapable of understanding how short their mortal lives are in comparison to their spiritual eternity. Yet . . . it is hard to watch them suffer when it comes out of true love."

"I do feel bits of empathy, but I wish they would just do their mourning and get on with their lives," responded

Ramuel who did not demonstrate the same compassion in his golden eyes. Ramuel stood tall. His tone was one that inferred *I am right, and don't argue with me.* Even in the presence of a Dominion like Doroniel, Ramuel was a strong personality. Alea realized that this particular trait of Ramuel was what made him the right angel to be a Principality. Ramuel's world was one of powerful people and influential decisions. A mistimed comment or a slow reaction could change a whole nation's future. Decisions had to be decisive and timely.

Ramuel had been assigned to high ranking officials in smaller, less influential countries when he had first completed his training to be a Principality. Stints in Austria, Paraguay and France were ones Alea had heard Ramuel refer to. During World War I, Ramuel was assigned to the Canadian Prime Minister and during World War II, Ramuel had been directed to aid Winston Churchill in England shortly *before* his promotion to Prime Minister. These were some of the most important international events of the last hundred years in some of the most critical countries with some of the most influential people.

The latest mission, President Mullen, was Ramuel's fourth assignment to a US president. Alea knew of Ramuel's assignment to the president, and she knew that he was in some way connected to her own mission with Brenden Tavis, but that was all she knew at this point. After listening to the scope of the unification project in Center Realm, it did not surprise her that leaders of nations would be involved. What continued to surprise Alea was the importance of Brenden to the whole mission. It shouldn't have been surprising. Most major events that affected the spiritual state of the world were perpetuated by people who were not famous or powerful or rich, at least not in human terms.

The Almighty knew every minute detail of His people. He alone knew who had the right gifts, sufficient abilities, enough faith, and the people to support them when they would need it most. Sometimes these unsuspecting heroes jumped at the chance to do something great. More often, however, they needed a little encouragement. Sometimes, every once in a while, they needed a sign that could not be ignored.

Brenden hadn't jumped into the project. Brenden had been encouraged. If he did not decide to join the unification mission soon, it would be time for a sign.

Inside the house, Brenden and Shawna went to bed earlier than usual. The clock showed 9:52 PM when the last lights went out. It had been a long day: an unexpected, stressful, draining, leave-you-exhausted sort of day. Yet husband and wife tossed and turned.

Not having Mom around would change the status quo, and this was the first opportunity to think through the reality of what had just transpired. How would Dad fare? What would next Christmas be like? Would Dad still take the kids from time to time? Would the family survive without Mom's cooking? What would all have to be done for the funeral? Did Mom have life insurance?

After all those questions had been pondered, the tougher questions began to creep in. Was Mom really in heaven right now? Death sure came quickly. How many years older was she? Only 25! How many years do I really have left? What is my purpose here anyway? Have I wasted my life? Jerry Moore? Pastor Phil?

Those names kept flooding to the front of Brenden's thoughts. Jerry. Phil. Jerry and Phil.

Alea had been saying the names repeatedly for over an hour.

Brenden's thoughts were all over the spectrum. *Yes, it is time to do something different! No, I can't risk it financially! Yes, I could feel alive and excited about what I was doing! No, I am not good enough to lead something like this. If I say no, they will find someone else. Everything will still work out OK.*

"Yes, yes, yes, yes! You can do it, Brenden! Believe in yourself! The money will work out!" Alea was bordering on frustration. If only she could transmit faith to people!

Maybe I should just say yes. I think I should. I don't know.

Then Brenden's breathing fell in sync with Shawna's. They were both sleeping. No clear decision had been made as far as Alea could tell. Alea threw herself down on the mattress between the two sleeping souls. Tomorrow would bring errands and concerns and phone calls and worries.

A decision would still not be made.

There was no more time to wait.

It was time for a sign!

CHAPTER TWENTY

Then the angel who talked with me returned and woke me up, like someone awakened from sleep.
Zechariah 4:1

The red glowing numbers on the digital clock beside the bed read 3:33 AM. Alea had thought through what was about to occur many times. Although angels usually held their emotions closely in check, Alea found herself anxious in an excited sort of way. Her actions had been delayed by one decision; she could not decide which option would be most appropriate in this circumstance.

Ramuel would, no doubt, have made a decision and acted on it a couple hours earlier if he had been in this circumstance, but Alea wasn't in a hurry and she wanted to do this right. Truthfully, she was very much looking forward to this.

Thousands of years earlier, Alea had been there when Elisha had prayed that a servant would see the angel legions that were ready to go to battle for him. When the servant's eyes were opened to the spiritual world, he saw the army of angels ready to fight on behalf of the

Almighty God. Alea had been there, sword drawn, and watched as the army of the King of Aram was struck blind and led helplessly away from the battle.

She had also had the huge honor of being a part of the hosts of angels singing in the sky when it was revealed to the shepherds in the fields that Jesus, their Messiah, had been born. That had been the most indescribable experience. The memories of that night brought a rush of energy and joy into the depths of her spirit. The proclamation of the Messiah! The birth of Jesus! The Almighty had not limited who could sing that night. Thousands of angels filled the night sky on that occasion wanting to be a part of the birth of Christ. The shepherds had seen many of them, but countless thousands were not close enough to be seen by human eyes.

Gideon had seen the angels, but it was the Power Glandiel, considered by many to be the greatest warrior angel of all, who had spoken to Gideon. The Archangels Michael and Gabriel had spoken with people. It was the Dominion Doroniel who had spoken to the shepherds near Bethlehem. This was different! This time, Alea would be doing the talking!

Doroniel had chosen grandeur, power and strength when he appeared to the people. He left no doubt that he was an angel of God. Even people of little faith knew an angel when it appeared glowing, tall, with wings spread and a brilliant sword in hand. Consequently, the reaction of the shepherds was fear. They listened all right, but they were scared spitless. Not all angels, however, appeared to people this way.

Other angels appeared before men more serenely. Wings folded back or completely hidden. Their height similar to that of the people they were addressing, sometimes even in human clothing. The initial reaction was, of course, quite different. In most cases there was surprise, even awe, but not the fear. In other cases, people did not even recognize that they were being addressed by an angel. How was it written in the Bible . . . "Be courteous to everyone as some have even entertained angels without knowing it"?

Brenden would not expect this visit, and it needed to be clear what was being asked of him. It would make sense to appear with grandeur and strength. Yet, somehow Alea felt that fear was not the emotion she wanted to convey in this situation. As was most often the case with this Virtue, she went with her feelings.

The transformation was sudden, instantaneous.

"Brenden Tavis." The voice was feminine, but powerful enough to fill the room.

Brenden's eyes opened with a jolt, but his body remained motionless. He found himself in a heightened state of awareness. Something was near. Something unusual. His heart was immediately pounding in his chest as he scanned the room to analyze how and if he should respond.

As his eyes adjusted to the dim light, it became clearly evident that someone was in the room. His first response was typical: a robber. Was there danger? Did the intruder know he was awake? It was in these few seconds of deliberation that his eyes adjusted fully to the dim light in the room, and the details of the intruder became more pronounced.

It was a woman. Tall, radiant, beautiful in a way he had never seen. She was not threatening. She was not holding a weapon. She was, in fact, just watching him. Brenden could still not force his body to move. If this was a robber and he remained still as though he were asleep, she may move on without harming anyone.

If she was not a robber, who was she? It was then that he saw her eyes. Even in the pale light from the streetlight, her eyes were clearly visible. They appeared to glow, not brightly, but noticeably. The glowing was not the strangest part. It was the color. They shone with such a golden hue that it was like part of the sun was in them.

"I am Alea, an angel of the Lord." There was silence. Brenden's mind raced, but no words came from his mouth.

"Brenden, you need to say yes to Jerry Moore and Phil Janzen. Great things will be accomplished. Have faith in the Almighty God." Alea's voice was strong and confident. It left no room for questioning or doubt. Brenden had still not moved. The fluffy, white comforter on the bed remained still.

Alea knew that her appearance and statement were most likely sufficient in convincing Brenden to finally say yes to the unification project. She could fade back into the spiritual realm and Brenden would lie awake trying to make sense of what had just happened. But she didn't fade away. Instead, Alea took a step forward toward the edge of the bed.

"Brenden, there is no reason to fear me."

Brenden cautiously sat up in the bed being careful not to wake Shawna. Afterward, he always wondered why he didn't just wake her up. It would have made things simpler.

"Why me?"

"You have read your Bible, Brenden. Surely I don't have to answer that question." Brenden recounted the story of Moses and the burning bush. The angel was right. There was no point in arguing that he was not the right person for the job. That particular argument never carried much weight in the Bible, so it was unlikely to be any more effective now.

"All you want me to do is say yes to joining Jerry and Phil?" Brenden's voice wavered.

"Yes."

"I will. As soon as the funeral for Shawna's mom is over, I will begin."

"Brenden, do not wait another day. Join this project to celebrate the passing of your mother. She was a woman of God. What choice do you think she would have had you make? Do not waste your life just to have it suddenly taken from you before you expect it. Your life is fleeting, but God is eternal."

"So Shawna's mom is in heaven now?" Brenden dared to ask.

"She is happier now than she ever was on this Earth. You have already mourned her loss, and you will continue to miss her, but do not waste away days for her sake. Celebrate her faith in God, and then allow the Almighty to do great things through your life."

"I will try."

Alea nodded and smiled back. She was about to leave when Brenden asked another question.

"Are you my guardian angel?"

"I have been watching over you for some time now, Brenden."

"So you are my guardian angel?" Brenden pressed for more.

"That is a more complex answer than you may think. Just know that the Lord God is watching over you. Be faithful, Brenden Tavis."

Alea stepped back. Brenden noticed only now that she was clothed in a single, white garment. He had been so mesmerized by her eyes that he had scarcely looked away during their conversation. Her clothing was seamless and made of a material Brenden certainly did not recognize. Again, beautiful was the only word that came to his mind.

This time, Alea revealed her wings. She gave one last, deep look into Brenden's brown eyes and then vanished. A shiver ran through him, but he remained in a sitting position on his half of the king size bed. He was wide awake!

Over the course of the next couple hours, Brenden wrestled with what had just occurred. He lay down for most of it, but sleep was not an option. He considered waking Shawna a number of times, but decided to think through what this meant and what he was going to do about it first. Besides, Shawna had experienced enough drama for one day with the passing of her mother. Surely a good sleep would be more beneficial in the long run. By the time Shawna got out of bed and wandered down the stairs with her fluffy, huggable white robe from the cruise ship, Brenden had made pancakes for the kids, fed them, and finished his second cup of coffee. Coffee was comforting, but he certainly didn't need the caffeine today.

He got up from the table, closed his laptop and wrapped his arms around his wife.

"How did you sleep?" he asked innocently.

"Pretty good."

They finished their morning hug which Brenden held for a little longer than usual. Shawna noticed, but attributed it to extra sympathy from the previous day. Brenden, however, felt more emotional than usual for a totally different reason. It wasn't every night one was visited by an angel!

"Do you want some pancakes?"

"Definitely."

"Coffee?"

"That would be good."

"Another hug?"

Brenden finished getting breakfast, placed it on the table, and proceeded to hug Shawna again. After a quick glance at the kids to see if they were still focused on Dora the Explorer on TV, he slid his one hand inside the neckline of her robe. He cupped her breast gently, and gave her a flirtatious smile.

"Good morning to me," he whispered in her ear.

"You must have slept well," was the fastidious reply, but Brenden saw the right sparkle in her eyes.

"I love you," he said as he gave her one last squeeze before removing his hand.

He went back to his laptop while Shawna broke her fast with two of Brenden's specialty pancakes. When she was done, she put her dishes in the dishwasher and glanced over at Brenden who had been absorbed by whatever it was that he was looking at on the screen of the laptop.

"What're you looking at?"

"Just reading some Bible verses." There was little emotion in his voice.

"Just because?"

"I was thinking about something and decided to look it up. Let me finish reading this and then I'll fill you in."

Shawna went to give the kids hugs which signaled the end of their interest in the TV, and soon the noise level reached normal household levels as all three kids talked, laughed or squealed about something. It wasn't until Tyler was on the computer playing a game and the girls were engrossed in an animal role-playing game which allowed their mom and dad to be the mom and dad horses but otherwise not be involved, that Brenden and Shawna were once again able to converse without interruption.

"So, what were you reading?"

Brenden sat down on the couch, turned the TV off, and turned to look at Shawna.

"Have you ever thought about angels?"

"Well, yes, sort of. How do you mean?"

"Have you ever really thought about them existing . . . like now?"

"Of course there are angels right now. Is that what you were reading about on the laptop?"

"Yes. I guess what I really mean is, do you think there could be angels here, right now, in our house?"

"Like a guardian angel or something?"

"Yah, or maybe angels that are just here watching over us."

Shawna let out a few horse noises for the girls who were checking in, and this sufficiently diverted their game back to the kitchen. "There could be angels here. I don't have any problem believing that."

"Do you think angels still show themselves to people like they did in the Bible?"

"I would think so. I guess I haven't thought about it much." Shawna looked at Brenden with a thin smile. "Why, did you meet an angel recently or something? Someone like me, perhaps?" She lay down with her head on Brenden's lap and looked up at him expectantly.

Brenden did give her a kiss on the forehead, but she could tell he was distracted. Her robe was still loose on top and she was still braless, lying on his lap. An undistracted Brenden would never have stopped with a kiss on the forehead! She thought about pursuing the "I'm your angel" angle, but thought better of it.

"What are you thinking about?"

Brenden took a deep breath and looked down at the beautiful face of his wife. "Last night, I was visited by an angel."

Shawna looked down to think a moment, and then looked back quizzically at Brenden. Her lips began to move, but no words came clearly to her mind so she decided to sit up. When she still said nothing, Brenden continued.

"At night, around three, in our bedroom. The angel spoke to me as clearly as I am speaking to you now." Again Brenden paused letting the words he had spoken sink in a little. "I know it sounds crazy, but there is no question in my mind that it was God giving me direction. It was real. I know it!"

Brenden was not sure why he felt the need to emphasize the point that it was real. He knew Shawna would believe him. The more he thought about it, the more he realized he wasn't saying those words for Shawna. He was saying those words to convince his own doubting spirit. It had been real, yet it still seemed rather unreal. Why was it so easy to believe things like this when you read them in the Bible, and so hard to believe them when they actually happened to you? Now that is irony, Brenden thought to himself.

He looked back at Shawna. She still hadn't uttered a word, but the expression on her face had changed slightly. There was less confusion now. Expectancy and excitement were taking over. She believed him, of course. He knew she would.

"And . . .?" One word said it all.

Brenden recounted every word. It came back so clearly. He could still see the golden glimmer in the eyes of the angel. She had said her name was Alea. A rush of endorphins sent a shiver down his spine as he revisited the experience.

Shawna stared. Her heart was pounding. Most of what she had just heard was incredibly exciting, but a part of her was becoming anxious at the same time. It took a while for her to figure out the contrasting emotions, but as Brenden finished speaking, it suddenly became clear. Her face tightened.

"Brenden, this must be hugely important for God to have sent an angel to you. Huge!" Her voice squeaked a bit as she said the last "huge", and she put her arms out as wide as she could in an attempt to convey her meaning.

"Scary, isn't it?"

"Uh, yah!" Shawna blurted with the heaviest "no kidding" emphasis she could conjure up.

"Do you think I should tell Pastor Phil and Jerry? Or should I just tell them I am going to join them? We are going to join them, right?"

"Uh, yah!" came the reply again. The emphasis remained the same, but the volume was louder this time.

"Is that yah we should tell them, or yah we are going to join them?"

"Yah, we join them. As for telling them, I'm not sure."

"I don't know either. Maybe we should just wait and see if it comes out. Maybe there will be a time when they need to hear something like that."

"Sounds good to me," replied Shawna as she finally relaxed a little. She leaned back into the brown, suede sofa and closed her eyes. Brenden just watched her. He hadn't been sure how telling Shawna would go. It was exciting. It was nerve-wracking. The previous seven hours were not really believable, yet he knew they had occurred. An angel of God had visited him!

Brenden's attention was brought back to Shawna's face. She had smirked momentarily, and made one of those mini-laughing sounds. "What?" he asked her.

"Oh, I was just thinking about how strange life is. One day, your heart can be ripped out of your body and total sadness can take over. You wonder if God really cares about you or if He even exists. Then the next day, God reveals himself in the most phenomenal way as if to say 'just trust me you bonehead.' I find it relatively amusing at the moment."

"I kind of doubt God would call you a bonehead."

"You never know."

"Maybe dumbhead, but not bonehead." Brenden moved back a little anticipating some type of physical reaction. It was a wise move. Shawna hurled herself at him, but he was already braced against the couch. Brenden held Shawna's wrists so they couldn't do any damage. She struggled some, but mostly Shawna was just looking for contact and a hug. She got what she wanted.

Shawna broke the momentary silence. "You were visited by an angel and the angel looked feminine. Has that ever happened before?"

"I don't know," Brenden grunted back.

Shawna looked up at her husband's face. "Well, next time wake me up . . . dumbhead!"

CHAPTER TWENTY-ONE

Put on the full armor of God, so that you can take your stand against the devil's schemes.
Ephesians 6:11

The Parthenon looked its age on this particular morning in Athens. Even lit by the early morning sunshine the cracks and fissures in the columns were depressing. Humans chose to remember the strangest things sometimes. Why preserve a decrepit building from an empire that created many gods but didn't know about the 'One True God'? The Greek Empire was an age of men with much knowledge for their time, yet it was a time when men could not see what was truly important. They had knowledge, but not wisdom. How many times had that mistake been made?

As soon as people believed they were in control, the nation around them collapsed. Religion could be everywhere, but spiritual poverty was abundant. It was another one of Satanael's powerful weapons.

Shamus avoided going closer to this particular tourist attraction. He was neither a tourist, nor was he attracted to the Parthenon. Shamus moved past the amphitheater. It was nearly devoid of people at this time of the day. He found a position that allowed him to see over Athens. If Shamus had been a tourist, the view of the city from the Acropolis would have been a much greater attraction than the ancient ruins. Angels, obviously, had quite a different view of history then people did.

As had been the case for the last three risings of the sun, Shamus kept his focus on one thing: Ygal. The dark Dominion had nearly circumnavigated the planet since fleeing the cruise ship in the Grand Caymans.

The battle had been fierce! Ygal was a skilled fighter. The dueling had taken them through many parts of the ship. Once, in the ship's liquor store, Shamus had knocked Ygal off balance. He spun his blade into position expecting to drive it through his enemy, but the formidable Ygal had anticipated perfectly. Ygal had concealed a secondary blade beneath his right wing. As Shamus' bright red blade bolted faster than lightning, Ygal spun his own body toward Shamus. Shamus' sword deflected off the hardened blade held in the Dominion's wing narrowly missing Ygal's side. By the time Shamus could counter, Ygal had his balance back, unyielding and unafraid.

The enemy was certainly arrogant. Shamus had diffused his impulse to be angry, and instead he used Ygal's arrogance to his own advantage. Shamus allowed Ygal to throw him through the bottles of flavored rum and just beyond the outside wall of the ship. Faking intimidation, Shamus retreated to a lower deck where countless angels and demons were engrossed in the battle for dominance of the ship. He pierced two unsuspecting demons before diving deep into the ship's passenger cabins and then out into the dark waters of the sea.

Ship dominance was now clearly moving in favor of the angels. Charcoal streaks of demons were dispersing in all directions. One battle weary demon had the misfortune of retreating down into the same watery depths as Shamus. Shamus's red blade emerged before the demon could react. The demon's form dissolved into what looked like ink in the dim glow of Shamus' sword. A stingray, somehow sensing a disturbance, fled through the ink dragging the demonic residue toward the Atlantic.

Another fleeing demon passed by, narrowly evading the same fate. Shamus, however, did not give away his position. Ygal was his primary concern. True to his character, Ygal appeared above the tennis courts on the ship looking as indifferent as ever. He turned to look at the fleeing demons with indignation. His posture alone portrayed confidence. He was daring any angel of light to attack. When no one accepted his invitation, he nonchalantly flew off to the south.

Shamus had followed. Although piercing the Dominion would be beneficial, finding out the true knowledge of the enemy in regards to the unification mission was more important.

Ygal had met with dark angels in many places. Orders had been given to three demons in a small town on the coast of Brazil. A fanatical pastor had been successfully teaching people about Christianity. Brazilian men and women by the hundreds were committing to follow the One God instead of dabbling in every religion that passed through.

Shamus heard plans for attacks on the community and the pastor. It would be a battle for the pastor to keep each new believer from falling back into his or her old ways. That was usually the case. The enemy's power on Earth, and the other six planets for that matter, was far-reaching and unrelenting.

Travel through New Zealand, China and India had taken the better part of two days. Ygal had met with a legion of demons under the command of a fallen Power named Brolon in New Delhi. One thing became evident after studying Ygal and watching the enemy in action. Satanael and his legions of dark angels were organized. Chains of command were strictly enforced. Any major offensive on the part of the angels would be reacted to quickly and with strength. There would be no easy victories.

Ygal had left New Delhi and Shamus had tracked him to Athens. Amazingly, following Ygal had been easier than Shamus had anticipated. In spite of the strength and organization of the enemy, arrogance surpassed confidence. *Confidence* was dangerous to attack against. *Arrogance* could be a weakness. Ygal was not careful. That was arrogance.

Unless Ygal was stringing him along.

Unless he knew Shamus was following him.

If that were true, Shamus was about to walk into a trap that even he couldn't fight his way out of.

Part way across the city on the roof of a rundown warehouse, Ygal waited. One roundish looking demon had met with him briefly before flying off. As per usual, this first demon would be the regional contact. He would be instructed to find and bring demons that Ygal needed to meet with. The regional contact would not be seen again. Satanael had learned many years earlier that protecting regional contacts was crucial. The angels would seek out and destroy regional contact demons to cause confusion, to delay communication and to make it easier to attack in a particular area. It had been an effective strategy.

To keep this from happening, the enemy used a contact in a region for one meeting arrangement only. The demon would immediately transfer to another part of the planet, or even another planet, and assume a different role. In a sequence thus far undecipherable by the angels, a new regional contact demon would be put on watch with a new destination for the next rendezvous point. Only high ranking demons were given the new rendezvous points.

Here in Athens, the roundish looking demon would contact those dark angels Ygal needed to meet with, and then he would be gone.

It wasn't long before Ygal had his expected company, but something was immediately different. The approaching demon landed beside Ygal, spoke briefly and was gone again. Ygal stood alone for a moment, as if processing what he had just heard, and then he too was gone. It took Shamus by surprise and he almost lost Ygal's trail. But he didn't. This could be the meeting Shamus had been waiting for. After three days of surveillance, hopefully Ygal was finally going to be meeting with the demons who would discuss the Tavis mission.

Clarity came quickly. Shamus dropped back as soon as he noticed Ygal's speed begin to slow. As usual, Ygal didn't once look behind him to see if he might be being followed. Arrogant again. Shamus found himself high up in the Himalayas. Miles of majestic, snow-covered peaks encircled their position. It was the kind of place people didn't go to. Maybe the occasional mountain climber would venture here. Maybe the occasional helicopter would scope the area. But for the most part, the area was desolate. Angels wouldn't have any reason to travel here, either. It was a perfect place for a meeting of high ranking demons.

About 100 yards in front of where Shamus stood, the mountain peak curled under itself creating a semi-sheltered plateau. It was clearly visible from Shamus' vantage point, but would not be noticeable from above. Unless an angel was searching specifically for this place, it would go undetected.

It had no doubt been used as a demonic base for some time. Shamus counted twenty-four demons of varying ranks, one of which was the Dominion Ygal. An enclosure, which appeared to be made of the same material as the garments worn by the dark angels, stood up against the rock wall in the back corner furthest from Shamus. A variety of benches and tables were scattered around the rest of the plateau.

Ygal was greeted by a small group of demons who had previously been in a light-hearted conversation that had left most of them laughing. Ygal continued past them and then hesitated slightly before calling whoever was in the enclosure.

"I am coming, Ygal. It is about time you showed up."

There was no audible reply from Ygal. He simply waited for the demon inside. Shamus sensed the fear immediately in Ygal's actions. Angels rarely expressed fear, but that was not the case for those fallen angels who were now under the command of Satanael. Satanael controlled his legions with one primary goal: to keep people from God. If it meant sending an army of demons to their demise over a seemingly insignificant cause, Satanael gave the order anyway. If it meant locking up demons for their insubordination, he did it. If it meant piercing a dark angel himself just to make a point, he would not waiver.

It meant, consequently, that fear crept in when demons of high rank were near. Ygal was a Dominion. If Ygal was experiencing fear, the demon in that enclosure had to be of the highest rank. Satanael himself had been the only Seraph to rebel against the Almighty. Nine Thrones and about thirty Cherubim had also joined the rebellion, and now were among the fallen. It was possible that another Dominion or Power held more power than Ygal, but it was doubtful that he would be fearful of a demon of similar rank.

The most likely scenario was that Ygal was about to meet with one of the top ranking demons in existence. Shamus had risked being captured for this conversation! If Ygal was aware of Shamus' presence and pretending not to be, then Shamus had already flown into a trap from which he would not escape. Either way, it was too late to turn back.

Shamus swiftly navigated behind the arching peak to a point directly opposite the enclosure. His hope was to slowly penetrate through the rocky peak and emerge behind the enclosure. As long as the material of the tent separated Shamus from the enemy, they would not be able to see him, but he would be able to hear their conversation. If he misjudged by even a few feet, Shamus' bright white figure would emerge from behind the cover of rock like a beacon for every demon around to see. Those same demons who appeared light-hearted and relaxed would be on him with such speed that escape was not even a logical possibility.

If this were a trap, they would already be aware of his presence. If this were a trap, Shamus would be surrounded by enemies no matter which piece of rock he eventually emerged from.

Somehow, he didn't believe that to be the case. The enemy *was* arrogant. Shamus was sure of it. Ygal had not considered the fact that he might have been followed for three days around the Earth.

Holding to that assurance, Shamus moved through the glacial ice and into the grey stone of the arched mountain.

CHAPTER TWENTY-TWO

They will enter Zion with singing;
everlasting joy will crown their heads.
Gladness and joy will overtake them,
and sorrow and sighing will flee away.
Isaiah 35:10

Shamus inched slowly but steadily toward the demon encampment. At any moment, his powerful angelic form would leave the visual protection of the rock. If he had calculated accurately, he would see the nearly translucent black material of the enclosure. At that moment he would stop, listen as long as he could glean information, and then retreat the way he had come.

If his calculations were off, or if Ygal had fooled him, Shamus' face would appear through the dark granite and he would immediately be thrust into battle. Shamus curled his fingers around the hilt of his sword in preparation for the worst, but his speed never changed. He needed to hear the conversation that was about to take place. He wasn't about to waste three days of careful tracking because he was worried about a battle.

The transition was instant. The scene before Shamus' golden eyes was neither the back of a tent or the open plateau filled with demons. What he saw, however, made him feel relieved that he had readied himself for battle.

A single demon of moderate stature was bent over maybe five feet in front of Shamus. In the partial second it took Shamus to decide how to respond, he surmised that the demon was tidying the area. Their eyes met. Surprise was the only emotion Shamus could read in the blackness of the demon's stare. It was the last emotion the demon felt before the sting of a red blade pierced right through his left eye. Shamus had been ready for battle. The demon wasn't even carrying a weapon.

Shamus found himself alone inside the enclosure. After a quick analysis, he realized that the material of the enclosure was attached directly to the rock in the back of the tent. There was no back wall except for the stone through which Shamus had just entered. That possibility had not occurred to him earlier. *"Foolish!"* he thought to himself.

Fortunately, only one demon had remained in the structure. Fortunately, Shamus had pierced him before any sound had squeaked out of his mouth. Fortunately, he could hear the conversation just outside the tent with ease. Unfortunately, he had nowhere to hide if any demon decided to come into the enclosure, and regardless of what Shamus heard over the next few minutes, the disappearance of the demon he had just stuck his sword through would alert the enemy to the fact that someone had been there.

None of those things could be changed, so Shamus turned his focus to the discussion outside where Ygal was giving his account of the battle on the cruise ship.

"The angels came without warning. They outnumbered us. We fought valiantly, but had to give up our position on the ship. The Power assigned to Brenden Tavis fled when he realized he could not defeat me. I do not know the fate of the Virtue."

"Was the seduction successful?"

"I witnessed willingness on the part of the Hollingsworth girl. She would have given herself to Brenden. He was strong in his faithfulness to his wife at first, but I believe he was about to give in. I was forced into battle before I could see the end result."

"Did you see him sin, Ygal? Did it damage the marriage?" The demon speaking was demanding. His voice echoed off the rock walls.

"I was not there long enough to know, Master."

Shamus could only hear the whistling of the wind. Presumably all the demons nearby were listening in on the conversation like Shamus was. There was no immediate response to Ygal's last statement. For one tense instant, Shamus expected the tent door to open and his cover to be blown. It was Ygal who spoke next.

"How are the other attacks doing?" The question was spoken without the usual arrogance Shamus was used to hearing from Ygal. It was inquiring and timid.

"The delayed death of Mrs. Montgomery was successful. The angels didn't see it coming in time. The Tavis' are in mourning. This should delay any decision by Brenden to join with the traveler and the pastor in this mission the angels are putting so much value behind. Attacks on Brenden's work partner and the little congregation in Alderwood are about to begin. May they be more successful than your failed cruise ship fiasco, Ygal."

"What would you have me do next, Master Kilael?"

"Find out if the Hollingsworth girl is still useful to us. If she is, use her. If she is not, then don't come back until you have figured out another way to destroy the family. Do not fail again."

"Yes, Master."

The discussion ended. The Dominion Ygal didn't wait for more reprimanding. He was gone. Shamus knew he should retreat through the rock just as quickly, but he risked a few more seconds to take one more look around the enclosure.

This was the temporary position of the fallen Throne Kilael. It made sense. The sheer size of the enclosure and its contents suggested that a Throne dwelled here. Kilael, second in command of all the dark angels, was standing only a few paces away. A surprise attack was tempting. Shamus knew that a well-placed thrust just as Kilael re-entered the enclosure would likely be successful in vaporizing the Throne. If Kilael was running the operation against the unification mission, this would throw the demonic enemy into delay and confusion.

Likely. The word rang too clearly in Shamus' reasoning. The attack would *likely* be successful, but there was plenty of room for failure. Thrones had the ability to see what was coming before any other rank of angel. Never underestimate a Throne. Many an angel had lost in battle because they underestimated Kilael. Shamus was not afraid to be pierced should he fail. His own demise was worth the risk of what could be gained by eliminating Kilael, but to know where the enemy was attacking next and to know who was in charge of the enemy's forces were potentially more valuable than simply delaying an inevitable opposition. If Kilael were removed, another demon would take charge. It would cause delay, but it would not end the war.

It was then that Shamus saw something that confirmed his decision. Laying on the table to his right was a scroll. Kilael would know by the fact that his servant demon had vanished that someone had been in the tent. There was no point pretending Shamus hadn't been there. He removed the scroll and vanished into the rock just as he sensed the flap on the door begin to move. It would take a few seconds for Kilael to assess what had just occurred. A few seconds was all Shamus would need to explode out of the back side of the arching mountain and be out of visual range. His spirit trail that could be traced, like that of Ygal which Shamus had been following for days, would likely dissipate before the enemy could pick it up. *Likely.*

The Power Shamus decided to look for cover among other angels. He would not make the same mistake as Ygal and assume the enemy hadn't followed. The Vatican. It was always good for cover. At any given time, angels of many sizes and ranks could be found there. The occasional demon would be there as well, but Shamus was confident he could blend in without being noticed. He would stop, wait and watch for any demon that might have picked up his trail before returning to the North Realm. If Kilael himself followed, Shamus would be caught before he reached a destination off the planet so Italy was a logical choice.

As the sun rose over the buildings of Rome, no sign of a tracking demon appeared. Although diligent in his watch, Shamus had let his thinking drift to Alea. Had she made it off the cruise ship? How had she handled Brenden and Shawna's reaction to the death of Mrs. Montgomery? Had she had time to return to Center Realm for worship? She probably needed it by now.

Shamus flew over St. Peter's square and then skyward.

Not once did he consider that the Virtue Alea might have transformed into non-spiritual form and appeared before Brenden during this same night.

৶৶৶

"You have done well, Alea! The unification can finally begin! What was it that finally convinced Brenden to commit to the project?" asked an excited Brand.

"Let's just say that the Almighty can be very convincing," Alea replied to Brand. She was not sure how much to say, or if it really mattered. She would let Doroniel decide whether her appearance before Brenden should become common knowledge. "Thank you for taking the watch here. I will return after worship in Center Realm."

Brand, realizing nothing more was to be said, nodded in acknowledgement, and took her post as sentry of the Tavis house. With the wall of angels outside still barricading any entry to the house, Brand was there to watch the details. The enemy could cause distraction through indirect means, like phone calls or visits from other people, without actually sending a dark angel anywhere near the house.

Brand would observe and monitor communications to eliminate as many surprises as possible.

Alea did not stop in North Realm. Word had been sent that Doroniel would meet with her in Center Realm. She was excited on many levels. First, Alea had revealed herself to Brenden with success! Second, the pressure of helping Brenden commit to the mission was finally over, although nothing had yet been accomplished. There would be many more trials to face. Third, she was going to worship. Finally, Alea was excited not to have to stop in North Realm because going there made her think about Shamus. She knew she shouldn't let herself be distracted from what was most important so it was just easier to ignore it and move ahead.

The golden glow of the Almighty began to brighten the path as Alea approached what the humans called

"Heaven". The Gate of Eden was about the same distance away as the gate she and Shamus had entered through the last time Alea had been here, but she chose the smaller gate. Something about the Cherub who guarded this gate drew Alea. She was glad to see a nearly empty archway as she neared the gate. A few angels were coming a short distance behind her, but there were no other angels in sight. If the chance to approach the Cherub presented itself, Alea would take the opportunity to do so.

She leveled off and looked for the guardian Cherubim angels, but the granite platforms on either side of the archway were empty. Alea felt disappointment, but didn't slow down. She gracefully entered through the light of the gleaming gemstones in the arch and touched down on the golden road that encircled the great realm.

Alea liked to stop and "feel" when she entered this realm. The fragrances of the flowers brought peace. The warmth of the spirit of the Almighty God gave joy. The purity of the environment brought contentment. Within seconds, reviving energy saturated her being.

She soaked it up for a bit and then allowed herself to tune in to the permeating music coming from the temple.

CHAPTER TWENTY-THREE

. . . how often I have longed to gather your children together, as a hen gathers her chicks under her wings . . .
Luke 13:34

Pastor Phil kissed his wife goodbye before getting into his Honda minivan that hadn't been black since sometime in fall. The dull brown of dirt and sand and salt was less than appealing. He knew better than to live in the northwest and drive a black vehicle, but when a deal this good had come about, color had made little difference.

A medical doctor who attended Alderwood Evangelical had got wind of the fact that the pastor was looking for a new vehicle. The slightly used Odyssey was soon in Phil's driveway; a brand new Lexus sat in the doctor's three-car garage. Phil had paid a fraction of the vehicle's worth, but the kind man wouldn't take a penny more for the van.

The salary of a pastor wasn't great, but there were times when generous individuals made life a little easier. Phil would never complain about his income. People didn't go into ministry if they were worried about income.

On the other hand, church pastors still had to pay the bills. Dirty or not, the van was paid for and reliable.

Movement in the living room window caught Phil's eye as he was about to back out of the driveway. Caleb would be waving goodbye. This was normal, and Phil loved it. Caleb still believed the best about people. Phil walked on water in his son's eyes, and Phil reminded himself constantly to enjoy it while it lasted. Church pastors had to pay the bills like everyone else; they were also imperfect just like everyone else. Someday Caleb would see that too, but for now, his son's sincerity was comforting. After a wave and the exchange of some silly facial expressions, Phil and his dirty van disappeared from Caleb's view up the quiet street.

Phil began the normal morning routine of focusing his thoughts on the day ahead. This usually began with prayer in the van while he was driving. It was between four and five minutes to the church, so the prayers were short and sweet, but they were effective in keeping Phil's priorities the same as God's priorities. Today, the drive would be closer to ten minutes, but today Phil had more to focus on and more to ask God about.

Today was to be the first official meeting at the new headquarters for the "idea without a name . . . yet," as Jerry had called it. Jerry, Brenden and Phil were meeting at the new office on Lonsdale Avenue. Everything was happening so quickly.

Helen Montgomery's funeral had been a great celebration of life. Preparations and plans had, amazingly, occurred without complication or delay. Some of the funerals Phil had officiated were full of doubt and sadness. Nice things were usually said about the deceased but the uncertainty of death put people on edge. The tone often felt fake to Phil. People would pretend to have their act together but inside there was anxiety about what happened after you died. Funerals caused people to stop and think about the things that were truly important. For many, that was not an easy thing to do.

Helen's funeral was not the least bit fake. It was clear to anyone who knew Helen that she loved the Lord. Sure, many tears were shed; it was difficult to have a loved one suddenly gone. But the tears were different. The tears at funerals like Helen Montgomery's were softened with joy and the full understanding that Helen was even happier now. Helen Montgomery had gone to be with God in heaven! Her death was not to be feared. Her death did not cause anxiety. Her death gave those in attendance hope for their own eternal spiritual lives. Phil actually enjoyed being a part of these funerals.

After the funeral, Brenden and Shawna had announced their decision to join Jerry and Phil. The preplanning and speculation were finally over. Within a few days, Brenden's realty connections had led them to the office they were about to meet at. A travel agency had shut its doors and there had been no offers on the retail space for months. After calling in a few favors, Brenden had obtained the office for only a few dollars a month "for as long as he needed it".

The strip mall parking lot was nearly empty at this time of the morning. The new office neighbors consisted of a take-out pizza place, a pet food store named the Fluppy Puppy, and a bakery. Phil didn't have a clue what "fluppy" meant, but he decided he would go in and check out the store one of these days anyway.

All of them had inspected the bakery the first day they had come to see if the office would be what they needed, and it was quickly apparent that Jerry, Phil and Brenden would become regulars and close friends of the older Polish couple that ran the place. Nothing won a man's heart and devotion faster than a flaky, fresh, buttery apple turnover. Mrs. Leskowski's turnovers were the best Phil had ever tasted!

"Be still my heart!" Jerry had commented after his first bite.

Brenden had replied with only one word. "Literally!"

Hanging out with Brenden and Jerry was certainly going to deliver some great laughs, but today was the day they were hoping to begin the actions that would deliver results. If lives could be changed for the better, if more people would be led to know God, if the world could be transformed one person at a time . . .

It was time to take away the "ifs"!

Phil parked the van just as Brenden's Tahoe pulled up beside him. Alyssa Gladstone was already inside with Jerry and soon the four of them were discussing décor and functionality. Alyssa was a fireball of energy when there was decorating to be done, and her expertise was so far beyond that of the three men that they gave her free reign to make it look good. Her perfect smile and straight, blond hair could sell more than houses!

Alyssa had asked many questions about what the three of them were hoping to accomplish. She had been sincerely intrigued by the possibilities of what the men shared with her, but it was Jerry's passion that truly won her over. Alyssa admittedly knew little about God, but she was excited about doing good things for others. Phil knew she was also excited about taking over an increased amount of Brenden's real estate deals. The more success Brenden attained in his new role, the less time he would have for selling houses, and consequently, the more commissions would find their way into Alyssa's black, Gucci purse that she had tossed into an open corner of the room. Another "win-win".

At this point, the built-in front counter, a small table and a few chairs Phil had brought over from the church were the extent of the furnishings. Alyssa began forming two lists. One was a list of things that would be needed. The other was a list of things that were wanted.

The men sat down to finalize how to get the ball rolling now that turning back was not an option. Jerry was more relaxed this morning then Phil had ever seen him. Jerry was being true to what he felt God was calling him to do. He had committed to it, he had set the vision before others, and now it was beginning to happen. The weight of uncertainty had shifted for Jerry. Before this point, he had been uncertain about himself and the idea. Now, uncertainty remained about how effective the venture would be, but Jerry had other people to rely on. It was a team now, and the whole team relied on God. The F.R.O.G. principle Phil called it: Fully Relying On God.

Leaning over the counter, Jerry prayed before any serious discussion began. Phil couldn't help but notice that even Alyssa stopped writing and listened during Jerry's prayer. She was curious about this Christianity thing.

"Help her to know you God," Phil prayed silently as Jerry concluded with an "amen".

Alyssa had bounced out the door a short while later with her Gucci purse, her pale yellow coat and her cell phone tucked against her ear under her long blond hair. She had an energy, Phil noticed, that brought life to a room. It was nice having her around. Phil hoped it would last.

Conversations about basics like setting up phone and internet service went quickly and efficiently, but when Brenden mentioned changing the sign out front to something other than "Travel Time", all went quiet. A few names had been thrown around, but never one that seemed quite right. All three men believed this would be a long-term organization. The name that was chosen would be voiced thousands of times over the years. "A name could be changed," Jerry had mentioned, "but it sure would be nice to pick a good one from the beginning."

"So what are we trying to accomplish? What is the focal point of this whole thing?" Phil figured now was as good a time as any to make a decision.

"Change the world? Help people spiritually and physically? Connect those who *have* with those who *don't*?" There was a pause after Brenden had voiced his thoughts.

"So we want to change the world by helping people physically and spiritually and we will do that by connecting those who have lots with those who have little. Sounds pretty simple doesn't it?"

"Yes," Jerry interjected. "That's what we want to accomplish, but we're really unifying people around a single cause. We can eradicate hunger and diminish poverty if we help people to see that it's possible. We unite people around a common goal with a vision big enough to include thousands. We start by unifying churches, Christian men and women, in wealthy countries with churches in need in poor countries. After that it might even spread to communities connecting with communities. There are over two billion people on this planet who call themselves Christians. If all we did was unify *part* of the Christian world around a common goal, we would change thousands of lives both physically and spiritually."

"So it comes down to connections and the unification of Christians? Is that what you see it as, Jerry?"

"Yah. I guess I do."

"I am just trying to talk this out here, but what I hear you saying is that our idea, our mission, our project, is trying to unite Christians around the world around a common goal?"

"Yes." Jerry couldn't help but smile as he responded.

"So, first and foremost, we are working on the unification of Christians."

This time Jerry just nodded.

Brenden looked up and met Phil's eyes. Then he looked over at Jerry. "So why don't we call it the Unification Project?" All three men let the words bounce around the room.

"What do you think?" Phil examined Jerry as he waited for a response.

"The Unification Project. The Unification Project." Jerry muttered the words a number of times in different tones before the same little smirk returned to his face. "I think I like it!"

"Me too!" said Phil with a broader grin.

"Does it keep us focused on the right picture?" questioned Brenden who still seemed unsure even though it had been his suggestion.

"I think so," Jerry responded.

Both Jerry and Brenden looked at Phil whose face was twisted in thought. Again a broad smile appeared on the preacher's round face. "What?" prodded Brenden. "What are you thinking?"

"I am thinking that our focus should always be God, right?" Nods by all. "I like acronyms. Look." Phil took a piece of paper and wrote "Unification Project". Underneath he wrote just two letters . . .UP.

"That should keep us focused. Is it settled then? This is the Unification Project?"

Jerry the traveler, Brenden the realtor and Phil the pastor nodded in agreement.

"Well, let's get the wheels rolling. Phil, you have already planted the seeds for a service trip in your church. Why don't you call a meeting to find out who might be interested in going. I have already set preliminary plans for projects in Kenya, Haiti, Guatemala, and Ukraine. Does one of those seem like the right fit for your church?"

"We have a couple in our church," Phil began, "who have been to Guatemala with a different organization. They shared with our congregation a couple years ago what was going on there. I am sure people would be interested in a project there."

"Start with Guatemala as a suggestion then. If someone in your church feels led to a different mission somewhere else in the world, we can easily adapt at this point. What is important is that people feel connected to the project. We don't want to just fly in a group of people, do some good stuff, and then just leave without returning again. Our goal here is long-term support. Remember, if each church in North America took on just one project somewhere else in the world, the effects would be staggering."

"I have also connected with four other churches in the Seattle area about the possibilities of starting a project." Jerry spoke quickly as though he had consumed too much coffee. "Actually, one of them has already sent a team to Haiti. Another church with some friends of mine about an hour outside of Columbus, Ohio has also shown interest. I will connect with the leaders in those congregations to see if they are ready to begin. If we can get the first few projects up and running with set timetables for their trips, we can all get a feel for how this will work."

Brenden had been listening. Jerry and Brenden would need to continue to support themselves financially for the first while. Money raised for the projects would go entirely to the projects. They all believed this was important. Jerry's travel expenses would be the only extra included in the total cost for the churches.

The first task for Brenden would be to find some financial supporters for the cost of the behind the scenes expenses. Things like telephone, internet, heat, and the cost of the office they were sitting in would need to be covered by people who supported what the Unification Project was trying to accomplish, but were not supporting a specific mission project.

Over time, as more and more churches began running projects, more help would be needed in the office, and more people would be needed to lead the teams to different parts of the globe. Jerry wouldn't be able to lead every team! These people God would have to provide.

Brenden would need to learn some things from Jerry about travel expenses, rules, regulations, laws and all the little things that would need to be taken care of so teams could focus on the mission they were doing and not have to worry about legalities. If the Unification Project could facilitate the trips and make it easy to send teams, Brenden was convinced that there would be an endless number of churches and organizations and communities who would be willing to join the cause.

How big the Unification Project could become was in God's hands. Brenden would do his part. The angel Alea had made sure of that!

CHAPTER TWENTY-FOUR

And we know that in all things God works for the good of those who love him, who have been called according to his purpose.
Romans 8:28

Fantastic progress was made over the next five months. Close to home, Alyssa had beautified the office beyond expectations. She had found deals at thrift stores and even had some things donated. Pictures and maps covered the walls while plants and decorations gave warmth to the counter space, desks, filing cabinets and large meeting table that filled the room. It was a comfortable place to work or socialize.

Brenden, Shawna, Phil and Jerry had spent many hours in the office. Four project teams were prepared to travel and minister over the summer months. Connections had been established with churches in Haiti, Guatemala, Kenya and Ukraine. The existing churches in these regions lacked resources to minister to the many people in need. Their church buildings were often falling apart or didn't even exist. In Guatemala and Haiti, basic medical care was needed as well. In Kenya, gardens would be planted and water wells would be drilled. In Ukraine, old, widowed ladies, the Babushkas, would be given basic hygiene supplies and food. Heating bills would be paid for the winter. An orphanage would be given aid and new windows to keep the many children warm at night.

On the spiritual side, people in the churches would be prayed for, encouraged and loved. Testimonies would be shared. People would be shown the love of Christ. Many would come to know God!

The members of the teams from the churches doing the ministry would also be changed forever! People would be stretched out of their comfort zones to minister and serve in ways they would hesitate to do in their own communities. Teams would pray more. The power of God would be displayed in many ways as money showed up from unlikely sources, as resources would be stretched beyond what was humanly possible, and as divine meetings took place that would extend missions and service to the people that would benefit most.

When God was behind a movement, Brenden had heard at a conference once, the hard part for the people involved was to stay out of the way enough that they didn't slow God down.

Keep the vision in front of people. Persistent prayer. Unyielding Faith. These were Brenden's goals. Another visit from an angel, Shawna had mentioned to her husband, would definitely help keep faith high, but he sensed this was about as likely as winning the lottery . . . twice.

Financial support for the Unification Project had been sufficient. A few committed monthly donors had taken the pressure off of meeting the bills, and another 25 to 30 lump sum donors had provided funds to purchase computer equipment, the meeting table, and other necessary supplies to get started.

At this point, house sales in the area had not been strong, but Brenden and Alyssa's sales had remained consistent and above average. The flexibility of both positions allowed Brenden to do what he needed to do.

The only part bothering him a little was that he had not spent as much time at home in the past few months. Shawna worked in the office a few times a week and often had one or more kids with her. That part had been good. Brenden quite enjoyed working on the same things as Shawna and having the same goals. Shawna was efficient and organized. She also had a knack for remembering details, and Brenden noticed that Jerry liked to make sure Shawna was around when he was discussing details regarding possible challenges teams would face when traveling to certain countries or legalities that had to be followed. She was definitely part of the team.

If things went well, direct personal financial support from others would soon allow Brenden to focus primarily on the UP and he would have more time with his family. He would keep his foot in the real estate world, but hopefully that would be all.

The buzz at church grew each week as Phil inspired the congregation with hope for change and a vision for what was possible. The team of 11 members was excited to go to Guatemala, and financial support from the rest of the congregation had been overwhelming. The team members had committed to paying their own flights, but the rest of the expenses for the trip plus an extra $45000 for ministry had been raised! This would help in the building of a school, provide many medical supplies, and renovate two homes for families living in extreme poverty.

Brenden had spoken at two of the fundraising dinners the team had put on. His charisma and passion had flooded the room and raised his confidence that he was the right person for the job.

In all reality, since the passing of Shawna's mom, things could not have gone better. The angels of God had been busy making sure of this. Brenden tried to remember to thank God daily because it was foolish to think Satan wouldn't cause problems sooner or later.

Hopefully it would be later.

Jerry Moore had felt the same optimism as Brenden. All the initial projects were moving along more or less as planned, and donations for these projects were exceeding expectations. Already connections had been started with other congregations in the Northwest.

The Baptist church in Ohio where Jerry's friend Chris lived was ready to take on a project as soon as Jerry could do his part to get it rolling. Jerry had decided to complete the trips already in place before booking the next set. Lessons would be learned over the summer that would be invaluable for future missions as Jerry traveled with teams to Eastern Europe, Africa, Central America and the Caribbean.

Jerry decided to fly to Columbus to meet with Chris and plant the seeds for what was to come. Chris was a worship leader with a voice that teetered around perfection. He would begin to inspire his congregation and instill hope in making change in the world. Jerry was confident that Chris' church would become the hub for The Unification Project in the eastern states.

The trip back to the West Coast, however, had been a disaster. The first flight from Columbus to Chicago had been late. Jerry had missed his connecting flight in O'Hare. That delay set him back six hours. Last minute mechanical problems cancelled the next flight and Jerry ended up taking a hotel for the night and flying out the next morning.

The only consolation was that the airline offered him an upgrade to business class for his trip to Seattle. Bigger seats and better food were a bonus on a four hour flight. Jerry had spent the better part of two hours eating and most of the last two hours talking with a young man named Conner who was seated next to him.

Conner had just finished speaking at a conference at Harvard about the book he had written. It just so happened that the book, *The Able Earth*, was about the world's capability to provide every living person with enough food and fresh water to survive comfortably. The resources of the planet were sufficient. The wealthy nations could even remain wealthy. It would just take coordination on an international level beyond anything that had yet been created to accomplish something of this scope.

Jerry had listened for the first hour and spoken for the second. By the time the plane circled for a landing at Sea-Tac, Jerry had unloaded his entire vision for the Unification Project on Conner. The two men had been mutually encouraged by their similar visions. Conner was visiting a friend from the University of Oregon who lived in Seattle before he would return to his home in Portland. The two men traded emails before saying farewell.

"A lousy trip, but a good conversation!" Jerry had mumbled to himself as he shuttled to his car in a lot near Sea-Tac International.

Unknown to Jerry, Maspial, the ever-present angel, overheard the words as he sat in the seat behind Jerry on the shuttle bus. "Nothing lousy about it, Jerry. It was a great trip."

CHAPTER TWENTY-FIVE

. . . in order that Satan might not outwit us. For we are not unaware of his schemes.
2 Corinthians 2:11

The mood in the chamber of Thrones was different this time. Throne Aziel had summoned Alea as soon as she had left the temple. She had entered the great doors of the chamber alone. It was startlingly quiet as the doors sealed behind her and the sound of music diminished into a soothing hum. The massive oak table at the far end of the room stood alone. On the couches to Alea's left, three angels were deep in conversation.

Facing Alea was Aziel. She quickly realized that he faced in all directions and that his human face was not the one engaged in conversation at this moment. Aziel's human eyes smiled at her, but he continued to speak to the other two angels with the face of the eagle.

She approached the couches confident that she was expected to join the conversation. The profile of Doroniel was clear, and he now turned to welcome her. It wasn't until she had formally greeted Doroniel that Alea looked across at the third angel.

The combination of surprise and relief were nearly more than Alea could contain. She wanted to fly in circles of joy, but instead, let herself float off the ground for just a second with a beaming smile across her face. "Shamus!"

"Surprised to see me?" he asked with a suppressed smile.

"Surprised at the timing, but glad to see you none the less."

"You were not the only one. Isn't that right, Aziel?" Doroniel, to the point as usual, gave control of the conversation back to the Throne.

"Not much surprises me, but yes, I was relieved to see Shamus return. Shamus was just debriefing us on his mission around Earth following that wretched Dominion Ygal. Why don't you continue, Power?"

Shamus recounted the battle in the Caribbean and his decision to follow Ygal. When Shamus revealed the conversation Ygal had had with Kilael and produced the scroll he had taken in the tent high in the Himalayas, even Aziel had to admit some surprise.

"So Satanael has the traitor Kilael investigating this mission. By God's direction we have escaped the destruction of this project to this point, but with Kilael leading the opposition, the battle is just beginning." Aziel's eagle eyes blinked in concentration. He unrolled the scroll on the table before them.

After a few moments of scanning and deciphering, Aziel looked toward Shamus and leaned so that his beak nearly met the nose on Shamus' chiseled face. "You have done well, Power. You have done well!" The high-pitched cry of an eagle echoed off the walls and domed ceiling of the chamber as Aziel declared his joy.

"Had you read this previously, Shamus?" The question was sudden.

"I have. I would not have bothered you with the scroll's discovery unless the information was useful."

"Useful! That may be an understatement!" Aziel turned his focus to Doroniel and Alea who now sat on the same couch. "The scroll contains the enemies planned attacks against this mission and, fortunately, we should have time to block these attacks."

"We should keep in mind that Kilael will now be aware that we are in possession of this scroll. His plans may already have been altered," added Doroniel as he leaned forward to look at the scroll.

"True, Dominion, but sudden changes at this point should not be as complex or effective. We must be sure to make these plans of the enemy fail. If they attempt something else, we will respond as we always do." Aziel and Doroniel read the scroll in detail before more words were spoken.

"I am now certain," Aziel spoke nodding his head, "that Kilael's plans would have had seriously negative effects on the Unification Project. These planned attacks on Alyssa Gladstone and on the members in the Alderwood church are well designed. Well done, Shamus. Well done!"

After a few minutes of strategizing, Alea and Shamus received their instructions and left the chamber through the great doors. Alea paused to gaze over the heavenly landscape from the lofty balcony. There was movement. There was always movement. But without the presence of evil, it was so different from the planets. The long awaited day would come when the Almighty would obliterate Satanael and his demons and the serenity felt here in Center Realm would be universal. That would be a great day!

Until then, however, it was the job of the angels to help people as God commanded and directed. Shamus had also been peering out over the realm. The two angels, reunited again, turned simultaneously, smiled at each other with a look of understanding, and took off through the Gate of Eden. They flew banking hard to the left off the balcony, over the river and out the massive, arched gateway to the rest of the universe.

Alea kept the inside track and narrowly beat Shamus outside. The race was over when cosmic travel began. Alea could have said something about her victory, but she was just happy to be back with her trusted ally. The two communicated many of the events of the previous days on the journey. The biggest shock to Shamus, of course, was Alea's answer to his question about Brenden. Shamus had figured out that Brenden must have committed to the Unification Project, but he certainly hadn't expected Alea to have taken on physical form and talked with Brenden.

"What was it like?" Shamus inquired. "Did you enjoy it? Would you do it again?"

"Exhilarating and yes," were the only words he got in response.

The next few days were spent on two primary tasks. One was making sure Alyssa Gladstone did not ruin Brenden Tavis' integrity as the enemy had schemed. The second was averting an internal rift within the Alderwood church that would likely have put the pastor's reputation in question. Confidence within the congregation would have been shrunk down to the point where an overseas mission trip would not have even been mentioned.

Phil would have spent countless hours putting out fires and trying to hold the people in his congregation together. The net result would have been little or no activity with the Unification Project and a disheartened group within the church.

The enemy was brilliant at using minor theological disagreements between followers of God to cause Christians to battle Christians. Satanael was entirely aware that when the people in a church looked inward, little was done outward. Evangelism stopped. Service, generosity and caring slowed drastically. Some followers of God would even turn away from their beliefs if the fight became personal enough.

The best way to combat a church that was growing and doing great things for the world was to direct the church's focus onto its own weaknesses. It was this point alone that made the Unification Project so exciting. If churches could work together on common projects to change the world without the internal battles caused by minor belief variations, progress and positive change would happen exponentially faster.

The Almighty had directed hundreds of angels to this project, and with the information gained in the demonic scroll, the angels were able to proactively stymie every attack the enemy attempted. The enemy must have been aware that the scroll had been taken because there were slight variations in the attacks, but with the general plan remaining unchanged, the angels of darkness achieved little success. The angels, thanks to Shamus, were winning this fight.

Success, however, was fleeting.

CHAPTER TWENTY-SIX

On reaching the place, he said to them, "Pray that you will not fall into temptation."
Luke 22:40

The four coffees in the tray Jerry was carrying released trails of steam as he entered the office. In Jerry's left hand was a bag full of freshly baked turnovers. Trips to Guatemala and Kenya were complete. Both teams had been successful. Inward growth was evident in nearly every person who went. The goals were met, although rarely on the time schedule that was expected. The teams bound for Haiti and Ukraine were in the midst of final preparations and would be complete within the month.

Jerry passed off coffees to Brenden, Phil and Alyssa before diving into the bag of turnovers. It was the first time in three weeks that the four of them had been together in the same place at the same time. Shawna would normally have been with them, but Marci had invited her out for a coffee on their own this morning so Shawna had pawned the kids off at her Dad's for a while.

Alyssa liked to help out when she could be of use and she tried to join in on meetings.

Across the front of the office, a row of angel guardians were in a discussion of their own. Had their forms stopped the rays of the sun, the room would have needed the lights turned on, but their presence was undetected by the humans. Zopheniel, Maspial, Alea and Shamus were listening attentively to the Principality Ramuel and the Power Brand discuss ongoings in the political world.

"Senator Reese will be on the front page of tomorrow's newspaper," Brand spoke solemnly. "A waitress at a Lincoln City pub is claiming the Senator slapped her on the butt and then asked her for sex. She claims he wouldn't stop asking and that he sexually harassed her the whole time he was in the pub."

"Is it true?" Ramuel asked.

"I was with him in the pub. He had been asked to go for a drink with some influential supporters. They ordered. She flirted. He flirted back. The other two men went to the bathroom. The waitress came back and, after further flirting, she waggled her butt at the Senator as she was leaving the table. He flippantly smacked her backside with his napkin. They both laughed. The two continued to be "friendly" the rest of the night."

"Is the damage to his reputation repairable, Brand?"

"It is doubtful. This one will take a while to sort itself out and by that time people won't remember the outcome; they will only remember the scandal."

"How do you think the President will respond, Ramuel?" Zopheniel inquired.

"The President trusts Senator Reese. They are close. We need to make sure Senator Reese and the President speak about what happened before it hits the public. Brand, how many people are aware of this?"

"The story was just given to the papers. The waitress in the bar has a friend who is trying to make a name for herself as a lawyer. The lawyer friend talked the waitress girl into making this public by practically guaranteeing a hefty financial settlement. I don't believe the paper will leak the story early. The Senator was only notified this morning that he is being charged."

"Are there any other people that could leak this early?"

"Not that I am aware of, Ramuel."

"Let's see if we can minimize the damage. Is there anything else I should know before I return to Washington?"

"The Senator and his wife will likely be turning to prayer within minutes. They were discussing the situation when I left a few minutes ago."

"Excellent! We shall await the Almighty's instructions."

Ramuel and Brand were gone. The trail of steam from Jerry's coffee swirled slightly as Ramuel raced past. The plan had been to discuss the Unification Project with Ramuel and Brand, but now they were gone and it hadn't even been mentioned.

"So am I to understand that Brand is assigned to Senator Reese at the moment?" Alea's eyes were open wide and her head tilted in a questioning manner.

Alea had expected Zopheniel or Maspial to respond, but it was Shamus who answered her question. "The Power Brand has been closely assigned to the Senator and his family for about a year now."

"So then why has she been involved with the Tavis' and the Unification Project?"

Shamus, Zopheniel and Maspial exchanged glances but no one spoke.

"They are connected. Aren't they?" Alea's face brightened with the realization.

"The Senator plays some role in the Unification? That more fully explains why Ramuel has been so involved."

Shamus flew directly in front of Alea, their eyes only inches apart. "There are many pieces in play here. Right now, you simply need to make sure Brenden and Shawna continue with their part in this."

"I know Shamus, but I can't help but be excited when I see the leadership of the most powerful nation in the world being connected to our mission."

"As I said a long while back, Alea, the bigger the mission becomes the bigger the attack from the enemy will be. Let's remain focused and effective in carrying out our Lord's plans."

The conversation ended with those words as Jerry began to pray at the table below them. The four angels listened as thanksgiving was given to God for the successes of the missions to this point. Jerry prayed for a number of people who had been significantly impacted by the trips. Jerry finished and only the sound of the noisy heels of two ladies walking by the front doors of the office broke the silence.

Brenden proceeded to pray next. He also offered thanks to God and prayed for continued success for the upcoming trips to Haiti and Ukraine. Then Brenden prayed for Shawna and, specifically, Marci.

Alea turned to Shamus. "Do we know what is happening with Marci? Why is Shawna meeting with her? I should be with her."

"I thought you knew why they were meeting." Alea shook her head.

"Zopheniel? Maspial? Any idea?"

Both angels shook their heads.

"With Brenden and Shawna being so busy lately, there has been little contact between the two couples in the past few months. The odd phone call. A coffee now and then. That's all. We stopped monitoring them as frequently."

"I will stay with Brenden. Go!"

Alea was gone before Shamus had finished the word.

CHAPTER TWENTY-SEVEN

Husbands, love your wives, just as Christ loved the church and gave himself up for her,
Ephesians 5:25

"I can't believe this! This can't be happening!" Shawna set her coffee down.

Marci was successfully keeping her emotions in check, but her eyes were red. "I know," was all she replied.

"How long? How long have they been having an affair?"

"Matt said it hadn't been more than a few weeks, but I haven't felt like things were quite right with Matt for months."

"Who is she?"

"Some skanky sales rep he met in Vegas."

The two women were sitting at a little table in the back of the dessert and coffee shop known for its amazing pies and warm atmosphere. Her cheeks were flushed. Anger was clearly brewing inside her, but her next words hid the emotion. "Now what?"

"I kind of just left. I couldn't look at Matt anymore. What if they made out in our house? On my bed?" Marci shook all over. "Yuck." She continued shaking.

"Well, you are welcome to stay at our place for a while," Shawna consoled. Our guest room is empty. Well, it's not empty. It is full of stuff we didn't know where else to put, but it will be empty enough for you to sleep in until we get this figured out." Shawna put her hand on Marci's shoulder.

"Thank you, Shawna. I stayed at the Best Western last night. I shouldn't have bothered paying for a room. I spent most of the night angry or crying anyway. I could have done that anywhere. Now I don't feel much of anything. I don't know. I don't . . ."

"Come. Let's just go." Shawna stood up and adjusted the front of her lime green tank top she had thrown on before coming. Beige shorts and sandals finished off her ensemble. "You need a proper sleep. Let's go." She pulled Marci up and started moving toward the door of the quaint coffee shop. She managed one step before Marci pulled her back and buried her face on Shawna's shoulder. She didn't break down fully, but tears trickled down Marci's smooth, tanned cheeks.

"Thank you, Shawna. Thank you for being there. I wish I were you sometimes. I wish I had it all together like you!"

Shawna felt like arguing. Nobody has it all together. Nobody is perfect. She was about to speak when a feeling flooded through her that caused her to stop. Shawna suddenly felt like the right thing to say was . . . nothing. She held Marci tightly a few moments before pulling back, wiping away a tear, and leading Marci out to the vehicles.

"Thanks for listening," Alea, the angel, whispered to Shawna as the two cars with the two women left the parking lot and headed back to the Tavis' house. Shawna hadn't checked in with Brenden about this yet, but she wasn't worried about that. Brenden would understand.

Marci was moving in.

A dark angel ran his gnarled hand over the rim of the cup that Shawna had just put down in the coffee shop. A sneer grew on his face.

Ygal would be proud.

Three weeks later, Jerry left with a team headed for Ukraine and Phil was swallowed by meetings and organizing for the fall. In a church like Alderwood Evangelical, kids' programs, small group meetings, and people's consistency in attendance all began again in September. It was a busy time for a pastor. Phil, consequently, hadn't been in the UP office with any regularity.

Life at the Tavis' had changed as well. Marci's stay had continued. She had been unwilling to make a decision regarding her marriage. Matt had told her that his relationship with Corinne, the skanky sales rep, was over and that he was sorry, but trust was never repaired that quickly.

As it was, Brenden was inwardly enjoying having two women in the house. Marci had always been easy to get along with, and she insisted on doing her part around the house. It was not uncommon for Marci to be running a vacuum while Shawna was taking care of the kids. Or Shawna would be making dinner while Marci would be out getting groceries.

It also provided built in child care when Marci wasn't working as a secretary for a financial planning company in Arlington. Brenden and Shawna had been able to go out on their own a number of times, spontaneously! They had even gone to an actual movie theater with popcorn and everything!

This particular night, the sun was shining, the air was warm and the three adults decided to take Tyler, Rachel and Amanda to the school park to let the kids play on the playground. They chose Fitzsimmons Elementary. It sat beside the Starbucks so the adults could enjoy a Frappuccino while the kids played. Brenden, as content as a turtle on a log, swung slowly with Marci on his right and Shawna on his left enjoying the colorful sunset.

There had been times when Brenden had thought of that night on the cruise ship and Marci's bikini incident. He couldn't help but picture her wearing only the skimpy, yellow bikini bottom from time to time. She was a beautiful woman.

She had come out of the bathroom a few nights earlier wearing a towel. Just a towel. Brenden had looked up at her and their eyes had met. Brenden was certain that she was thinking the same things as him. It made him feel momentarily awkward, but the look she gave him was relaxed and confident. Either she was good at hiding her feelings or she still felt the same way she had on the ship. She *had* openly asked him to touch her breasts.

Brenden had no intentions of pursuing anything sexual. He loved Shawna with all his heart. He would never jeopardize his marriage. That being said, it certainly wasn't a hardship living with two beautiful women every day.

"What are you thinking about?" Brenden glanced over at Shawna who had asked the question.

"Why?"

"You were totally lost in your thoughts and you looked happy. That's why. I want to know."

There was no reason to say anything but the truth. "I was thinking about you and how wonderful my life is."

"That's a good answer. Now what were you really thinking about?"

"No, really. I was thinking about how happily married we are, how lucky we are to have three healthy, beautiful kids, and how well the Unification Project is going."

"You do have it pretty amazing," Marci broke in. "There aren't many families like yours. You guys never really even fight! You just seem to be on the same page and if you're not, you work it out without getting angry. It was never like that with Matt."

"We have worked on it for years, and we still need to work at it all the time," Shawna responded. "We decided right from the start that we would always try to keep God the focus. If we make decisions with the other person in mind instead of thinking selfishly, things work out better. You always have to remember *what comes around, goes around*. It all works out fairly in the end."

"So what does that have to do with God?"

"That is the model God teaches in the Bible. Love the Lord your God with all your heart, soul and mind. Love your neighbor as yourself. So if we try to make decisions that are in line with how God wants us to live, and then if we treat others respectfully and with love, things tend to work out fairly well. When they don't, at least we did the best we could."

Marci turned to Brenden and Shawna. "But then you have to follow all of those rules all the time!"

"So, which ones are difficult to follow?" Brenden gently prodded.

Marci was about to speak, but hesitated. Brenden found himself trying to answer the same question. Finally Marci spoke, "Every time I think of something that I think you have to give up for God, it doesn't seem that important." She looked over briefly at the other two on the swings.

"There really aren't that many rules. Don't murder. Don't follow other Gods. Don't steal. Some of those are just common sense for anyone. The other things all fall in line with loving God and loving and respecting others. Don't lie, don't use God's name in vain . . . I can't even think of anymore right now." Brenden looked at Shawna to see if she had more to add where he left off. She just shrugged her shoulders.

Amanda started yelling, "Mommy! Mommy!" A glance at the playground revealed that she was stuck at the top of the slide. Her legs were hanging down the slide, but her arms were holding on for dear life. Obviously her courage to go down the slide had left her part way through the adventure.

Brenden jumped up and went to her aid. He helped her back up and then decided to go down the slide with her between his legs. With the fear of the unknown now gone, Amanda worked her way back up and slid down the slide on her own. Brenden chased Tyler and Rachel around the monkey bars before returning to the swings.

The conversation at the swings had turned to Matt and whether Marci could see getting back together with him.

"Why don't we invite him over in the next couple days," Shawna suggested. Maybe Brenden can have a man-to-man talk with him and see how sincere he is. If things go well, we can leave you two alone to talk it out."

"Do you think I should take him back?"

"Do you love him?"

"Yes."

"Do you think what he did is forgivable?"

"No!"

"Really? You could never forgive him?" Shawna kept her tone calm and non-judgmental. "I am not suggesting anything here, but I just want you to think about this.

Have you ever been tempted physically by another man? Can you understand how it could happen?"

Brenden was often surprised at how Shawna could ask the tough questions without jeopardizing relationships. In this case, he was glad Shawna had asked. After Marci's words and actions in the cabin on the cruise ship, Brenden had wondered how Marci could be so hard on Matt. Unless he had misread the situation terribly, Brenden touching Marci's naked body could easily have sent hormone levels out of control. Once those hormones get moving, it is incredibly difficult to stop. Brenden had experienced that a time or two when kids had unexpectedly needed help or the doorbell had rung when he and Shawna had been somewhere in the midst of physical intimacy.

Marci never turned to make eye contact. "I just don't understand why he would do that to me?" A tear rolled down her cheek as she spoke.

"What do you mean?" Shawna continued.

"I didn't realize that I wasn't good enough for him. I didn't realize that I wasn't satisfying him sexually." Marci's words were soft, but clear.

"So you think it was your fault?"

"Why else would he do it? I know I am not perfect. I know we fight sometimes. But most couples do, present company excluded of course!" She managed a slight smile to ease the tension.

"Have you asked him why he did it, Marci?"

"It was one of the first things I asked him, but I was so mad at the time, I can't remember what he said. I don't really think he gave me a solid reason."

"Maybe it is time to ask him. Don't blame yourself, Marci! You are a wonderful person. You are gorgeous! Matt is a very lucky man to have you, and he messed up royally! But . . . I believe he still loves you. Let's at least find out for sure."

Marci went back and forth on the swings three times without a response.

"OK?" Shawna was persistent.

Two more times Marci swung back and forth without a reply. Finally she dropped her head slightly and said, "OK."

Brenden called Matt and he agreed to come over the next Wednesday.

The demon Ygal listened to the conversation without displaying any outward sign of emotion. He didn't interfere. With the Power Shamus and the Virtue Alea on constant watch, it was not the time to start a confrontation.

The conversation was frustrating, however. Firstly, the Tavis couple had tried selling Marci on being Christian, and had done a remarkably good job of it. Secondly, there were only three days left before Matt and Marci might potentially put their relationship back together. It would be impossible to use Marci to break down the relationship between Brenden and Shawna if that happened, especially after the annoying Shawna got the whole adultery topic out in the open with Marci.

Still, all was not lost. Ygal was certain that Brenden found Marci attractive. It wasn't even necessary to coax Marci and Brenden to go all the way and actually have sex with each other. He just needed to create the possibility that something had happened. Trust was so easily broken among humans. If Shawna started to suspect something, damage could be done. If Brenden felt guilty about something, even more damage could be done!

Marci had not committed her life to God and, consequently, was in Satanael's domain. Shamus and Alea could keep Satanael away from the Tavis', but they couldn't keep him away from Marci.

"Adultery always seems easier to forgive if both parties are guilty," Ygal said out loud to himself. A month without sex! It would be easy to ignite the passion in Marci. Brenden would be the harder one to convince, but the right moment would come.

He would make sure of it!

The dark Dominion Ygal flew right over the swing set Brenden, Shawna and Marci had just been sitting on. Alea and Shamus watched until Ygal was well beyond visual sight.

"I thought that conversation went well, but it still makes me uneasy having that Dominion so clearly interested in this situation," Alea spoke still watching the evening sky where Ygal had disappeared.

"The Unification Project has been successful to this point, but it is only in its infancy. The foundation for success has just begun. Satanael and his followers will attack again. They will attack often and they will attack with strength. This time we will not have the scroll telling us of their plans. You should be uneasy, Alea! This is what the humans like to call the calm before the storm. We need to inform Doroniel of what we've just seen and heard."

Alea nodded and then proceeded to join the Tavis family, and their guest Marci, as they packed into the Tahoe. Soon after returning home, Brand and three angel sentries came to stand guard until Shamus and Alea returned from speaking with Doroniel.

Ygal's opportunity came sooner than even he expected.

CHAPTER TWENTY-EIGHT

To the pure, all things are pure, but to those who are corrupted and do not believe, nothing is pure. In fact, both their minds and consciences are corrupted.
Titus 1:15

"Tucking in three kids with three adults is great!" Brenden said as he poured three glasses of Pinot Gris.

"We don't have to get up early, so hot tub anyone?" Shawna was already making her way to the stairs to go get changed.

Marci had turned on the TV and was flicking through channels, but hit the power button while replying, "Who can argue with wine and a hot tub?"

"I'm in!" Brenden added. "Well, I'm not in yet, but I will be shortly. I'm in for the idea but not yet in the tub, in case that was confusing for you."

"Your brain is confusing for me!" Marci bantered back.

"I know. How are you supposed to understand perfection when you are not perfect? I wouldn't expect you to understand me."

"Oh, I am only confused because you fail to understand how far from perfection you really are!" Marci was now right behind Shawna ready to go upstairs.

"If you were really perfect," Shawna decided to join in, "then you would have the cover off the tub and some snacks ready to eat with the wine. That is what a perfect husband would do." She batted her eyelashes.

"It just so happens that I was going to take the lid off and have snacks ready, but now that you asked for it, I have decided, in all my perfection, that you need to learn your manners. You shall, therefore, have to take your own lid off and apologize before I will bless you with my presence in the hot tub."

Shawna and Marci looked at each other, back at Brenden, and then back at each other. "We are so sorry, your majesty!" both women said in unison. Shawna continued. "Please forgive us, your humble servants, and bless us with your presence."

After a slight bow, Brenden spoke with a serious, almost stern face. "Apology accepted. Now hurry off before I change my mind. You are dismissed." He slurped at his wine with his pinky finger raised toward the ceiling.

"Stuck up and pious! What a man!"

"And humble!" Marci said.

"Don't forget perfect!" Brenden reminded them.

After changing and getting cheese, crackers and chocolate, Brenden was still the first outside and decided it was in his own best interests to take the lid off so he could get into the 103 degree, bubbling water. He was taking his first taste of wine when Marci and Shawna strolled out in their bikinis and joined him.

Brenden thought about saying something witty, but decided instead to put his head back and stare up at the stars. It was truly a beautiful summer evening. The girls eased their way in and did the same. All three sat quietly in corner seats looking up at the heavens.

Barely audible over the sound of the bubbling jets came the words, "Thank you guys." Marci was stretched out toward the empty corner of the tub. Her hair was back in a ponytail. "This really means a lot to me. I don't know who I would have turned to if you weren't here. My family, I guess, but . . ." She left the sentence unfinished.

"You're welcome. It has been fun having you around actually. I just wish you were here for different reasons."

"Me too."

Brenden nodded but didn't add his own thoughts. He felt the same way. He had really enjoyed having her around. In fact, he was feeling guilty about that. It wasn't that he had done anything wrong. She was staying at their house out of circumstance. Shawna was a great friend, and Shawna had invited Marci to stay.

The part that bothered him inside, just a little, was that he liked the freshness, the newness, of having another beautiful woman in the house. He liked looking at her. It didn't change anything about how he felt about Shawna. He loved her just as much as ever. She was still just as beautiful. They were best friends. Their relationship was stable and strong.

What man wouldn't enjoy this situation? It was natural, wasn't it? To find a woman attractive wasn't a sin.

He didn't lust for Marci. At least he didn't think it would be considered lust. Granted, the picture of her mostly nude body was firmly imprinted on his brain. His brain had filled in the rest of the picture sometimes, the picture of Marci entirely nude. It wasn't much of a stretch from what he had seen. Remove the little yellow bikini bottoms and replace them with "au natural".

But picturing a woman nude was not the same as desiring to have sex with them. He had, if he was honest with himself, let his mind imagine what it would be like with Marci, but he had never really desired it or seriously wanted it. The New Testament said that even desiring to be adulterous was sin, even if you didn't ever physically cheat on your spouse. He hadn't done that. He hadn't *desired* to be intimate with her.

So why was he having this internal struggle? Was his conscience just keeping him honest? He knew he was close to the line, but he hadn't crossed it, had he?

"I am doing nothing wrong enjoying the company of a gorgeous woman." He repeated the thought a few times to himself to put the struggle to rest.

"Well I hope things can get somewhat back to normal soon," Marci continued.

"Whatever normal is. As much as I love it here, I want to go home. I want my old Matt back." She paused. "Do you think that's possible?" Marci looked at Brenden this time.

"I think it'll take years for you to regain entire trust with Matt when it comes to him cheating on you. Neither of you will forget that it happened. That doesn't mean, however, that you can't make it work with him. Everyone makes mistakes. If you believe Matt is really sorry for what he did, I believe forgiveness is an option. Focus on what is right in your marriage, and don't blame yourself."

"What if he isn't sorry?"

"That would be tougher. Let's reserve judgment until after Wednesday."

Again the mellow, relaxing sound of the jets was all that could be heard.

"I have a question for you," Shawna put her feet up on Brenden's lap as she continued questioning Marci. "I know both you and Matt had other relationships before you got married. You both had sex with other people. Was that weird? Do you ever think about that when you are with him?"

"Not really. It just seemed normal. I don't know very many people who didn't have sex before they got married. Until I met you guys, I don't know if I knew anyone who hadn't. That's why I think it must be weird for you!"

"That is why I am asking," Shawna smiled. She couldn't imagine having this conversation with anyone but Matt or Marci. "In nearly every way I am not sure what it would feel like to be in your position."

"Are you asking if it makes it easier to forgive and forget what Matt did because it isn't the first time he has had sex with someone other than me?"

"No!" Shawna backpedaled a bit. "I am not trying to minimize what he did. He still broke trust. He committed to being with only you when you got married."

Brenden was surprised that Marci didn't appear offended. Marci's tone remained the same. "I guess in some ways you might be right," Marci responded. "The act of sex probably doesn't bother me the same way it would you. We are sexual beings. I haven't had any physical contact in weeks and it's nearly killing me! It makes me horny just thinking about it!"

"It is not like I am afraid Matt will constantly compare me to "sleazy sales girl". Matt dated a lot of girls before me. I didn't marry him for his purity." She even managed to laugh at her last comment. "I guess the same could be said for him marrying me. Matt wasn't the first man to get these," Marci cupped her breasts and gave them a couple shakes. They all smiled at the confession.

Brenden couldn't help but notice how firm her breasts still were.

After a few moments, Shawna kept pushing the conversation further. "Is that why you are struggling with blaming yourself for this? Do you think you weren't living up to his expectations in some other area?"

"I think so. If I was sure this was just a random loss of control of his hormones, I wouldn't be as concerned. That could happen to any of us, couldn't it? But what if this is the result of other parts of our marriage being messed up? What if he doesn't love me anymore?"

Again, Brenden was amazed at the lack of emotion in Marci's voice. It was the first time she had simply spoken her thoughts out loud. Brenden couldn't help but think Marci was finally ready to deal with the situation logically instead of emotionally.

"I guess you know what questions you really have to ask Matt about then," Brenden offered.

Marci nodded slowly. "I guess so."

"So let me get this right. If Matt just had a fling because his sex drive got the best of him, but he is totally happy with your marriage, you are ready to forgive him?" Shawna was good at getting to the point.

"Well I wouldn't make it that easy for him, but yeah, I guess that would be right."

"What would you do to not make it easy for him?" Brenden had to ask.

"I don't know," Marci looked up at the stars in thought. "Maybe give him some of his own medicine. Right now we are broken up. I could have a fling of my own to show him what it feels like and then forgive him," she laughed, but Brenden sensed the comment was not entirely innocent.

Brenden glanced at Shawna. The look in her eyes told him that she was concerned about the statement as well. It was obvious to both of them that Marci didn't make decisions with the same moral set of standards that they did. Certainly neither did Matt.

It wasn't the first time Brenden had clearly understood the differing view Marci had about what was considered okay physically even though she was still married.

It wouldn't be the last time.

CHAPTER TWENTY-NINE

Great is our Lord and mighty in power;
his understanding has no limit.
Psalm 147:5

"I'm concerned about an outright attack, Dominion Doroniel." The tone in Shamus voice was serious and urgent. "After all that's occurred, after all that we've seen, and after seeing that evil Dominion Ygal, I believe the enemy is poised to strike."

Shamus and Alea had found the Dominion in one of the gardens in the North Realm. Alea was sitting beside the Dominion on a bench under a massive oak beside the path connecting the Hall of Red with the angel combat training headquarters. Shamus was standing. Alea knew the Power well enough to know he was anxious to return to Alderwood.

"Prayer has diminished, Shamus."

"Then it is time to inspire some prayer!"

"The Unification has begun smoothly. More people are involved, but apathy has already set in. No "major problem" means only "minor prayer". We do not have the same power we had at the beginning. Unless the Almighty commands more numbers to join in protection, we must be ready to protect with the angels that are assigned to the mission." Alea noticed a look of distress on Doroniel's face. She hadn't seen that before.

"Do you think the Almighty will make that command?" Alea asked.

"The Unification is important to Him. He knows the situation as you have explained it to me, and He knows things we do not yet know. I believe an attack is imminent, Alea, but what the strength of that attack will be . . ." Doroniel left the question hanging.

"Where do you suggest we focus our strength, then?" Shamus spoke the words with little emotion. Alea sensed the warrior side of Shamus taking over.

The question about where to send angels for protection was answered.

Not by Doroniel.

The alarm in the training headquarters sounded. Shamus, Alea and Doroniel flew to formation without hesitation. It took a moment before instructions were given to the thousands of warriors that had assembled in front of the headquarters.

Shamus looked into Alea's golden eyes.

He didn't speak audibly, but Alea knew.

The attack had begun. The enemy was one step ahead.

"What timing!" Alea commented as she and Shamus began the cosmic travel back to Earth. "We were only gone a matter of hours."

"Ygal will have been waiting for us to leave. It was perfect timing, Alea. Perfect on their part."

Few words were spoken on the remaining journey. Both the Virtue and the Power were running through possible scenarios they'd encounter when they returned to

Alderwood. Their mandate was to protect Brenden and Shawna from attack. That was the easy part. Exactly what the attack would be directed at and what the size of the enemy force would be were unknown.

Alea would find the Tavis' and assess the form of the attack. Shamus would find Brand, if she still fought, and meet the demon force with the power of a second red blade. A contingent of warriors Shamus had counted at five hundred and sixteen was following his lead. As with most battles, the goal was to break through the enemy force and interfere with the attack before it caused serious damage to the people involved. Vaporizing enemy demons was inevitable, but not the goal. Even vaporized demons returned at some point in the future.

Similar size angel armies had been directed to other points of attack. Zopheniel would be protecting Pastor Phil, but that attack was occurring indirectly at a house in the Everett area.

A third demonic interference had been centered on Jerry, the traveler, and his team in the Ukraine.

A fourth force had been sent to Oregon.

The angels behind Alea and Shamus moved into attack formations as the army slowed. They were entering the outer atmosphere. A feeling of déjà vu swept over Alea as she saw the mountains below. The last time she had approached Alderwood from this angle, she had almost been captured by the dark Dominion Ygal. She did not look forward to seeing Ygal's sword again, but inwardly she expected the demon would be front and center in the battle they were about to enter.

As they neared the rooftops of their destination, Alea's suspicions were confirmed. Awaiting the attack from the angels, the menacing form of Ygal looked skyward from the back deck of the Tavis house.

It was night. Lights were on around the hot tub, in the kitchen and in the master bedroom upstairs, but the illumination from the bulbs was hardly visible through the wall of black demons that covered the house like tar.

A glint of red broke through the dark mass.

The red of an angel sword.

The Power Brand still fought.

CHAPTER THIRTY

It is more blessed to give than to receive.
Acts 20:35

Jerry's back was sore, and he couldn't wait for a proper sleep in a prone position. The Ukraine team had flown to New York and then on to London. After a five-hour layover and another flight to Kiev, the team had gotten into a large passenger van and driven for nearly ten hours before reaching their mission headquarters in the town of Nikopol, Ukraine. Jerry was used to flying and the rigors of travel, but this trip had worn him out.

The team of 11 had been welcomed with hugs by the host families in Nikopol. Three of the couples would be staying in one host house while the other two couples and Jerry would be in a second house a mile down the potholed road.

Ukraine was an interesting mix of old and new. Most houses were old and crumbling. The paint was peeling. Wood was rotting. The effects of years of communist rule were everywhere. The people now owned the land, but many had little or no money to live. In contrast, brand new gas stations would sit on a street corner. McDonald's in Kiev was not much different than the McDonald's at home. Even the poorest of widows carried a cell phone for communication.

The government of Ukraine continued to wrestle with corruption. Social programs did not exist. There was no welfare. There was no health care program. In fact, doctors went hungry without getting a second job. People were in need physically and spiritually.

Jerry could envision his own bed in his recently purchased apartment in Alderwood. It was the middle of the night in Northwest Washington. If he were home, Jerry would climb under his heavy, blue comforter and try to finish his prayer time before he fell asleep. His body was shutting down and ready for a good night's sleep. The problem was that it was noon in Nikopol. The other ten members of the team were all as exhausted as he was.

The plan was to rest today and start working tomorrow. Work would begin with purchasing supplies for the hampers that they would be leaving with the Babushkas during their week-long stay. The team would provide flour, sugar, soap and other household items with the widowed Ukrainian women who were often alone and left to fend for themselves. So many men had died during World War II and the Communist era that followed. Many more had simply left their wives and children rather than try to take care of them with limited means. Alcoholism and suicide were common ingredients in the recipe for poverty.

It was early afternoon the next day when the team went out to buy supplies for the bags they would pack after dinner. The goal was to make 200 packs. 200 would be a good start. It reminded Jerry of a story he had once heard. A young couple was walking down the beach hand-in-hand. The shoreline was covered with fish that had been stranded by the receding tide. As they walked, they saw an old, bearded fellow picking up fish and throwing them into the sea. The young couple approached the old man and laughingly commented, "Why do you bother throwing fish into the sea? You will never get them all. Look how many there are!"

The old man heaved one more fish into the sea, paused to see it swim away, and then looked at the young couple. "Well, it may not make a difference to them all, but it made all the difference in the world to that one!"

Jerry told the story to the team as they were sampling some of the many Ukrainian candies the host family had provided for them. He was sure many of them had heard the analogy before, but he told it anyway. "We won't get them all, but those hampers could make all the difference in the world to the 200 women and families that get them."

He believed in that concept. The others did, too. That was why they would spend thousands of their own dollars and a bunch of their own time to travel halfway around the world to buy groceries and fill plastic bags.

It wasn't until they were loading the bags of flour into the back of the van that Jerry noticed the pain in his chest. He wasn't sure what the tightness meant, but it was an instant pain he had not encountered before. He let the rest of the team load the remaining supplies. The pain diminished as he sat in the front seat of the van on the way back to the host houses. He went to use the bathroom, which was actually a North American style toilet instead of a hole in the ground, while the team unpacked. Jerry didn't bother to tell anyone about the pain. He was tired. It might have just been a tweaked muscle. He would wait and see if it happened again before worrying too much.

Four angels had accompanied Maspial on the journey to Nikopol. The team, from his angelic perspective, was strong in its faith. The members had incorporated consistent prayer and they had the right mindset for a trip of this nature; they were relaxed and expected a few complications along the way.

One rogue demon had attempted to derail the team as they were passing through customs in Kiev by heaping suspicion about the team on the customs officer that watched as the team approached. Maspial had expected an attack here. He managed to foresee the problem and touched the mind of Brice, a thirty-two year old team member, so as to create an urgent bathroom stop before taking the team through customs. The team turned to find some seats and wait the few extra minutes.

Maspial could tell the delay bothered Jerry. Jerry just wanted to get through this part. "It is all right, Jerry," he whispered. "Patience is a virtue. Sometimes delays are necessary." Jerry relaxed a little. Humans had such a hard time understanding the full scope of the spiritual realm and how it affected their lives.

The extra minutes provided enough time for two of the other angels, Panthielle and Jalel, to dispose of the demon. At the same time, Brice's wife Jan was silently praying that all would go smoothly through customs. Three other angels, strengthened by prayer and sent by the Almighty, brought words of wisdom to the group as they passed through customs. With God's help, the team passed through without raising any alarms or causing any delays.

Outside of that event, the trip had gone smoothly. More resistance from the enemy was expected, but with the five of them assigned to protect the team, and with consistent prayer support by the team and from a steadfast congregation back in Seattle, Maspial was ready and confident.

So it wasn't as if the enemy caught Maspial and the others off guard when they attacked, but the sheer size of the attacking force *was* unexpected.

Including the van driver, the interpreter, the host couple and the eleven foreigners, there were fifteen immediate targets for the angels to protect. In the larger scope of the Unification, Jerry needed to be given primary protection. His vision went beyond the team he now led, and his experience and connections around the world would take time to replace. Maspial did not know what the demons' intent was, but delay, injury or emotional stress were the most likely; anything that could stop or demoralize the good that was being done by the team.

A wave of black evil hit Maspial before any other thoughts were formed. He managed to deflect any blades intended to pierce his spiritual being and kept his larger form completely around Jerry. A second wave approached. This time Maspial was ready and not only parried any blows, but managed to catch the lead demon through the wing as the enemy charged by like the flow of electrons in a copper wire.

The demon was not vaporized, but lost balance. In that fraction of a second, Maspial could have finished him. The dark eyes of the demon met Maspial's and opened wider acknowledging the same fact. But Maspial did not strike.

It was as clear as the water in the pool of Eden that delay was the only option for victory the five angels had against such a force. Help would already have been sent by the Almighty. The brilliant stream of God's army would overtake the present darkness . . . eventually.

The question Maspial could not answer was "when"? Rush after rush of Godless angels hit Maspial. He staggered once, but recovered in time to surprise the thick, feminine demon that had narrowly missed his left shoulder with her dark greenish-hued blade. All Maspial's force was behind the thrust that drove his silver weapon directly through her thin-lipped mouth. She shrieked as she vaporized. The space that had been filled by her large form allowed Maspial the opportunity to see if his angel companions were still holding out in their own battles.

About twenty feet away, a sphere of black encircled the others. Maspial counted three silver swords shimmering as they struck with blinding speed at the prison around them. It was likely that the fourth angel had been pierced. Eight humans were within the sphere of black, and Maspial spotted the six other team members with a peripheral glance.

It was a containment sphere. It was meant for delay, not attack. If the demons had not attacked the six unguarded humans, and were not after anyone in the sphere, only one further option remained. Jerry was the target!

Another wave exploded down upon Maspial and the human body of Jerry Moore. Again the clashing of blades drowned out any other sounds. This time, however, the wave was deeper. The attack became constant. With the companion angels blocked from providing any aid, the enemy could focus all its attention on fulfilling the mission. Blade after blade and demonic face after demonic face streamed into view.

Then came the demon Power with his toned, hulking form. Maspial diverted the first blow that came from the once red sword of the Power, but the second blow came with such strength that Maspial could not hold his position. Maspial's form wavered backward exposing the flesh of the traveler he was protecting. The dark Power continued to attack. The grinning face of another follower of Satanael stopped directly in front of Jerry who was standing behind the van with a bag of flour in his hands.

Maspial attempted to lean forward, to regain his position, but the Power did not allow it. The second demon dropped his eyes to the chest of Jerry. A serious expression erased the grin on his face as he carefully directed the tip of his sword into Jerry's chest.

A wall of light met the evil darkness in the parking lot of the Ukrainian grocery store. Help had arrived. Both demons felt it. The dark Power turned to fight the angels of God. The second demon, only momentarily slowed by the distraction, looked back at Jerry intent on completing his task.

With a flick of the wrist and inhuman accuracy, the tip of Maspial's silver blade was thrust through Jerry's back and precisely into the tip of the demon's sword. The sword of evil fully left the flesh of the man standing between the two spiritual beings. Maspial withdrew his own blade while simultaneously grabbing a double-tipped knife from beneath his wing. He flung himself through Jerry and landed the knife into the mid-section of the demon. The demon watched as Jerry bent over in pain.

The ugly grin on the demon's face reformed as he evaporated.

The sound of battle filled the parking lot as the team from Seattle, entirely unaware of any of it, went on with their task of carrying and loading the van with supplies. No one noticed Jerry flinch, and he did not let on that anything was wrong. Maspial knew that damage had been done, but he did not know to what extent.

His priority was to make sure Jerry was okay, but with the angel attack from above, the enemy mass was being forced right on top of Maspial. Most of the demons were facing away, but it would only take one to notice an unsuspecting Maspial and vaporize him. He would do it if he thought there was immediate danger to the traveler. He glanced once more at Jerry, and then began vaporizing defenseless enemies. Maspial had pierced seven demons before the black crowd around him realized the danger.

When the initial surprise of attack was over, Maspial cut straight through the mass above him until he surfaced out of the dark sea of evil. His allies above had seen him coming and made way for his retreat.

Maspial turned to survey the scene. A quick count revealed several hundred angels and nearly that many demons. Black demon swords met the angels' silver ones as the enemy morphed into a dome defense. The dome was holding in most areas, but was caving in near the van after the damage Maspial had just caused to the demon formation.

The Archangel Raphael who reared the only platinum colored sword in the fight was, by all signs, leading the attack. He approached Maspial.

"Could you determine the goal of their attack?"

Maspial kept an eye on Jerry as he responded. "They were after Jerry Moore, the man in the front passenger seat of the van. I held them off as long as I could, but the enemy has inflicted some damage. I didn't have time to investigate Jerry's health, but I did see him bend in pain."

"We were sent to protect the entire team," Raphael replied. "Are you certain there were no other targets?"

"The enemy created a containment sphere around eight members of the team. The four other angels trying to protect Jerry with me held their ground as long as they could. I saw no other attacks. I did not see any demon contact with the other six members of the team outside the sphere. I cannot be certain, but I am confident Jerry was the sole target."

"I fear with these numbers that the demon force may not be finished. If we don't penetrate their defensive position, they may try a secondary attack. I'll coordinate the angels to take control around the van. Retake your position beside Jerry. With your sword and mine, it shall not take us long." Raphael relayed his commands.

Without delay, the two flashed toward the van. The angel attack knifed through like a harpoon into the blubbery mass of a whale. Raphael's platinum sword and many other silver ones filled the void that was created. Maspial took position beside Jerry confident in his safety as the blade of the Archangel defended the position. Maspial hadn't noticed any high-ranking demons apart from the Power who precipitated the attack on Jerry. The dark Power was directing the enemy defense in full view of Maspial, but it was clear that the demon position was collapsing in spite of his efforts. The opportunity for a secondary attack by the demons had passed.

All the team members were now in the van. The entire battle in human terms would have lasted less than three minutes. The team would go on with their day oblivious to the spiritual chaos that had surrounded them.

All except Jerry.

The van drove away from the battle scene. The angel force had now created a wall between themselves and the van. As other buildings blocked the scene from view, Maspial saw the dark Power signaling for retreat. He took to diagnosing the damage to Jerry's body as the van bumped its way along the road.

CHAPTER THIRTY-ONE

The night is nearly over; the day is almost here. So let us put aside the deeds of darkness and put on the armor of light.
Romans 13:12

Alea got close enough to the house to see that Brand was in the master bedroom fending off demons. Shawna was the only human in the room. Alea turned toward the hot tub, but her view was instantly obstructed. Ygal had been expecting Alea and Shamus, and he moved into Alea's path. Shamus had forced his way into the bedroom with a large contingent of the angel force.

Alea was supported by her own group of angel warriors, but Ygal's black eyes ignored all but the Virtue. She pulled out her blue blade in spite of the fact she had no intention of battling one-on-one with Ygal.

Ready for this moment, a hundred demons filled the space behind the dark Dominion, their blackened blades sucking hope from the air around them. Ygal's lack of concern was understandable.

The feminine angel's blonde hair flew sideways as she glanced toward the kids' rooms where the rest of the angel army had been directed. Tyler, Rachel and Amanda could easily be targets for the attack. Any demons in those rooms would have been met full force by the angels of light. If there was no imminent danger for the children, many of the angels directed there would return to aid in other areas.

Alea would know in seconds if the children were safe.

Giving a nearly imperceptible signal with the tip of her right wing, the warriors behind Alea tore into the demon force before them. Ygal was met with the onslaught of silver. Three angels were erased into a stream of white smoke at the hand of the Dominion, but more filled the space.

Alea didn't want to get caught alone, but she needed to get to the hot tub on the back deck of the house. She could retreat and attempt an alternate route, but she didn't trust Ygal. He had anticipated the angel arrival. He had cut off her path once. He would expect Alea to try to reach Brenden who, Alea was confident by this point, was in the hot tub.

Her mind raced. What would Ygal not expect? Her slender form moved before her mind had committed to a plan. Blond hair streaked toward the master bedroom and the bulk of the enemy force. She needed Shamus or Brand.

Alea bowled full force into the wings of a gangly demon knocking him off balance long enough for another angel to seize the moment and pierce the fallen being. Shamus acknowledged Alea with a spark in his golden eyes and he ruthlessly turned his energy on the wall of black separating himself from Alea. Other angels noticed the movement and joined in clearing a path for the Virtue.

The demonic enemy saw it too, but did not react quickly enough to stop it.

The battle was one the enemy was trying to win with delay. Even with the influx of 300 angels, little ground was being gained where it needed to be gained. The children were safe as the angels sent there had returned, but whoever was in the hot tub was unguarded and it was all the angels could do to keep the enemy away from Shawna.

Alea had hoped to team with Shamus to break through to the back deck from the upstairs bedroom where they now were, but it was obvious that Shawna would be in danger if Shamus' sword were not part of the force protecting her from evil.

"Can we get to the back deck?" Alea asked her allies in hope of a solution she had not yet thought of.

"Not without losing ground here." Shamus answered as Alea had expected.

"Brand, what should be our priority?"

"I still don't know what we're trying to stop. I suspect they need influence with Shawna and they're certainly isolating Brenden and Marci outside. We don't appear to be gaining an advantage anywhere. Are more angels coming?"

"Not that we're aware of," said Shamus as he disposed of three more demons. Brand pierced two more and a slight gap opened. Alea wasn't being attacked, nor was she attacking. It was decision time again. Alea surveyed the area. Ygal had separated himself from the swordplay and was looking over the battle. His narrowed eyes met with Alea's. He continued to stare, waiting for her next move.

Shawna Tavis was opening the closet door in the bedroom and retrieving her housecoat. The water drops on her naked body sparkled like jewels under the pot lights in the ceiling. Her wet bikini lay on the floor.

If she and Shamus moved quickly, she was confident they could reach Brenden. She began to open her mouth to suggest to Shamus that they try it when the Dominion Ygal raised his sword and yelled to his demon soldiers, "Now!"

The demon movement was immediate. Every dark angel other than Ygal himself converged on the bedroom. The angels did not anticipate fast enough. A spike of black drove at the two Powers and the Virtue angel separating the rest of the angels from them. The number of demons was similar to the number of angels, but the coordination of the enemy movement gave them the advantage.

The demons fought with their backs to the middle, their swords out in front of them, in a long semi-circular formation that was designed to take control of an area quickly, but not necessarily for a long period of time.

"This is it!" yelled out Brand as she lashed out at the line that was trying to come between her and Shawna. Shamus followed the lead and forced the line of demons through the closet wall. Alea took the opportunity. She flew up beside Shawna and whispered into her being.

"God is with you. Your marriage is . . ." The last word was not clearly enunciated as the line of demons burst through the wall and knocked her tumbling back. "Strong!" she yelled. "Your marriage is strong!"

Alea was at least eight feet away, and the buzz of demon voices drowned out her words.

The enemy line tightened its arch around Shawna. A path between demon soldiers, like a fashion model runway, led from Shawna to the patio doors of the bedroom. A demon approached the beautiful woman who had just secured her robe around her waist.

"I wonder what they are talking about?" he yelled. "Go listen on the deck. Go. Aren't you curious? You have no reason not to listen."

Shawna paused. Her eyes blinked as her mind filtered through the information it had just received. It wouldn't have been a strong communication, but she would have heard it.

Alea looked at her ally Powers. They drove forward, swords swinging in unison. Green haze filled the room as demons vaporized.

Shawna walked toward the patio.

Alea could see Ygal descend outside past the patio down toward the back deck and the hot tub.

A group of about twenty angels broke off toward the dark Dominion, but they were cut off by the demons who were in perfect position to protect Ygal.

The line of demons folded back, filling the space between the Powers and Shawna. Many were pierced, but Shawna had already reached the patio door. She turned the handle and stepped out, silently, onto the deck.

There were too many demons.

The angels wouldn't reach her in time.

CHAPTER THIRTY-TWO

Do not be misled: Bad company corrupts good character.
1 Corinthians 15:33

"It feels like we were just on that cruise." Marci sat up on the edge of the tub to cool down. Her hair was back in a ponytail and she was leaning back on her hands. Brenden noticed how small her feminine body was. Small, almost fragile, but beautiful.

"I so enjoyed that trip! I would go back in a heartbeat!"

"Me too." Marci spoke the words with less vigor then Brenden and he assumed that had to do with the fact she and Matt were not together anymore. "Watch your towel. It might get stolen again."

"It wouldn't surprise me," Brenden said with a smile. "Some rogue raccoon will leap into the yard and run away with my towel!"

"At least this time you can't get locked out of your room."

"And there is another woman in the house who can fix your broken bikini clip!" The words slipped out before

Brenden had considered whether it was wise to broach the subject. "*Too late now*," he thought to himself.

"True. This one works though." Marci unclipped her top and then reattached it in order to make her point. Brenden's heart sped up and the water felt warmer. Marci was so free with her body. She lacked the embarrassment, or the worry, or whatever it was that most women had about their bodies. It was confidence, Brenden concluded. Marci just knew that she was beautiful.

They were quiet again for a bit. Both of them stared at the stars. Shawna was pretty, too, but Brenden couldn't imagine her actually undoing her top with other people around. Brenden knew Shawna didn't even like to sit on the edge when other people were around because she was insecure about how she looked.

It was flirtatious. That was all there was to it. Marci was flirtatious around Brenden. She was probably like that with other men, too, Brenden presumed. He was intrigued by it, though. He liked it, he admitted to himself.

"It is more fun to sit in a hot tub without any annoying clothing on. You and Shawna must have skinny-dipped out here before?"

"Yup."

"And . . ."

"A very freeing experience!" Brenden remembered numerous times he and Shawna had slipped out of their bathing suits once they were in the tub. There were too many windows of neighboring houses to just strut out of the house naked, although Brenden was pretty sure that wouldn't have stopped Matt or Marci.

"It sure is more convenient," Marci continued. "Grab a towel, whip off the clothes, jump in. After you're done, you dry off, throw your clothes back on, or not, and you're done. No wet swim suit to take care of and it feels more natural in the water."

"That is true. There's nothing more annoying than putting on a freezing cold swim suit because it is still wet from the last time you were in the water."

"I might just try it next time." Marci was flirting again. "Do you think it would make Shawna uncomfortable if I was naked?"

"I think so. Especially the first time."

"I already know it would make you uncomfortable!"

"What makes you so sure?"

Neither of them noticed the upstairs patio door open or Shawna, changed and in her housecoat, step out onto the deck.

"Well the last time I was naked in front of you, I could barely get you to look at me!"

"What do you mean? I helped you take your bikini off!" Brenden's face dripped of sarcasm as he said the words.

"You are an expert bikini remover!" Marci admitted.

"Amazingly, I am a fast learner."

"I bet you say that to all the girls."

Brenden shrugged. It was a bit awkward flirting with another woman, but he was just joking around. They both knew it. "I only say that to the girls I undress."

They both laughed. Brenden was glad to have finally spoken about the cruise ship incident with Marci. It had happened. It was an innocent act on his part. He hadn't done anything he wouldn't tell Shawna about if he felt it necessary to do so. It was one of those things that could happen when you had friends like Matt and Marci.

"Speaking of undressing, I think it's that time again." Marci stood up and began toweling off. Brenden took a long look at the lines of her body as she stood facing the other way. "Matt was crazy to leave such a beautiful woman," he thought to himself again. Hopefully the two of them would get back together soon.

He got out of the water as the patio door clicked shut on the deck above.

CHAPTER THIRTY-THREE

Therefore do not let sin reign in your mortal body so that you obey its evil desires.
Romans 6:12

The Dominion Doroniel stood behind the glass lectern of the Alderwood Evangelical Church, but his head was turned down. He was not speaking to the congregation of angels before him. He was listening as the angels debriefed the recent attacks by the enemy.

Maspial had just outlined the events in Nikopol, Ukraine. Major catastrophe had been averted, but Jerry had suffered a minor heart attack. Jerry was unlikely to have it checked until he got back to the States, and Maspial was uncertain as to what the doctors would order for recovery. It was likely that Jerry would have to take it easy for a while even in a best case scenario.

Otherwise, the mission trip in the Ukraine had been a success. The elderly were being cared for. The orphans were being given love and hope. The people who had traveled to Ukraine were growing in their spiritual maturity. Fourteen people had accepted God as their

Savior and given their lives to Him! This news was met with cheering and shouts of "Praise the Lord Almighty" by the other angels in the sanctuary.

Before Maspial, the Power Brand had similarly given a review of the attack on the Tavis house. Some of the angels trying to fend off the demon attack had been close enough to overhear the conversation in the hot tub that Ygal had "orchestrated". Many of the other angels, including Alea, Shamus and Brand, had seen the devastated expression on the face of Shawna Tavis as she reentered the bedroom from the patio. Shawna had heard every word and feared the worst.

The demon attack had been successful. The potential for serious damage to the relationship of Brenden and Shawna and to the Unification Project was extreme.

Zopheniel spoke next. "Pastor Phil conducted marriage counseling for a young couple in this area back in April and May. The young man's parents attend this church and he has come occasionally. His fiancé is not a believer, but agreed to the counseling to appease her soon to be in-laws. By the end of the sessions, Phil had warned of potential difficulties the couple would face in light of their conflicting spiritual beliefs and the young lady's fear of commitment in marriage."

"Two days ago, the young man called off the wedding. His fiancé was furious. She threw a DVD at him on the way out the door, which by the way, was a copy of the movie "The Break-Up". Zopheniel paused to smile. "She blamed the split on Pastor Phil. Last night, the still hostile young lady met with another bitter friend at a local bar called *The Next Pint*. This is where the enemy attack occurred."

"With no Christian presence around, the dark angels focused the discussion on hatred and revenge. A phone call was made to a lawyer friend suggesting that Pastor

Phil had inappropriately touched her when he gave her a hug after one of the counseling sessions. There were also comments about Phil flirting with her when her fiancé was not around. The bottom line was that Phil was being accused of sexual harassment. Not true. Lies aimed to hurt. We all know, however, that even when accusations are totally false, they can ruin careers and the integrity of those involved."

"The lawyer friend, who had just finished her third glass of wine at home with her new boyfriend, spilled the story on him with little regard for confidentiality. An angel named Carmelle was present at the time because of the prayers of the ex-fiancé. Carmelle relayed the details of what was happening and the danger that was apparent."

"The angel Carmelle and I," Zopheniel continued, "encouraged the angry woman's only other Christian friend to call and invite her to come over and watch a movie. By the end of the evening, the two had watched "The Princess Bride" which reminded the angry woman of an old boyfriend she still cared for deeply. She told her Christian friend the whole story including the break-up from earlier in the evening. The friend talked her out of the law suit and encouraged her to find her "farm boy" from the past and move on." Zopheniel smiled again.

"At this point, the law suit has been called off and disaster for Pastor Phil has been avoided. The emotions of people can be their strength and their weakness all at the same time."

The other angels in the church nodded.

The Principality angel Ramuel had been flying back and forth up near the projector on the ceiling of the church. He, like many of the angels at the gathering, had only listened up to this point. "My turn," he called out as he lowered himself to sit on the top of the black, baby grand piano.

"Now the details of attack number four. Not all of you understand how my connection with the President and Brand's work in Portland connect with the Unification Project, but you will by the time I'm done."

"There's a marriage set for this coming Saturday between a young lady named Alana Reese and a young man named Conner Harris. Alana is the daughter of Senator Reese. Conner is the man Jerry the traveler met thanks to a few delays on a trip back from Columbus. Conner has written a book called *The Able Earth* that parallels the Unification Project in many ways. He is a passionate young man both for his cause and his soon to be wife."

"Conner was highly impressed with Jerry's vision for the UP and is soon to be related to a personal and close friend of the President, Senator Reese. This is how it all comes together. If it remains the will of the Almighty, and if the President and Senator continue to seek God for wisdom, and if the enemy can be kept out of the equation, the President will hear about *and* support the work of the Unification Project in a number of important ways. There are many steps still to be taken before this comes to fruition, but it's still on track even after the latest attack from the enemy."

"We're presently unsure of how the dark angels learned of this connection, but as the other three attacks were happening, a fourth contingent of demons converged on Senator Reese in a restaurant in Lincoln City where he was meeting with some supporters of his. The Power Brand was at the Tavis', a fact the enemy was well aware of, and the angels who had been left to protect the Senator were overcome by the vast number of demons."

"The Senator has been known to drink too much from time to time, and he fell to temptation on this occasion as well. With high levels of alcohol in his system, Senator Reese began driving himself back to Portland. By the time the legion of angels sent as reinforcements could fend off the demons, the Senator was less than a minute from an alcohol road check that would certainly have resulted in an arrest."

"The Senator has been charged with drinking and driving before. Another criminal charge would most likely have resulted in his dismissal as a Senator." Ramuel paused long enough to let the angels connect all the dots. If the Senator lost his position, then all the work that had been done to connect the Unification Project with the President would have fallen apart.

"The Virtue Para was able to get close enough to the Senator to convince him to pull into the next hotel he passed to sleep off the effects of his drinking. A huge setback was narrowly avoided."

Ramuel made eye contact with every other angel in the sanctuary, the last of whom was Doroniel. It was obvious he was finished speaking.

The Dominion Doroniel put his massive hands on either side of the lectern as though he were the pastor about to let loose the words of God on his people. He did speak, but as was usual with Doroniel, concisely and with controlled emotion. "The enemy has been successful in two of four attacks. Brand, do not leave the Senator's side unless specifically called to do so."

"Zopheniel, keep an eye on the angry woman. We don't want her changing her mind and going after Pastor Phil again. She's not a believer, but we can at least keep from being blind-sided by her. Encourage prayer for the UP from the Pastor and his congregation."

"As for you, Maspial, let's wait for further direction from the Almighty. Stay with Jerry. Keep him encouraged."

"Shamus and Alea, this will take wisdom, skill, patience and direct instruction from the Almighty to diffuse. We will return to Center Realm. The rest of you," Doroniel scanned the large room in front of him, "you know your missions. The Almighty hasn't changed them. Immanuel."

The word was echoed by the other angels.

"Immanuel".

A curtain by one of the closed, tall windows of the sanctuary wavered ever so slightly. The sanctuary was empty.

CHAPTER THIRTY-FOUR

Do not let the sun go down while you are still angry
Ephesians 4:26

"Guess who I talked to today?" Brenden was sitting at the table with his laptop in front of him.

Shawna shrugged her shoulders. Over the past three days, she had said few words to her husband. She pretended to watch TV. She spent extra time with the kids. Shawna had even tried to read, but if Brenden had been watching closely he would have noticed that she never read more than a page or two. Usually she read them over a few times and still had little idea what the words were telling her.

Shawna had replayed the words Brenden and Marci had spoken in the hot tub hundreds of times. They were clear as day.

The last time I was naked in front of you, I could barely get you to look at me.

What do you mean? I helped you take your bikini off!

I only say that to the girls I undress.

Never in the many years of being married to Brenden had Shawna worried about him cheating on her. He had met for coffee and shown houses to many good looking women over the years in real estate, sometimes alone. He had taken a little long to get home a few nights. With all the exposure to cheating and broken marriages on TV and in movies, Shawna's mind had considered the possibility from time to time, but it rarely lasted more than a moment.

Brenden appeared happy. She never felt like he was hiding anything. A part of her could not believe he would cheat.

I only say that to the girls I undress.

The cruise had been nine months ago. Marci did say it was the last time he had seen her naked. Maybe it had just been a one-time thing. Maybe that was why Brenden didn't appear to be hiding anything. It had been months ago.

Maybe nothing happened. Maybe he just saw her naked somehow.

It was this possibility that had kept Shawna quiet the past days.

On the other hand, maybe something had happened. The picture of that in her mind . . . a cup slipped out of her hand and bounced on the floor. Good thing it was plastic. Shawna bent over and picked it up as though nothing were wrong. Brenden glanced but refocused on his screen.

Marci? Her friend? She *was* beautiful. Maybe Brenden had become bored with the same old Shawna. She was getting older. She had birthed three kids. Marci's perfect little body hadn't had to deal with childbirth and nursing!

Here she was giving Marci marital advice!

I am an idiot! The words hit her hard. *I am such an idiot!*

I have been giving marriage advice to my close friend about her cheating husband when my close friend has been cheating with *my* husband! Wow! Now that really does sound like a movie!

The surprising part to Shawna was that she wasn't furious with Brenden. She had been angry at times. At one point after they had gone to bed on the night of the hot tub discussion, when Shawna had pretended to be sleeping, she had fought off the urge to sit up and start screaming and punching with reckless abandon. Barely.

She had been totally relieved the next morning when Brenden had gone to work early. She had entertained the thought of locking him out of the house and putting a note on the door telling him to stay out! The problem with that plan was that Marci would still be living in the house!

Facing Marci was easier than facing Brenden. Somehow Shawna could forgive Marci. Why was that?

It was then that Shawna noticed Brenden staring at her.

"Are you alright?" he asked softly.

"Yes . . . sorry. Who did you meet?" Shawna recovered quickly.

"When I was in the outlets earlier, I stopped for some lunch. It was packed as usual so I joined a guy at a table. He was waiting for his wife and we got to talking. His name is Allan and he is a pastor in British Columbia. I told him about the Unification and he got all excited. His church is considering sending a mission team to the Philippines, but it hasn't got off the ground. There are some missionaries there they support. Anyway, he'd love to hear more about what we could do to help them put a mission trip together."

"I'm going to send him some information and he's going to talk to his leaders, but . . . this could be our first international connection! If we can facilitate groups from Canada that would be great!"

Again, no sign of remorse. No sign of . . . anything. Shawna found herself not caring about the Unification and some pastor from Canada. If Brenden and Marci slept together, then the Unification would break down just like her marriage. How could you be the spokesman for a project like the Unification and commit adultery? Brenden would have to step down.

How could their marriage ever be the same? A rise of anger and a flood of heat was smoldering just beneath Shawna's skin. She knew she should respond to his excitement. She should be the supportive wife. She should smile and cheer and congratulate her husband.

She didn't want to!

But she didn't *know* that he was guilty!

She should just ask him. She knew it. Another night of keeping this inside was likely to result in some sort of dangerous explosion that would result in someone getting hurt.

What Shawna was concretely aware of, however, was that if she asked Brenden what happened that night on the cruise ship, she *would* get an answer.

If Brenden were guilty, she would know immediately. She would know, and she would have to deal with the unthinkable consequences of it.

At least now she could lean on the possibility, however slim it was, that Brenden and Marci had shared an awkward moment, or something, and that everything was going to be okay.

It was going to be okay! Think positive! Think positive!

"That's great!" she managed before opening the fridge and moving stuff around without any real reason except to appear busy.

Brenden hit a few more keys and then closed up the computer. He leaned back and stared at his wife with little expression. Shawna noticed but went on with the dishes. Tension spread though her shoulders. It wouldn't be surprising if Brenden noticed. He had always read her like an open book with big printing and lots of pictures.

Not now! She pleaded with him silently. *Don't ask me what's wrong!* The clock on the microwave flipped to 6:45 PM. She used the thought to change the subject.

"Matt's going to be here in fifteen minutes. How do you think that's going to go?"

Brenden hesitated before answering and transitioning his mind to the new topic. "I don't know, but I think they'll work it out. She still loves him, and I'm pretty sure he feels the same."

"Hard to imagine," Shawna replied.

"Which part?"

"Going through something like that."

"Yes. I guess we'll find out how solid their relationship was. Or maybe how fragile?"

"Is sexual desire so strong that people would ignore the fact that it might ruin their marriage just for a good night? That I find hard to imagine. It's hard to understand." Shawna had worded the sentence carefully. Her eyes were fixed on Brenden waiting for a sign. Maybe he would flinch or blush or try to make excuses for Matt or something. Anything. If he were guilty of the same crime they were currently discussing, surely he'd give it away.

The response was silky smooth. "I don't get it either. I guess it's hard to understand how people think when they don't have God in their lives. At least we don't have to worry about that."

Unbelievable. Either nothing did happen between Marci and Brenden, which Shawna realized she was having trouble believing, or Brenden had become an incredible liar.

Innocent and loving husband or adulterous and lying scumbag? The thought bounced around in Shawna's brain like a bullet in a steel room.

CHAPTER THIRTY-FIVE

For in Christ all the fullness of the Deity lives in bodily form, [10] and in Christ you have been brought to fullness. He is the head over every power and authority.
Colossians 2:9-10

Doroniel, Shamus and Alea had expected to get direction from Throne Aziel and then return to Earth to do what they could to save the marriage of Brenden and Shawna and continue aiding the progress of the Unification Project. Even before entering Center Realm, however, the Cherub at the gate had motioned for Doroniel, Alea and Shamus to approach him.

The deep voice of the Cherub was recognizable now to Alea. As it turned out, this Cherub named Kron not only knew her name, he knew everything about the Unification Project. A few words had conveyed his understanding of the mission as well as the fact that Throne Aziel had been directed to go to Annaxis.

Apparently, the enemy had correlated the efforts on Earth that had occurred in the early stages of the

Unification with similar actions on Annaxis, the first human planet. This time, the angels of darkness had launched a massive offensive against any and every person they anticipated being involved in a similar type of mission on Annaxis. At this point, the mission was salvageable, but the window was small and shrinking. Throne Aziel had not entered a battle for many years, but it was expected that his presence, along with the three Cherubim that accompanied him, would be enough to alleviate the enemy threat on Annaxis.

"And NO, Shamus, you may not go to Annaxis to join the battle," the Cherub had answered before Shamus had even moved his lips. Shamus, predictably, didn't like to miss a fight, but Alea guessed that Kron was feeling the same way. The Cherub's body was quivering as its muscular, lion-like frame gave every indication it was ready to strike down its prey at any moment.

The Power Shamus and the Virtue Alea were to wait in Center Realm until Throne Aziel contacted them. Doroniel stayed to speak with Kron alone. With nothing else urgent, the angel tandem proceeded directly to the temple and were soon engrossed in worship.

Alea's focus kept moving toward Jesus who was sitting at the right hand of the Almighty. He had actually *been* man in the flesh. He had felt the flow of blood and the beating of a heart. Jesus had lived and died as a human. Alea had found the ability to show herself to Brenden as a novelty. It was the closest she had come to feeling the world as people did. But Jesus! Jesus fully understood both the physical and spiritual. The Almighty was not only the creator of the heavens but also a lover of them. He loved the angels! He loved humanity! He was worthy of praise!

Praise the Lord God Almighty! Praise the Lord God Almighty!

Blessed is the name of Jesus! Blessed is the name of Jesus!

The words poured out of her. Her love of God emanated from her spirit.

When the message came to Alea, it wasn't the Throne Aziel who relayed the instructions. Directly and clearly, the pure eyes of Jesus had met with the golden eyes of Alea as she continued her worship. Then the voice of God had filled her!

"Go to Annaxis. You will be given your orders there. I do love you, Virtue Alea. You are a good and faithful servant!"

There was no misunderstanding. There was no need for confirmation or question. Alea turned toward Shamus who was already staring at her. He had also heard. With a flick of their wings, the splendor of Center Realm and the radiance of the Almighty quickly faded as the two angels sped toward Annaxis.

Annaxis was fifty percent larger than Earth, but its surface had similar amounts of land mass as the oceans were more expansive than those on the Earth. It was a planet with less elevation change. There were hills, but nothing the people of Earth would consider mountains. The overall temperature, conversely, was higher which together with no mountains, translated into much of the land being usable for farming or development.

Cities sprawled in every direction. Shamus and Alea approached the surface above the city of Gerolix, but veered over the coastline and out to one of the hundreds of islands nearby. It was on one of those islands that they were to meet with Aziel. The Throne was there. The Dominion Kana stood at his side.

"Immanuel," Throne Aziel called through the face of the eagle.

"Immanuel," replied the visitors. Kana acknowledged the Power and the Virtue with a tip of his head, but Alea could see concern in his golden eyes.

The group of angels spoke underneath the canopy of a grove of massive broadleaved trees similar to the palms of Earth, but twice as high. A mother and her two blond girls were exploring a stream that babbled along near the trees. One of the girls walked through Aziel's leg, but remained unaware of her brush with the spiritual world.

"Things haven't gone well here," Aziel began. "The enemy anticipated every attempt we made to aid the people involved in the mission here. Even my presence and that of the Cherubim appeared to be planned for by the dark angels. Satanael himself commanded his legions. At every entrance into the battle, the enemy retreated. This would normally have been the desired result, but the enemy remained one step ahead in the attack. By the time we had determined the actual objectives of the dark angels, we were too late."

"Many angels fell on both sides, but in the end, the process of unification on Annaxis has been delayed substantially. The intended leader, a woman named Hannah, has succumbed to apathy; she rejected any responsibility claiming she was too busy to take on any other projects."

"Busy with entertainment, and busy with cooking, but never busy with things of eternal importance!" interjected Kana.

"As is usually the case, Dominion."

"The rest of the details here aren't your concern, Alea and Shamus. They will only slow you down. What's most important is that the Unification on Earth does not suffer a similar delay. We fear that the enemy will pull many of their demons from Annaxis back to Earth in light of their successes here." Kana paused and looked at the Throne as if deciding how much to say.

Aziel was the one to continue. "We expect a massive attack on Earth, Alea and Shamus. Legion upon legion of demons focused on stopping the progress of the Unification. In all likelihood, Satanael will direct the attack."

"How soon?" Shamus wasn't caught unexpected by this news. He had been predicting huge resistance since the beginning.

The eyes of the eagle along with hundreds of eyes on Throne Aziel's body peered at Shamus. His booming voice uttered the words Alea feared. "We know little more than you do, Power. That's why we called you here. We need to know every guess, prediction and hunch you have. We need to know them immediately. Then we'll let the Almighty guide our next steps and encourage more prayer on the Earth than we've seen in years. Only with the added strength of prayer and the omniscient eye of God can we hope to be successful."

"Then we shall not delay," answered Shamus. "Where would you like us to begin?"

"Alea, why don't you answer that question. Where are we the most vulnerable?"

The contemplative human face of the Throne and the serious face of the Dominion analyzed every word Alea poured out.

Although light years from Earth, Shamus' hand instinctively formed around the hilt of his sword as he listened to the Virtue speak.

Battle would come.

CHAPTER THIRTY-SIX

So watch yourselves. If your brother or sister sins against you, rebuke them; and if they repent, forgive them.
Luke 17:3

Matt Hollingsworth felt anything but charming as he parked in front of the house that his wife had been living in for the past month. On one hand, he was brimming with energy and hope. Marci was finally ready to talk.

Hopefully, she was ready to listen.

Matt had never planned to have an affair. Was that called second-degree adultery as compared to first-degree? It should count for something that it just . . . happened. Matt would be the first to admit that he was a fool for the beauty of women. Marci knew that. Everyone knew that! Since Marci, however, he had always kept his hands off the beauty that his eyes saw. Until Corinne.

Matt had been in Vegas at a business convention. He had been at many business conventions. He had decided not to join the guys for a drink after dinner. That should've been the first clue that something weird was going on! When had he ever turned down going out with the guys?

His plan had been to go back to the room, watch either a sporting event or a movie, and then enjoy the king size bed at the Bellagio. He had actually planned to sleep in the city that never sleeps. That, Matt figured, was his second mistake.

His third mistake was deciding to drink coffee instead of alcohol! He had popped into a little coffee shop, ordered his Americano, and gone to add a splash of cream.

From the moment Corinne had swept into the café, her wavy hair and glamorous smile had put Matt into a trance. Only two drops of cream had dribbled out of the empty stainless steel carafe, but Matt found himself taking his sweet time asking for more. Even Corinne's voice was smooth and intoxicating. She had ordered a large coffee, added a pack of sweetener, and was searching for the cream.

"I think they are bringing more." That had been Matt's inevitable pickup line. From there, his irresistible charm worked its magic. A five-minute wait for cream led to slow sips of coffee and an hour of flirting. Corinne had been at a networking conference by herself fresh off a breakup with her boyfriend of four years.

They were in Vegas. She was on the rebound and feeling betrayed. Matt was ensnared by her beauty, and she had been the one to suggest he come check out her room. He knew he should have declined, flashed his wedding ring, and left the encounter forever.

He just didn't.

It would just be a one night stand, he had justified.

Corinne revealing that she lived in Tacoma had thrilled him. It had also doomed him. It was too easy to see her again, and he had.

That was the story. There was no more to it than that. He still loved Marci. He had no intention of ever leaving her. She wasn't perfect. Their marriage wasn't perfect, but marriages weren't meant to be perfect! Matt fully expected to tell Corinne that their affair couldn't continue. They would part ways. Life would go on.

Marci having a friend from the gym who happened to be in a sushi restaurant near Sea-Tac airport while Matt and Corinne were having an early lunch was also not part of the plan. Having the friend sit close enough to eavesdrop on the entire conversation Matt and Corinne had that day was not only *not* part of the plan, it was inconceivable!

Matt walked past the koi fish in the pond in front of Brenden and Shawna's house. He missed coming here. There was always something warm and inviting about being in this house. Part of it was the house itself. The colors, the decorations, and the accents created a coziness that made you want to stay. The real warmth, however, was different. Matt had been in many houses over the years, many of them as beautifully decorated, but few instilled the peace and comfort that the Tavis' house created. The only reasonable conclusion Matt could come to was that it was Brenden, Shawna and the kids that made the difference. They had a level of modest confidence that was uncommon. Matt had always felt welcome.

He only hoped today would feel the same. It was obvious that Matt had been the villain. He knew it, and he would admit it!

In previous, happier days Matt would have walked right in without knocking. Not today. He rang the doorbell. The sound of excited children and little feet running followed. Tyler opened the door with a smile followed by an explosive shout to anyone who was listening, "Uncle Matt is here!"

At least Tyler was excited to see his "sort of" uncle again.

Brenden rounded the corner into the entry. He, too, was smiling as he offered his hand for an informal handshake. "How are you doing, Buddy?"

Matt grabbed his hand and pulled Brenden close enough for a manly, pat-on-the-back hug. "It is good to see you!"

"It is weird having you ring the doorbell," Brenden muttered as they stepped back from each other.

"Yah, well I wasn't sure who or what would greet me on the other side," came the reply. Brenden noticed immediately that Matt's tone was sincere, not sarcastic or joking as it would normally have been.

Tyler, Rachel, and Amanda led the adults back into the great room with non-stop chatter. Shawna swept in, greeted Matt as though nothing had changed since the last time he had been in the house, and whisked the kids off to finish getting ready for bed.

"How are things going?" Brenden asked with a light enough tone to allow Matt to respond with either shallow conversation or real emotion.

"Work is work. House is lonely." Matt shrugged. "I guess life sucks."

"Understood." Brenden wasn't sure whether to pry more before Marci came down. "Well, this is a start."

"And hopefully not an end. How 'bout you? Selling any houses?"

"It's been steady. Enough to keep me going which is all I can ask for. It allows me to focus on the Unification Project at least."

"How's that going lately?"

"Mostly good. We have impacted a bunch of lives in a positive way! Our friend Jerry isn't doing great however. We just found out that he had a heart attack in Ukraine."

"Is he going to be okay?"

"We think so at this point. He was such an important part of the team, though. I hope it doesn't slow everything down too much. Things never seem to go as fast as I would like."

"Tell me about it," Matt replied and then let the words hang in the air as Marci, clothed in her grey workout gear, casual yet beautiful, entered the room. Brenden noticed that Matt had come in wearing black slacks and a lavender dress shirt that, judging from the wrinkles, had just come out of the package.

"Hey you," Matt spoke with a calm tone.

"Hey." Marci's reply mirrored the emotionless comment.

Brenden wasted little time jumping into the dead air. "We need to put the kids to bed. The coffee is made. There is some wine on the wine rack. Whatever you need, help yourself. Let us know if you need anything, otherwise we'll be upstairs for . . . awhile."

Brenden waited for any quick objections. None came. He poured himself a coffee and was about to help with whatever was left of the putting kids to bed routine. Marci stepped beside him in the kitchen. She pushed a mug over to Brenden.

"Make it a double?" she said, a thin smile on her face.

"Double cream, double sugar and double caffeine?"

"No. Just double the luck." She whisked away the cup, still black, and with her shoulders set, strode confidently into the living room to join Matt.

"Do you want one?" Brenden looked at Matt for a response.

"Can you pour a triple 'I'm a stupid idiot' for me?"

"Coming right up." Brenden poured another mug full, and without a hesitation, grabbed the notepad and a pen. He soon presented Matt with the now paper-covered mug. The words "I am a stupid idiot!" encircled the cup three times.

"Thanks, Buddy!" Matt offered his own smile as he accepted his drink.

Brenden left for the stairs confident he had at least broken the ice. The rest was now out of his control.

A small group of middle-aged men and women sat around the living room of Pastor Phil and his wife. The care group met weekly to pray, study the Bible, and worship God.

"Let's spend some time in prayer," offered Phil after a heavyset woman sitting on the recliner in the corner had shared about her struggle finding a job.

A number of mugs were set on the coffee table as people bowed to pray.

Zopheniel stood behind Phil as he began to pray, "Where more than one are gathered in my name to pray."

The Holy Spirit filled the room. Three other angels entered and took up positions behind the praying believers ready to carry out the commands of the Almighty.

All but the heavyset woman in the corner offered up prayers over the next twenty minutes. A number of the prayers were for the people in the room, but more were directed toward the Unification Project. Prayers for Brenden and Shawna were vague, but offered in sincerity. The feeling that prayer for the Tavis' was needed overwhelmed the minds of the group of believers.

Zopheniel nodded as he looked around. Two of the other angels departed. The presence of the Holy Spirit remained.

Shamus and Alea stood in the corner of the master bedroom in the Tavis' house. Shawna was folding some laundry on the floor. Brenden picked up a book from his side table although he had no intention of reading anything.

"Prayer. Time to Pray." Shamus spoke the words sternly.

Shawna looked up momentarily, but went back to her pile of socks and underwear. Brenden didn't even move.

Alea moved beside Shawna. Her tone was gentle. The words were clear. "Healing. God heals. It is time to think of others. It is time to think of your friends downstairs. God heals."

Shawna's hands stopped midway through a fold. Her mind was racing. She knew she should pray for Matt and Marci. She knew she should pray with Brenden.

Of course, she didn't want to!

Shawna spoke the words to herself over and over. She didn't want to pray with Brenden. She didn't even want to pray! The furrowed brow on her forehead and deep stare clearly revealed her dilemma to the angels watching.

"God loves you, Shawna! Pray, pray, pray!" This time Alea spoke as sternly as Shamus had.

Two other angels entered the room. They wore expressionless faces; their silver swords were drawn. It was a sign that someone was praying for the Tavis'. The presence of two more angels was encouraging, but at this point it appeared to Alea that they had no directive.

Alea turned her attention back to Shawna who had finished folding the pair of boxers now. Her expression was beginning to soften. Shawna's forehead had smoothed out. Her brown eyes were warmer. Shawna turned toward her husband, but did not say anything. Instead, she turned away again. This time, however, she closed her eyes. She had begun to pray!

The Holy Spirit filling the room was an even bigger lift to Alea and Shamus. The prayers of other believers were strong and full of faith. Brenden had felt it, too. He turned toward Shawna, but her eyes were turned away.

"You know, we should pray for those two downstairs and then go see how it's going. If we wait too long, dishes might start flying."

Shawna's response was slow. When she did turn toward Brenden, a tear slid down her right cheek. "I've already been praying. So yes, I agree with you."

"Sorry," Brenden replied apologetically. "I won't interrupt. I'll do the same." He sat on the bed, dropped his head slightly, and began to pray.

The power of the Almighty filled the entire house as the prayers continued.

Brenden and Shawna soon joined Matt and Marci in the living room. Tensions were still low, and the conversation between Matt and Marci flowed easily.

All four angels surrounded the people in the living room and waited to see what would happen next. Any darkness from the enemy had been pushed far from the room.

The spirit world was poised for healing! It was now up to the people in the room to open their souls to it.

CHAPTER THIRTY-SEVEN

But look, you are trusting in deceptive words that are worthless.
Jeremiah 7:8

The words came from Shawna. She looked Marci straight in the eyes. There was no wavering. It was just a question that needed an answer. "Have you ever cheated on Matt?" The question surprised everyone because of its directness, but surprise turned to intrigue as Matt, Brenden and Shawna waited for a response.

Shawna was impressed with her own calmness. She had known the only way for her to help Matt and Marci was to find out the truth about what happened with Brenden and Marci on the cruise ship. Somehow there was a peace inside her now that prepared her for the answer. That being said, Shawna still decided to focus on Marci instead of Brenden at this point. If Brenden had cheated, she would rather hear it from Marci.

Marci opened her mouth to speak, but no words came out. The fact that this was difficult for Marci to answer sent ripples of pain though Shawna's chest, but she refused to let her emotions show. Matt leaned forward, his own expectations changing.

"I guess it depends on how you look at cheating," Marci began. She spoke the words with firmness. There was no hint of remorse.

"I would think knowing if you cheated should be simple, Marci." Matt was almost squirming with anticipation. Shawna figured that as much as it would hurt for Matt to hear that Marci had been unfaithful, the confession would ease his own conscience.

"I do feel some guilt about what I did once, but I'm still not sure I cheated on you Matt."

Matt looked up from his hands to his wife's face. He said nothing, but his eyes signaled for Marci to keep going.

"You swept me off my feet pretty fast back in Chicago, Matt. I guess I wasn't totally sure where it would all lead in the beginning. So, I've never told you this, but I did get together with an old friend of mine a couple times after you and I started dating."

"Got together?" Matt needed more.

"Yah, and one of those times we had a few drinks and I was still a little confused and I stayed the night at his place."

"So this was before we were married."

"This was before we were engaged," Marci clarified. "So I know I shouldn't have done it, but I'm also not sure if that was really cheating. We were just dating. It wasn't like it was the first time I had been with this guy. He and I had dated for almost a year before that."

"So that's it?" Shawna asked the question in stunned confusion. Marci sleeping with an ex-boyfriend before she and Matt were married was not the confession she was expecting.

"That's it."

Matt was quiet. He leaned back and looked up at the ceiling fan hanging in the vaulted room to let the information digest properly.

Brenden hadn't said a word.

Marci was evidently finished answering the question.

That left Shawna. She alone moved forward and pleaded for more. The question slipped out as fast and as bluntly as the one she had asked earlier.

"So you and Brenden have never slept together?"

"That should get to the bottom of it." Alea was smiling as the angels watched in anticipation.

"Whoa!" was all Brenden could get out.

"What're you talking about?" Marci's eyes doubled in size as she stared her friend down. "Of course not!"

This time, for the first time in many days, Shawna knew the truth. The shock of the question on everyone else in the room left no doubt. Whatever had happened on the cruise ship had been innocent, or at least had been mostly innocent.

"Why would you ask that, Shawna?" Brenden found himself much more involved in the discussion suddenly.

"I heard you and Marci in the hot tub the other night talking about the last time you undressed her, and how you're such an expert bikini remover. What would you think? And, if you didn't sleep together, then please fill me in on what did happen."

This time it was Brenden who looked up to the ceiling fan. Digestion of what Shawna had said began immediately, and the beginning of nausea set in. It was Marci who answered the question, as it probably should've been.

"Oh, that!" Marci laughed. She was both relieved that there was an honest explanation for the question, and that the focus had quickly moved away from her sleeping with her ex-boyfriend. "That's easy to explain. Remember when Brenden lost his key and you guys went to the show. My bikini clip broke and Brenden helped me get it undone. I think he got a little sneak peak at my girls in the process. That's all that happened. No cheating."

Only Marci could make it sound that matter-of-fact and meaningless, Brenden thought to himself, but at this point he was glad for the simplicity of the explanation. He saw no reason to explain the whole conversation in the ship cabin that day. It had, after all, been harmless. Then another thought occurred to him. He voiced this one out loud.

"So you've been holding this in all these days thinking that I slept with Marci?" The words were spoken with compassion, not aggression.

Shawna nodded slowly, but little expression was visible. Now it was her turn to consider the information she'd just been given.

"That explains some things," Brenden said as he recalled a number of cold and distant responses from his wife over the past days along with the fact they hadn't shared any meaningful physical contact for a while. "Why didn't you just ask me about it?"

"What if you had cheated? It sure didn't sound promising. I didn't know how I would respond. It almost killed me holding it in."

"I'm surprised you didn't kill *me*! How is it that you didn't punch me in the nose or poison my coffee before today?" Marci put her arms up as if to block a punch.

"You might not want to drink any more of that coffee!" Shawna's response time on the comeback was impressive. All four of them laughed this time. In a matter of a few minutes, a number of bombs had been dropped in the conversation and all parties were ready to lighten the mood.

A few more details about the cruise incident were asked for and shared. Matt pushed Marci for more information about her ex-friend. A bottle of wine was opened and emptied. It wasn't until 9:30 PM that the conversation came back to the main event for the evening.

Again it was Shawna pushing the conversation. "So, what now?"

The humor in the room was instantly suffocated by a fog of tension. Many events in the future hinged on what the answer to that question would be. All four people knew it.

All four angels knew it. Even with the calming presence of the Holy Spirit, Alea stood straighter as she awaited the response.

"I've said my part," Matt looked expectantly at Marci.

"I still don't know if I can trust you, Matt. Once someone has cheated, they're more likely to do it again."

"All I can do is give you my word. I want you. I want only you. It won't happen again."

After a nervous pause, Brenden asked, "Do you want us to leave again?"

"No," Marci jumped right in. "Actually, you have helped me greatly with this decision. It just occurred to me, and by that I mean I am a little slow, that Shawna actually believed that you, Brenden, the perfect husband, cheated on her. I can see you not trusting *me* fully, Shawna, but not trusting Brenden? He did everything he could not to look at me with a bikini on much less off."

She chuckled to herself before continuing. "If couples like you believe temptation can get the best of you, how can I be so hard on Matt? Even though it was stupid!" Marci stared Matt down and furrowed her brow in disdain. "You two have the relationship I wish Matt and I could have! Whether God exists or not, living with moral standards like you do works. As much as I've missed you Matt, I've loved living in this house even if I was the third wheel."

Matt nodded at the last statement. "I don't doubt that. I've always loved coming to your house." Matt then directed his attention to Marci. "So does that mean you'll give me another chance?"

"Can I poison your Vegas girl?"

"Just don't tell me."

It was clear Marci was going to forgive Matt, but she still waited what felt like an eternity to say the words. "Yes. I want to come home."

"Thank you." Matt's words dripped relief. Brenden had never seen Matt be serious for this long at a time. He decided he liked this Matt, too. Now that things would hopefully return to semi-normal, he would see more of this Matt.

CHAPTER THIRTY-EIGHT

Trust in the LORD with all your heart
and lean not on your own understanding;
[6] in all your ways submit to him,
and he will make your paths straight.
Proverbs 3:5-6

All the members of the care group had gone home, the kids were in bed, and the pastor and his wife sat watching sports highlights on ESPN. They had both needed a few minutes to calm their minds before sleep would have been a viable option. For Kathy, Pastor Phil's wife, the slam-dunks, the hole-in-ones, and the great catches were something interesting to watch even though the teams involved in the games were inconsequential. Phil was personally attached to every sport in one way or another, so sports highlights were a routine.

Kathy couldn't get the evening meeting out of her mind, nor did she want to. The power of the prayer that night sent shivers down her spine each time she thought of it. The presence of God had filled the room. The desire to pray for the Unification and for the Tavis' was undeniable. It was comforting and scary all at the same time when God made his presence so clear. Obviously, having the Almighty God on your side was comforting, but knowing that the prayers that were spoken and that the decisions that were made had eternal and spiritual consequences brought importance and a new level of seriousness.

Often prayer felt empty. Often God felt distant. In times like those, it was easy to go through the motions without really believing it made a difference. Nights like tonight left no doubt of the importance of prayer.

"I still get emotional thinking about tonight," Kathy turned from the tennis on the screen to look at her husband in the recliner beside her.

Phil's immediate response was a clear sign he had been thinking about the prayer session and not the match on the TV. "Pretty cool, isn't it?"

"It makes me excited, but also nervous. What do you think we were specifically praying for? Do you think something is going wrong with Brenden and Shawna or with the Unification Project? Why would God so clearly put it on our hearts to pray for them?"

"I don't know. I was tempted to call Brenden right after the meeting, but it was already quite late. I wish now that I'd called him."

"Are you worried?"

"For some reason, no. I don't claim to understand the ways of the Lord, but I think the Unification can change a lot of lives. If lives are going to be changed, Satan won't like it. If anything, it clarified how important it is for us to focus on prayer and worship and not to take things for granted. The Bible wouldn't talk about praying without ceasing if it were pointless. I need to encourage more of this in our congregation."

The pastor retrieved his laptop from the bedroom and resumed his position in his chair. His fingers could barely keep up with the constant flow of inspired words as his sermon for the next Sunday took form. "Worship the Lord your God and lean not on your own understanding. In all your ways acknowledge Him and He will direct your paths."

It was so clear all of a sudden. The best way Phil could help the Unification was to help heal the church in North America. He could inspire people with stories of need in other parts of the world. He could appeal to people's sense of serving and kindness. These things were good and somewhat effective.

The problem in North America, however, wasn't a lack of sermons. Christians and non-Christians knew how to help. It wasn't a lack of resources either. The problem in North America was a lack of urgency. Intentions were good, but few acted on their intentions. The best sermon, the most amazing speech, the finest story that Phil could give could never measure up to the inspiration God could give. When the hearts of men and women were right, and they gave themselves in worship to the great and mighty God of the Universe, faith increased. Belief increased. Activity increased.

Phil was humbled at the realization. Once again he had been relying on himself instead of God. It was worship. It was praise. It was prayer. These were the keys to overcoming apathy.

The poor and needy in the world had to rely on God. They had nothing else. The poor and needy of the world had faith that dwarfed the faith of the average North American Christian. Increase the faith of the wealthy! Increase the faith of the people!

The beginning of another set of sports highlights caught Phil's attention. He was surprised at the fact that he'd only been typing for twenty-five minutes. Kathy was still on her chair. Nearly his entire message for Sunday was typed out in front of him.

He turned off the TV. "I can't wait for Sunday!" Phil broke the silence in the room. His wife just smiled at him. She didn't have to speak. She believed in Phil. She knew God had spoken to him.

Zopheniel couldn't help but smile in relief. "Finally!" he shouted as the pastor and his wife made their way to bed for the night.

The days on Earth raced by while the spiritual world remained poised for the inevitable battle over the success of the Unification Project. The Senator's daughter Alana married the author Conner Harris. It was a beautiful wedding at the Senator's grand estate with friends, family and many dignitaries in attendance. The greatest of these was the President who brought with him an army of security personnel who amazingly blended into the gardens of the estate as though they themselves were part of the beauty.

After the bride and groom had boarded a plane bound for Hawaii and their much anticipated honeymoon, Senator Reese and President Mullen had found time to speak as friends without the formality of public impressions driving the conversations between them. Conner's book, *The Able Earth*, was discussed and the Senator had brought up all he had heard about the Unification Project. Conner had anticipated the chance for his new father-in-law to make an appeal to the President before the wedding and had provided all the necessary information. Conner had also contacted Jerry, who was recovering rather quickly from his heart attack, to check on the progress of the UP. The correlation between the

Unification Project and Conner's book would be a win-win for both parties as they looked for exposure and, ultimately, success in eradicating poverty and hunger from the planet.

The angel Maspial had stood in the corner of Jerry's apartment living room when Conner had called to talk. "Praise to the Almighty!" He had muttered the words to no one in particular. It was always uplifting to see the Lord's plans coming to fruition.

Potential global change initiated by the people of the United States was certainly something the President opened his mind to. Tax breaks for individuals or groups who were involved and positive publicity for the Unification Project were mentioned. Details would be hammered out at a later date, but the foundation for support had been poured. There would be some outcry that this was a "Christian" initiative, but the President was confident that the focus on feeding the hungry and helping the poor would overshadow the fact that it was a Christian ministry.

The Principality Ramuel and the Power Brand, surrounded by hundreds of angels, had guided the discussion. The President was a believer and the prayers for the nation uttered in churches all around the country that Sunday morning had given power to the angels through the Almighty.

The expected attack by Satanael and his demons to interfere with this discussion never materialized. Four legions of demons had been mobilized and prepared for attack, according to angel sentries, but the enemy had not offered resistance. Demonic spies had been sent to the edge of the angel perimeter around the Senator's property. Angel reinforcements were ready to assist if the attack became reality, but the spiritual realm sat quietly by as the political discussions that were needed to precipitate the widespread growth of the Unification Project occurred.

The President and his entourage returned to Washington. Senator Reese and his wife took a trip to Cabo while the clean-up of the wedding took place. Alana and Conner enjoyed the exhilaration of being newly married with a whole life before them. Perfect weather and the luxurious Grand Wailea topped off a vacation of a lifetime.

The church in Alderwood began regular worship services on Sunday evenings. With Pastor Phil more excited and passionate than ever, the church building was filled to capacity on many a Sunday morning and night. Brenden, also inspired by his pastor, contacted other churches who had been involved in the UP or who had expressed interest and encouraged the same focus on worship and prayer. Within a couple months, Sunday night worship was gaining momentum among those who believed that God was starting something great.

The phone was ringing with consistency in the little office in Alderwood as word about the Unification was spreading.

"Who was that?" Shawna asked her husband after another phone call. It was a Sunday afternoon, but Shawna's dad had taken the kids in exchange for Brenden and Shawna bringing dinner later. Another win-win. Somehow being in the UP office never felt like work. It was a positive, comfortable environment, and it was usually peaceful on a Sunday.

"Pastor Ron in San Diego," Brenden replied. "He had heard through a relative in Miami about a mission trip to Haiti that had been orchestrated by some organization called the Unification Project. He had checked the website, liked what he read, and called to find out more."

"You know, calls like that used to make you leap out of your chair and fly around the room like a little school girl excited about a lollipop."

"I am excited."

"But . . ."

"But . . . we miss Jerry. We have plenty of interest in sending out teams, but I have to tell them all that we need time to organize the location and the project. Without Jerry hopping around the planet, we're moving too slowly."

"How is he?" Shawna was looking out the window into the parking lot.

"Jerry?" Brenden received a nod. "Progressing, but it will be a while before he is flying again. He has made a few calls, but it's not the same."

"Do you think you could do it?"

"Fly around meeting with people in strange countries to organize and facilitate missions?"

Another nod.

"I could try. I've seen a fair bit of what Jerry has done to put these together. With his support and contacts, it's a possibility. But then who'll do what I do? Someone still has to talk to the churches. Someone still has to speak at fundraisers. Someone still has to be the voice of the UP."

"We need to grow." Shawna's comment was simple and to the point.

"Another Jerry?"

"We need another Jerry, we need another administrator, and we need to think bigger!"

"Who's out there that would raise his or her own support to join us?"

CHAPTER THIRTY-NINE

That if you confess with your mouth, "Jesus is Lord," and believe in your heart that God raised him from the dead, you will be saved.
Romans 10:9

"Alyssa."

Brenden tilted his head as he stared out the window beside his wife. "Have you ever talked to her about it?"

"I'm way ahead of you, Honey." Shawna spun around with a smile. "Alyssa has been waiting for us to need her. Ever since she became a Christian, she's wanted to be a part of this. She would be great in here. She's here half the time anyway."

As if on command, Alyssa Gladstone parked her Hyundai Genesis in front of the office. It was true. Alyssa had spent a lot of time around the UP office since its inception. Brenden had not necessarily understood why at the beginning, but it became clear that Alyssa was interested in more than just the missions. She was searching. She was searching for truth. She was searching for God.

She had found Him!

Alyssa had asked if she could come to church one day seemingly out of the blue. When Pastor Phil had invited anyone who wanted to accept Christ as his or her Savior to pray with him that morning, Alyssa had prayed. She filled Brenden and Shawna in on that fact like it was just another event on another ordinary day the next Monday at the office. "I asked God into my life yesterday." The words had just come out. It had been a great day in heaven and on earth!

Since that day, the innocent, pure belief of Alyssa had rubbed off on everyone. She loved God! She wanted to bring other people to know Him! She wanted to make the world a better place!

Brenden had not contemplated a formal position for Alyssa within the UP before this moment. It was a fact he was ashamed of as he looked absently back at his wife. Shawna waited for it to sink in to Brenden's brain that it should have been obvious. It was Brenden who spoke next.

"You would be okay working with her?"

"We would get along just fine."

"What about raising support?"

"Why don't you ask her that question?" Shawna said it just as Alyssa had entered the room, loud enough to be "accidentally" overheard.

"Ask me what?" Alyssa threw her purse and jacket down on the counter and plunked down in the nearest chair. Brenden gave Shawna a subtle glance easily interpreted as, *"Thanks a lot!"*

In spite of the coaxing, Brenden looked up at Alyssa and said, "Ask you whether you have ever considered joining the UP?"

"Of course I have." Alyssa rolled her eyes as though it were the dumbest question she had ever heard, and once again Brenden was surprised by the simplicity of the answer.

What was it about the women Brenden found himself around? The three of them, Shawna, Marci and now Alyssa, spoke their minds so clearly. Brenden had always been under the impression that communication with women was supposed to be a complicated thing. Apparently he was the one hard to communicate with!

"And?"

"What do you want me to do?"

"I'm not totally sure yet, but it wouldn't surprise me if the two of you have already written up a job description." Brenden was trying to mock the two women. It didn't work. Shawna was already opening a desk drawer and pulling out a paper that she unfolded with over-exaggerated movements. She cleared her throat before reading.

"Alyssa's assets: organization, people skills, financial management, loves to travel, committed believer. This is in no particular order of course." Shawna looked up for emphasis and effect. "Would you like me to go on?"

"What about financially? Can you make it work?"

"I'm here almost daily as it is, Brenden. I have the time to help without changing my work. I know I would sell more houses if I spent more time advertising, but I can make ends meet. Besides, I've been dating this great guy I met at a fundraiser dinner a couple months ago. He makes more money than I do and I think this might be going somewhere good."

"A couple months ago? You have been dating a guy for a couple months and you didn't tell me?"

"It's OK, hubby. She told me about him. I even met him. He's cute." Both women laughed.

"Well, thank you," Alyssa replied formally. Then she looked at Brenden. "Don't worry. He's a Christian and he lives in Mount Vernon. I'm not going anywhere."

"We could use you around here." Brenden was serious, his voice sincere. "Are you sure?"

"Yes, Brenden. I'm sure. What do you want me to do?"

"I guess that means welcome to the UP!" Brenden got up and gave his business partner a hug. Shawna stepped in for a hug of her own before all three sat down again. "I want to give Jerry the good news, and I'll talk about where he sees our greatest needs right now. I'm sure you have some things that you'd like to help with too?"

"Sure do, but first we pray." Without a hesitation, Alyssa jumped up, grabbed a hand from each Tavis, and began praying. "Thank you, God! Thank you for starting this project and thank you that I can be a part of it. Help us make decisions that change lives around the world and bring people to know you. Amen."

Before the "amen" had even ended, Alyssa's cell phone signaled a text. "Probably work." She peeked at the screen. "Nope. It's my man! I can't wait to tell him. He's interested in learning more about the Unification, too. I should get him out here one of these days!" With that, she grabbed her phone and threw a text back.

Brenden's phone rang next. It *was* work. He had some house showings scheduled for Monday afternoon and was waiting for confirmations. He called Jerry after replying.

Shawna called her dad to make sure all was good with the kids. It was a while before all three had hung up their phones and were able to focus on each other again.

"A toast!" Brenden declared while raising his coffee. The girls lifted their own cups. "To a fantastic day!"

"To a fantastic day!" Shawna and Alyssa declared in unison before all three took a swig.

"To top it all off, Jerry says he is doing great and could be cleared to travel sooner than expected. And, there's still more. Wait until I tell you what he told me about Conner Harris and his father-in-law Senator Reese."

Brenden's phone rang again to his ringtone of the familiar Christian song "Mighty to Save". He sang a few words before answering.

"Hey, Matt. How's your day?" He paused to listen as Shawna and Alyssa watched.

"Sure." The word was spoken slowly. "A Bible?" Another pause. "Sounds good. See you in a bit." Brenden pushed the button to end the call with a look of consternation and confusion.

"What was that about?" Shawna asked.

"That was Matt. He and Marci want to come by. He asked if I had a Bible close by."

"Have we waited too long, Master?" The demon Dominion Ygal asked Kilael, his master, as Alyssa Gladstone turned left onto Wester Street out of the UP office parking lot.

The second-in-command of the demonic forces pursed his lips without turning to look at the questioning Dominion. "Of course not, Ygal. We are stronger. We know the plan. We will prevail."

Ygal made sure Kilael was finished before daring to question his superior again. "Then we'll be attacking soon?"

"I don't like the new girl's naïve excitement. It's potentially dangerous. The rest of them, however, no longer feel enough pressure to do anything quickly. Things are again appearing to go well for their "unification". This is how Satanael has wanted it. We shall delay where we can. We will watch their faith dwindle.

When the prayer has slowed, we'll finish off this poor excuse for a mission." Kilael now turned to look at Ygal.

"Satanael is confident that we can undermine the Christian church through the media in the end. Anytime the President can be connected to anything evangelical, it's easy to turn the wolves on a deserving prey."

"In fact, their unification just may be successful for us. I do believe we can unite the unbelievers against this in such a way as to turn many souls from their God and heaven. Waiting, Ygal, is exactly the plan."

As surprised as Ygal was by the sincere and almost cheerful tone of Kilael, the decision to delay attack bothered him. He nearly voiced this displeasure. The arrival of four demons, all of whom were obviously nervous and bearing news, stole Ygal's opportunity to voice his displeasure.

The shortest of the four demons stepped forward, his eyes downcast. "Master Kilael, we have news from Satanael."

"Well, then. Proceed." Kilael looked past the demons and down the street where Alyssa had just driven.

"Satanael would like all available legions gathered and mobilized for battle. He has asked to speak with you immediately."

Kilael turned to the demon who immediately dropped his gaze downward. Kilael stared a moment and then turned to Ygal. "I was mistaken, Dominion. It appears your desire for a fight shall be fulfilled sooner than I expected. I wonder what's changed." Kilael looked back at the four demons.

"What are you waiting for? Lead me to him."

Ygal didn't wait for an invitation. He followed the demon contingent, and was soon standing on a large, wind-smoothed rock overlooking a forlorn landscape in Afghanistan. It was another common meeting place for the dark angels. Few angels occupied the faithless lands in this part of the world. Satanael and his demons had steered most of the souls here away from God. Few people had hope. Even less prayed.

The amassing army already numbered in the thousands. Legions were taking formation. The angels would detect this gathering, but it wouldn't be immediate. The time gained could be invaluable in the outcome of a war.

Kilael and Satanael stood alone about 40 yards in front of Ygal. Their conversation was short-lived. Satanael confidently raised his scepter to call for the leaders. The Dominion Ygal leaped to join the others. Twelve legions had already assembled on the dusty plains.

The highest ranked demons formed a perfect circle around their leader waiting in silence for Satanael's instructions. The Dominion Ygal felt his sausage-like fingers stiffen and he flexed them in anticipation of what was to come.

Many angels would be pierced today! Perhaps Ygal would be able to finish off the Power Shamus this time!

Christianity would suffer!

It would be a day to remember!

CHAPTER FORTY

He threw him into the Abyss, and locked and sealed it over him, to keep him from deceiving the nations anymore
Revelation 20:3

Only four circular drops of coffee wobbled on the countertop beside a relieved Shawna. In Brenden's excitement from the phone call from Matt, he had hurried over to his desk to be sure his Bible was there, and in so doing, had bumped Shawna's coffee.

"I can't believe it stopped on the edge like that!" Brenden eyed the familiar "to go" cup from the bakery next door which sat at what appeared to be more than halfway over the lip of the counter. He moved the cup back onto the counter and quickly wiped up the splashed coffee with a tissue. "I was sure you were going to be covered in steaming hot coffee."

"Lucky," was the only word Shawna could muster.

"I guess so! I bumped it solidly."

Shawna methodically reached for the cup and took a careful sip before placing it back in a safer spot on the counter. "It tastes even better now that I realize I could've been wearing it!"

"I'm glad I could help you enjoy your coffee more then," Brenden quipped before actually retrieving his Bible from his desk.

"How quickly they take credit for 'good luck'," Shamus said as he watched Alea move back from where she'd just blocked the fall of the coffee. "They pray for protection, they pray for success, they ask the Almighty for help, and then they take credit for good luck when disaster is averted."

"Shawna needs to be here when Matt arrives," Alea spoke without condescension. "Shawna trusts God. She just doesn't comprehend the full expanse of His power. We didn't need her rushing home to change coffee-stained clothing."

"I agree with you, Alea, but I've never understood how believers can be fully confident in the Almighty's ability to carry out miraculous events like turning water into wine or protecting someone from fire, yet don't have enough faith that He can stop a cup of scalding coffee from falling. Humans give far too much credit to their 'luck'!"

"They underestimate the Almighty's love."

"That they do."

The wings of Zopheniel closed behind him as he entered the room and came to rest by the front door. "I bring news."

"As do I," came the deep voice of Ramuel as he also entered the room. "Please, go first," he motioned to Zopheniel.

"Matt Hollingsworth has opened his soul. He desires the fulfillment of the Almighty God!"

"Praise the Lord!" echoed around the room as the Principality, the Power and the Virtue shouted their excitement.

Ramuel wasted no time adding his news. "The President is sending representation to meet with Jerry and Brenden about the Unification. If his expectations are met, the intent is to bring national attention to the project."

"That will exponentially increase the amount of missions and changed lives!"

"Yes, Alea," Ramuel continued. "These phones will be ringing without ceasing."

"How fast can it grow with only these few people involved?" Zopheniel asked as he sequentially looked at the handful of desks in the room. "Jerry's not even fully recovered."

"That's not our concern at this point, Zopheniel. The Almighty has directed us this far. His vision far exceeds my own. Here I see only four angels, yet the Almighty has many others carrying out orders in connection with this mission. We may only see a few people, but the eyes of God may see hundreds or thousands more."

Zopheniel nodded in agreement.

"As exciting as this news is, Ramuel, your presence suggests there is more for us to discuss or you would have simply sent a messenger to inform us of this."

"You are as perceptive as you are powerful, Shamus, and you'll need both of those qualities for what I'm about to tell you. The Dominion Doroniel informed me that Satanael was not expecting some of the current developments. An angel of the Lord witnessed the "fire of the dragon" as Satanael reacted to news about developments with the Unification. Obviously, he wasn't anticipating these events to occur at this point."

"I always love hearing about the Fallen One losing his temper," Shamus said as he watched Brenden open his Bible.

"I'll only *love* hearing about it when we rise with our Lord and lock that Dragon into the abyss where he belongs. Satanael's separation from the Almighty was a start, but I'll only cheer when the believers are separated from the Fallen One for all eternity. That event cannot come soon enough."

Ramuel's eyes brightened as he spoke. He withdrew his purple sword and ran through several attack sequences with ease and coordination. Had his sword been meant for earthly matter, the stapler on Jerry's desk would have been carved up like a mini jack-o-stapler on Halloween. As with Shamus, Alea rejoiced in the fact that Ramuel would be fighting at her side against evil in that final battle against the dark angels.

"What are we to expect?" she asked.

"A fight." Ramuel chopped up the phone with equal precision.

"Soon?"

"We're attempting to find that out."

"Where do we focus our defense?" Shamus was now pacing, energy pulsing through his muscular angelic form. Alea expected the red sword of Shamus to fly out like Ramuel's had, but it remained at his side. "Or do we attack?"

"I expect that report at any moment. What's clear is that we must be ready to protect our people." Ramuel sheathed his sword and spoke with his usual calmness. "I will be protecting President Mullen. You will not let the enemy reach these two." Ramuel raised his eyes to the Tavis couple. "The traveler and the pastor are obvious targets. Alyssa Gladstone, the Hollingsworths, Conner Harris and his wife and anyone who would like to see the

Unification succeed is a target. If this attack meets my expectations . . ."

Two messenger angels formed in the room. They waited, still as statues, for a chance to convey their information.

Ramuel never did complete his sentence. Instead, he glanced at the two messengers, looked back at the others and voiced, "I'm thinking this will be that report I was expecting." He looked back over to the messengers.

"We have news that the enemy is mobilizing in the Middle East for a large scale offensive. A Christian Afghan man who had been beaten and left in the sand to die called out to the Almighty for help. The angels that were sent to attend to the believer caught sight of the dark angel force nearby. The angels were fortunate to escape with the information. It's unlikely we would have spotted the gathering army in that location by chance."

"The Almighty leaves little to chance," Ramuel responded. "Praise the Almighty!"

"You've been instructed to protect the people you are assigned to," the second of the two messengers continued. "An angel army is being called together as we speak to you now."

"Who was commanding the enemy force?" Shamus asked with some trepidation.

"Satanael was there."

Shamus nodded before asking another question. "Does Satanael still believe he has the element of surprise?"

"No, Power Shamus. The angels who spotted the enemy escaped, but not before being detected by demon sentries."

"How much time has elapsed since Satanael gained this knowledge?"

"Nearly two Earth minutes," the messenger responded.

"Immanuel," said Ramuel.

"Immanuel," was the response. The messengers departed. Ramuel disappeared just as quickly. Zopheniel delayed long enough to offer a personal farewell to Shamus and Alea before he flashed to the side of Jerry, the traveler.

Shamus, perfectly trained for situations like this, took position at the front of the room. Alea moved directly behind the chairs of Brenden and Shawna who were discussing what they hoped to accomplish with the rest of the day.

In the White House, the president was enjoying steak and prawns with a baked potato that, from Ramuel's vantage point, had more toppings then potato. Ramuel stood alertly behind the president's shoulder.

A BMW SUV cut in front of Conner Harris' car as Conner and his wife traveled down the I-5 on their way home on a Friday afternoon. The angelic form of the Power Brand stood on the backseat. Half of her form rose above the roof examining every detail of the spiritual and physical worlds.

Pastor Phil was at the hospital in Alderwood visiting Mrs. Jepsom, a sweet, 80 year old widow from the church, who had suffered a mild stroke the day before. Maspial, informed about the impending attack, held his sword in front of his chest. His body was unwavering, but every angelic sense was prepared to respond to attack.

The angel Jillia, recently assigned to the new believer Alyssa Gladstone, walked at Alyssa's right shoulder into the Safeway. Three demons glared at Jillia as they accompanied a sharply dressed man on the way out of the grocery store. The demons held formation and Jillia lost sight of them as Alyssa rounded a produce table stacked full of apples. With a nearly instantaneous glance from up at the roofline, Jillia acknowledged four other angels and only two demons in the massive building.

Zopheniel hovered in the middle of the apartment where Jerry the traveler was watching a recording of *The Amazing Race.* An open bottle of water sat on the table. Nothing was moving but the images on the screen. Sunrays broke through the clouds and the light bounced off the silver sword that was protecting the man below it. Colors not identifiable on Earth glimmered off the wall as Zopheniel methodically turned the blade.

Car doors slammed as Matt and Marci got out of their vehicle in front of the UP office.

"How is this going to go?" Alea asked as Shamus lifted his sword to avoid having Marci walk through the blade.

"In the end, we win. Today, I'm not so confident." Shamus lowered the red blade as the sun broke through the clouds.

CHAPTER FORTY-ONE

. . . he looked and saw the hills full of horses and chariots of fire all around Elisha.
2 Kings 6:17

"What do you suggest?" The Archangel Michael hovered about 100 feet off the ground beside the Dominion Doroniel. Below the commanders, fourteen legions of angels waited in perfect formation covering the grassy Whidbey Island field. The front of the formation stood motionless at the edge of a sharp drop from the field to the crashing waves of the inlet below.

They glimmered in plain view of any spiritual being that might have been looking for them. There was no need to hide. There was no element of surprise on behalf of the angels. The cards lay in the hands of the enemy.

Had the angels not found out about the demonic gathering in Afghanistan, the war would have already begun. The angels would have been reacting to an unsuspected attack that would have put the odds of victory in the zero to slim range. Satanael would have been a step ahead in every battle.

"At least we are ready." Doroniel responded without really answering the question.

"Do we know the size of the enemy force?"

"The force in Afghanistan was slightly smaller at the time it was spotted than what we have assembled, however, I expect more demons were being summoned."

"How many more do we have on alert?"

"There are none on alert."

"Then we shall win with what we have."

The timeless warrior Michael had led the angels of the Almighty against Satanael's rebellion in the greatest battle in eternity. Satanael and a third of God's angels had betrayed the Almighty and attempted to gain power. Many great angels fell that day. They fell not to a mortal death, but to a fate far worse. They were banished from the presence of God in Center Realm with the promise that one day they would be locked away from everything beautiful in the universe. It was called The Abyss. Satanael and his legions would be thrown down for eternity. Their existence would be forgotten. They simply would not be.

The enemy didn't believe that, or course. Satanael, the great deceiver, had convinced his armies that in time they would be strong enough to once again challenge the Almighty God and win! Fools! Some of them had been great angels!

It was with that hope the demons fought for every human soul. They believed every human that rejected God would join in the battle against God and weaken the power of the Almighty and his angels.

As if he had been thinking the same thoughts, Doroniel replied. "It will not be long now, Michael. The Final Judgment is approaching. This fighting will end. That's why we must protect the Unification Project. The eternal fate of many people depends upon it. It will take many missions before we see the full results of the

Unification, but right now its success is still too unstable. The Almighty knows it. Satanael knows it."

"Will the foundation of the Unification be strong enough after we win this battle?"

"That's the expectation."

Doroniel and Michael once again surveyed the scene before them in silence. The angels were ready. A flock of gulls, Michael counted 306, flew off the ocean riding the updrafts of the cliffs. The birds sailed right above the heads of the thousands of angels, unaware of their presence.

A pod of orcas surfaced in the inlet. They had come upon a school of salmon and were feasting mercilessly. The water churned with energy.

Beauty. Life. Death. It is creation. Michael smiled as he watched.

Praise the Almighty!

"OK, slow down, Matt. I didn't follow all that." Matt had begun talking before the door had closed behind him. The stream of information flowing from Matt's mouth lacked context for Brenden and Shawna who stood dazed and confused in the UP office. "Oh, and Hi! By the way."

Matt paused, faked a smile and a "Hi" of his own, and went on talking. Marci plopped into a chair, rocked back and forth a few times, and watched her husband with interest.

"I forgot who I was talking to. My apologies. I will keep this simple." It was sarcastic belittlement from Matt as usual. "Marci." Matt stopped to point to his wife. "Baby!" This time Marci put her hands on her stomach that looked just as tight and flat as ever.

"Really? That's fantastic!" Shawna jumped up and gave Marci a hug.

Brenden gave Matt a manly nod and then shook his hand in congratulations. "Well done!"

"How far along are you?"

"Not very. We just found out a few days ago, but we had to tell somebody. Officially I'm about six weeks."

"This is a life changer," Matt added.

"It sure is!" Brenden replied. "But a great one!"

"I was just starting to wonder what we were going to do with all our baby stuff."

"You could have another baby, too." Marci suggested. "Haven't you always wanted another one?"

Shawna glanced at Brenden, and then back at Marci. "I think we're done. I know Brenden wants us to be done, and I'm really starting to enjoy sleeping through the night, no diapers, no bottles, no diapers, more freedom, no diapers . . ."

"Is this your way of trying to encourage an abortion?" asked Marci. "You know the word "diapers" has always been a swear word for me."

"Well get over it! There are plenty of diapers coming and you better get used to it!"

"Just get Matt to change the really smelly ones," added Brenden. "I took care of most of them at our house."

Shawna broke out laughing hysterically and it contagiously spread to the others. Brenden laughed at his own expense.

"I think I can handle changing as many diapers as you did, big guy!" said Matt as he punched Brenden in the shoulder. "You had super mom on your team!"

"What are you trying to say?" Marci stared down her husband with eyes that sparkled and burned at the same time.

"Just that I have a super mom on my team, too, so it should be about the same."

Nodding in admiration at the quick recovery, Brenden punched Matt back. "Nice catch! You could play for the Seahawks!"

Looking quizzically back and feigning sincerity, Matt responded. "What do you mean?" His face remained emotionless.

"Oh, give it up!" Marci said emphatically.

Matt turned his serious look to Marci. "You're cute when you get angry. Do you want to have my babies?"

Brenden expected Marci to throw something hard and pointy, but Shawna responded with a verbal blow of her own. "I'd say you might consider it, Marci, as long as the babies look like you and not him."

"I'm not sure I'm willing to take that chance. A baby that looked like Matt would bring a whole new meaning to 'a face only a mother could love'."

"The child could only hope to be so lucky as to look like his father. And to have my charm. And my athleticism. And my genius brain . . ."

"And your humility . . ." Shawna added.

"It's hard to be humble when you're as great as I am!"

"I think I'm going to puke but I'm not sure if it's morning sickness or husband sickness." Marci faked heaving. "Actually, I'm quite sure it's husband sickness."

The angel Alea moved close to Brenden and whispered, "The Bible". Brenden giggled one more time before his attention left the conversation and his focus turned to the Bible lying on his desk. The red, digital clock beside the book read 4:49 PM. He picked up the Bible and absently flipped it open and closed.

Shawna watched Brenden pick up the book. Matt and Marci had noticed as well. By the time Brenden looked up, everyone in the room was staring at him. He held up the Bible.

"You did ask for a Bible, right?"

Matt lit up. "I sure did. Weird, isn't it?"

Matt flicked his eyebrows just as the shrieking of countless demons polluted the spiritual world around him with a thick cloud of evil.

CHAPTER FORTY-TWO

Set your minds on things above, not on earthly things.
Colossians 3:2

As was usually the case with spiritual warfare, peace became chaos faster than Jesus had turned water into wine. The attack was expected. The angels were ready. Supporting armies were close by. Yet the immediate onslaught was nearly insurmountable. The flashing blades of the demons came from every direction. Alea held her position until it was obvious escape would have to be immediate or it would not happen at all. A few seconds of delay could be enough for the angel legions to arrive and join the battle, and with that inspiration, Alea blocked and parried several more demonic blades before she retreated through a slight gap toward the front of the building.

The blur of evil shielded Alea from any glimpse of Shamus, but to her relief, he appeared beside her outside the glass window at the front of the building.

"I couldn't hold my position any longer," Shamus said as he pierced three demons in succession who had followed the two angels out the front of the office. "It wasn't long enou . . ." Alea never heard the rest of the word as the front of the arriving angel army smashed into the demon force with a noise like a train hitting a rock wall.

With perfect anticipation, a second demon force hit the angels from the north side virtually eliminating any momentum the angels had created. The angels were caught in a "V" and, at this point, were obviously outnumbered. A feeling of hopelessness swept through Alea, but this too, would not last.

This time it was a second angel force that changed the shape of the battle. The Archangel Michael and an angel mass swept in behind the second demon force causing the demons to fight front and back. It was a tactic that would be useful in the long term, but in the short term, the demons still held position in the UP office.

The consequences of the demon attack were immediate. Brenden's phone rang. It was a client looking for a piece of land to build a new house on. It would be a long conversation.

Matt had realized it would be a while before Brenden would be back so he began telling Shawna about the reason for the Bible. That's when *his* phone buzzed. He heard it and ignored it, but Marci, wanting to stop the incessant "mooing cow" ringtone on her husband's phone, picked it up to see who was calling. Her intent was to reject the call and send it to voicemail, but the name on the call display changed that. Matt noticed the expression change on his wife's face and paused halfway through a sentence.

"Who is it?" he asked with curiosity.

Marci answered by tossing the phone, with some aggression, at Matt. He caught it, showing off his excellent coordination, and glanced at the screen.

"What's she calling about?" There was a definite edge to Marci's tone that hadn't been present a few seconds earlier.

"I don't know. I have nothing to say to her!" Matt replied directly. He turned off the phone and took a deep breath.

Marci had crossed her arms. She was tapping her foot against the desk. She spoke no audible words, but communicated volumes.

Shawna, who had observed the entire scene, leaned forward. "Is that who I think it is?"

"If you mean sleazy Vegas girl, YES!"

"That's who I meant."

Matt watched the two women, his mind working so fast he was sure smoke would begin pouring out of his ears. The words *less is more* were running through his head as he tried to decide how to respond. *Less is more, less is more. Don't say something you will regret!*

"It's over with her," he said quietly and calmly. "I have not talked to her since I called to tell her it was over for good. I have no desire to ever speak to her again." Here he stopped. *Less is more. Keep it simple.*

Marci waited for more. She was sure he would argue his position of innocence. When Matt responded firmly and confidently, however, she had to admit she almost believed him. She looked at Shawna and figured by the look on her face that Shawna felt the same way.

Matt's phone made another "moo" signaling the receiving of a voicemail. He made every effort to ignore the phone. The moment was awkward. Marci, unsure of whether or not to let Matt off so easily, decided to lighten the mood. "The voicemail even sounds like her."

After opening his mouth to speak and then thinking better of it, Matt looked at his buddy Brenden who was still working out details with his client. Matt put the Bible back on the desk and stood up. He walked over to the front window of the office and stared out at the parking lot. He turned to Marci. "You are the only one I want, Marci."

This time Marci got up. She didn't respond to Matt's comment. She *wanted* to trust him. She did, strangely, at this moment trust that he was telling the truth, but she didn't want to be foolishly played as the naïve, unsuspecting wife again. She walked to the door. "It's almost dinner and I'm getting hungry. Correction. *We* are getting hungry!" Marci patted her tiny stomach.

"What are you guys doing later?" asked Shawna who had also got up and was putting stuff away and tidying the desk she had been sitting at.

Matt answered. "Not much." He glanced at his wife who nodded a confirmation.

"Well, we have to bring dinner to my Dad's, eat, visit a bit, and will probably be home around 7:00 PM. Do you want to swing by after that?"

"Are you going to the worship service tonight?" Matt responded.

"We weren't planning on it. It's been a long week, and we have to get the kids to bed in their own beds at a reasonable hour."

"Then we'll be there."

"Sounds good," replied Shawna. "Oh, do we still need a Bible?"

Matt crossed over to the door before indicating his reply. "Yeah," he said with little emotion. "Later Buddy!" he called to Brenden who acknowledged the farewell with a wave.

The door closed.

White vapor, left by the piercing of no less than a dozen angels, clouded the space around the Hollingsworth couple as they left. Alea flew from the office in retreat. She turned to survey the battle when she was far enough away to reduce the chance of conflict.

She analyzed the vapor and her eyes closed involuntarily. A trail of scarlet was mixed in with the pure white vapor that had been left behind by the angels who had felt the cold blades of the demons. Ygal's crooked smile centered the ugly scene.

Shamus.

Masking and shutting out emotion, Alea reopened her eyes and focused again on the task at hand. This was a war. It wasn't a time for an angel to be hindered by emotion.

Alea had been successful in reaching Shawna at the last moment. Shawna had felt the urging of God through his angel Alea to invite the Hollingsworths over later. More importantly, Shawna had acted on that feeling. Matt and Marci were going to visit Brenden and Shawna later to discuss the Bible. There was still hope of victory.

With the departure of the Hollingsworths, the demon attack shifted. The UP office was quickly deserted. Brenden was hanging up his phone. Shawna was filling him in on the turn of events.

Alea saw Michael and a great following of angels streak off to the south at the heels of several thousand demons.

Another legion assembled and vanished to the east.

The only other remaining legion, that now numbered in the hundreds instead of thousands after being decimated by the confrontation, reorganized above the office. They smoothly, flawlessly, took up a defensive position in the event of a further attack on Brenden and Shawna.

Realizing that she was the only Virtue that had been present in the battle, a new experience being that this was only her second mission as a Virtue, Alea remained motionless. She inwardly believed she should remain with Brenden and Shawna, but in circumstances like this, with a full protective force already surrounding the Tavis', Alea found herself uncertain of her next action.

She needed guidance from the Almighty. It came via the Dominion Doroniel who had directed the battle to this point from a position of observation. "Well done, Virtue Alea. Your quick reactions and even quicker thinking created the only positive outcome of the battle."

"So many were lost," Alea replied solemnly. "Shamus."

"You will see him again, Alea."

Alea knew the Almighty would return Shamus to his former state, but in light of the ongoing battle for the success of the Unification Project, immortality brought little joy. Shamus would not return during this small segment of human history. She had enjoyed his companionship and found courage from his blade. In fact, the two angels might never be assigned together again, even in the face of eternity.

Alea would miss the Power Shamus. A heaviness remained. In Center Realm, in the presence of the Almighty, there was no heaviness like this, but on the planets where Satanael and his demons still ran rampant, the angels could feel the sense of loss. It wasn't the same sorrow that people felt. Even believers who believed in eternity with God in heaven had difficulty with the apparent finality of death. In training, Alea had been taught that it was the mortality of the human body, even in light of the immortality of the soul, which was to blame for this. It wasn't an emotion *that* strong, but Alea, nevertheless, felt loss, the loss of a companion. It was something like a person on earth might feel about a loved one who suddenly moved to another country.

There was no time to dwell upon it. It just was.

"You must remain with Brenden and Shawna."

"I will."

"This legion," Doroniel inclined his head at the nearby angels, "has been assigned to aid in protection of the Tavis couple. This clash with the demons, although potentially disastrous, was simply one point of attack. Satanael wasn't even present. Your skills will be needed again, Alea, in ways only the Almighty knows. Immanuel."

Doroniel didn't wait for response. Brenden and Shawna were locking up the office and preparing to get in their Tahoe. Alea dropped in behind Shawna in the vehicle. The eight hundred sixty-two angels assigned to protect them, moved in absolute unison as they flew in the shape of a three-dimensional cross over the vehicle.

The ride from the office to get the three Tavis children was only ten minutes on a Sunday afternoon, and for the human passengers, the drive was relatively uneventful except for a quick stop for fast food and a couple of cell phone calls.

For the spiritual world around the moving vehicle and in the Northwest of the United States, it was quite the opposite. Demons and angels clashed with both sides striving to affect the outcome and relevance of the Unification Project.

One of these strikes by the enemy attempted to quash the possible spiritual discussion between the Hollingsworths and the Tavises. Obviously Satanael would not let this meeting happen uncontested. The enemy attacked the Unification Project with another solid weapon: conflict. When people were dealing with conflict, even of the slightest and most insignificant kind, they were rarely willing to take on anything new or to stretch their boundaries. Conflict aided apathy. If the enemy could get people to argue over something small, the possibility of major decisions being made was minimized.

A second call by the Vegas girl to Matt, consequently, precipitated an argument between Matt and Marci. Matt had answered the call with the intention of telling the woman that their relationship was over and that she was to never call again, but Marci, listening to every word, felt Matt was too soft and that he had not "crushed all hope out of the useless wench". The argument brought back tension which ultimately led to Matt making a call to Brenden and Marci to cancel the meeting scheduled for later that night.

Alea was forewarned about the incoming call to Shawna's phone by another angel, so she encouraged Shawna to change the radio station. It worked momentarily as the Hillsong United song "Mighty to Save" was on the Christian radio station she tuned in to. Brenden turned up the volume, and both husband and wife started humming along.

The sound of the phone was masked.

It was possible that without talking to Brenden and Shawna, Matt and Marci might cool off long enough to go ahead with the meeting.

When the demons rammed into the angels as the Tahoe rounded onto Cedar Street, however, the brunt of the blow was strong enough to force an opening into the vehicle. A sleek demon interrupted the radio signal long enough for Brenden to turn down the volume on the radio due to the static. Shawna heard her phone.

The meeting was cancelled.

The angels pushed the demons back after Shawna had answered the call, but the damage had been done. As the truck parked at Grandpa Montgomery's house, the angels set a perimeter around the house. Every sword was drawn. Every angel expected another attack. Alea quickly realized that her sword was not *her* best defense against the enemy. She dropped her arm and the blue glow of her weapon disappeared. Shamus had been the brute strength. Shamus fought with the sword. Alea was here on an emotional level. She would leave the fighting to the legion above her.

As Tyler, Rachel, Amanda, Grandpa, Brenden and Shawna sat down to enjoy the burgers and fries that had just been picked up, Alea evaluated the situation. The family prayed for the meal. Actually, it was Grandpa who prayed. The rest bowed and listened. The prayer was not rushed even though the food was spread before them on the table. He thanked God for the food, his family, and for sending His son Jesus to die on the cross. Then the man, his mostly bald head nodding slightly as he spoke, prayed for renewed courage and strength, and that the family sitting at the table would be able to make a difference for God in the world. He paused before saying the "amen", after which time the table flew into a frenzy of noise and eating.

The prayer sent a rush of energy through Alea. There was a rush of wind, and two angels, standing tall, appeared before Alea.

"The Almighty is directing you to encourage Brenden to attend the service at the church tonight," the angel nearest the table uttered. Another rush of wind followed. The angels were gone.

Without hesitation, Alea moved close to Brenden and spoke the words, "Alderwood service. Go to the service tonight, Brenden."

She then moved to Shawna's side. "Brenden needs encouragement. He should go to the church tonight."

As the sound of voices decreased and the amount of chewing increased, it was clear to Alea that both Brenden and Shawna were considering the rest of the evening. When after several minutes had passed and no mention of church had been mentioned, Alea tried Grandpa. "Church service. Mention the church service."

Grandpa had barely swallowed his mouthful of hamburger when he spoke. "Is there a service at the church tonight?"

It was Shawna who responded. "Yes, Dad."

"So are you going to go?"

"Well, we were supposed to be having our friends Matt and Marci over later. They wanted to discuss the Bible. I really think they're looking for answers! Unfortunately, they cancelled on us just before we got here. So, we hadn't planned on going tonight. I'm going to go home and put the kids to bed. Right kids?"

All three children groaned in unison before offering alternative suggestions to going to bed. Shawna smiled, but didn't respond to her pleading offspring. She looked at Matt. "You can go if you want, Brenden."

"Yes, go Brenden," Alea shouted.

"I guess I could. I hadn't really contemplated it until now." Brenden dipped a fry in ketchup and shoved it in his mouth.

Alea knew he wasn't being honest. Brenden had been contemplating her suggestion to go to the service over the previous minutes. A response like this meant he had decided not to go, but was not directly coming out and saying it. It was easier for people not to go. Without prior commitment, apathy usually won out.

The Almighty had made it clear, however. Brenden needed to go to the service. Was there going to be another attack? Where would it be? Was the Almighty removing Brenden from danger, or putting him in the middle of it? It wasn't Alea's job to question the Almighty's orders, but she was unsure of how far to go in her "encouragement". The possibilities hung before her. Alea chose.

Pastor Phil was already in the church when Alea found him. Zopheniel stood tensely; his eyes softened when he realized it was Alea and not an attacking demon army. The church was surrounded by angels who expected an attack as Zopheniel had. To this point, the demon armies hadn't disturbed the pastor.

"The Almighty wants Brenden here tonight. I haven't been successful."

Zopheniel nodded and moved directly to Phil who was rearranging mics and music stands on the stage. He spoke only one word. "Brenden."

Phil stopped moving. He put down the music stand in his hands, looked up to the heavens, and prayed. "Oh God! You have done great things. You have blessed Brenden with many talents and gifts. Touch him tonight, God. Wherever he is at, lead him here tonight. I pray in the powerful name of Jesus. Amen."

Phil picked up the music stand again and continued his preparations for the evening. Again Alea felt a surge of energy as the pastor had prayed. Zopheniel stepped in front of Phil.

"It's you, Phil. You need to call him. You are God's messenger." Again, the pastor froze. In the silent sanctuary, the prompting of God through his angels was unmistakable to the believer.

"What was I thinking?" Phil whispered to himself. "If I want him to come, I need to ask him to come." Phil nodded to himself as he pulled his cell out of his pocket and dialed.

Alea was already back at the family dinner when the phone rang. Brenden checked to see who it was before answering. Seeing Phil's number, he answered. Many other callers would have been left to go to voicemail, but Brenden respected Phil too much to not answer.

The conversation was short. Phil's smooth and silky manner combined with encouragement and love left Brenden with little option but to attend the service.

"I'll see you there. Thanks. Bye." Brenden hung up and Shawna and her father smiled.

"I guess that means you're going?" Shawna prodded.

"I guess so. You can't lie to the pastor."

"You could, but I wouldn't recommend it," chimed in Grandpa with a smile.

It was good to see him smile, Shawna thought to herself. Her dad still missed Mom deeply.

"Can I come?" asked Tyler who evidently still had notions of staying up later then his mother wanted.

"Me too!" pleaded Rachel.

Amanda, who had just stuffed her mouth with food, echoed her siblings' sentiments. Sounds that resembled "Me too!" came out of her mouth along with a few pieces of fry.

"Not tonight, munchkins. It'll go too late, and it starts in twenty minutes. I need to eat quick and go."

Alea left the room. She surveyed the angels outside. Status quo. The enemy hadn't attacked since the meeting with the Hollingsworths had been squashed. She moved back into the house. Brenden was in the bathroom and Alea saw little reason to remain in the bathroom with him. She went to the kitchen where the meal was being cleared from the table. Her job here was done for the moment. She fluttered up to the angel contingent guarding the house and informed them about Brenden's decision to go to the service at the church.

At the command of Argem, an angel with thick, rippling muscles, the angels reformed their position. Two-thirds of them would accompany Brenden to the church and then join the protection around the service. The other third would remain in defense of Shawna and the kids trying to ensure their safe return home without negative interference from the dark angels.

The kids had forgotten their disappointment about going home at the mention of being able to ride in Grandpa's car, so as Alea left with Brenden to the Alderwood Evangelical Church, Tyler, Rachel and Amanda were racing to get their shoes on so they could get the best seat in Grandpa's Volvo.

It was just another day for the Tavis family. They continued on with life with relatively little stress. Alea often wondered how humans would react if they actually understood how much happened in the spiritual world around them. She decided that they probably wouldn't handle it very well or else the Almighty would have given them a clearer understanding of it.

It didn't always seem fair that the angels had to fight, strategize, plan and protect, often risking everything for the humans when the humans didn't understand it or appreciate it. Shamus had just been pierced for them. Many other angels had been turned to vapor. A war was going on!

It *was* the order of things. It *was* the way of the Almighty. Alea understood that, but even with suppressed emotion, she found it just a bit frustrating that people were often so removed from it. The importance of eternity and the importance of salvation outweighed everything else on Earth or any of the planets but people rarely treated it that way.

One thing Alea was sure of. The Almighty was patient, and the Almighty God loved his people!

CHAPTER FORTY-THREE

But do not use your freedom to indulge the flesh; rather, serve one another humbly in love.
Galatians 5:13

Every pew was occupied. Brenden sat in the back beside Reg and Annie Dornville who were long time members at the church and committed to everything the church did. They were the definition of loyalty and Brenden admired that. Sitting beside them in the pew was no big deal and he wouldn't be distracted during the service. The only challenge with the Dornvilles was that if they started conversing with you, it bordered on the miraculous to keep the conversation short without feeling like you had insulted them by cutting off the sincere, but continuous, stream of words that flowed out of their mouths. Brenden had often shook Reg's hand or made eye contact with Annie just to be friendly, and found himself listening for ten or more minutes without getting a word in edgewise.

Although Brenden felt guilty about it, his mind had already scoped out John Rigg in the row beside him and formulated his plan of escape when the service had ended.

He would quickly stand and turn and say something to get John's attention without hesitating or opening the door for the Dornvilles to catch his eye. With that thought tucked safely in his brain, Brenden shook hands with Reg and Annie and whispered a polite good evening just at Pastor Phil took to the stage to begin the evening meeting.

Phil was dressed casually in jeans and a red polo. His calm, warm demeanor filtered through the crowd and Brenden was immediately grateful he had come. Phil's greeting was short, the band played a few worship songs, and then the pastor returned to introduce the speaker for the evening. Brenden spotted Jerry a few rows in front of him. Beside him was Alyssa with, he presumed, her man. Again, Brenden was glad he had come.

"I can see the building is full," began Phil. "This is good! This is good!" He paused and smiled. "Our speaker was born in Guatemala. He's been living in the U.S. for about three months with his new wife Jennifer who, regretfully, could not be here this evening. A number of you met Diego in Guatemala on the Unification Project trip our church participated in. I know he had a profound effect on you then. I'm confident he will do so tonight as well."

"I'd say more, but what I have to say is not as important as what he feels led to share with you this evening. Come up here Diego." Phil motioned with his arm and a short, dark haired man skipped up the stairs from the front bench. "People, this is Diego Tuarez. May God be praised for bringing him to us today to share his story. Let's pray." Phil put his big arm around the small man's shoulders.

"Our great God, thank you for Diego. Thank you for bringing him to us this evening. Fill his mind with the things you would like him to share and say. May each one of us be drawn closer to You tonight. Amen."

Phil descended the steps. The stage felt larger than usual with only the small figure of Diego standing in the middle of it. The feeling evaporated, however, as soon as the first words echoed in the sanctuary. The words of Diego poured out with energy, with passion and with power. Brenden was convinced the man on the stage grew at least a foot as soon as he began to speak. For a third time in only a few minutes, Brenden was glad he had come to the meeting.

Phil's prayer, combined with the sheer number of angels in and around the Alderwood church, equated to a formidable power around the gathering of believers. Alea felt it. The presence of God permeated the people by filling their spiritual souls like water would fill a bucket. Alea was also confident that Diego felt it. The dark-haired man told his story and shared how the Almighty God had raised him out of despair into a life of meaning.

A collection of angels encircled him as he spoke. Their presence was meant to keep away distraction and the negative influence of the enemy. They also worked to keep his mind focused on the message he was meant to impart on the people in the room.

North Americans liked to use the phrase "the speaker was on fire up there" when they referred to a particularly effective presenter. Alea felt this was a fitting expression for Diego Tuarez of Guatemala. The eyes of the congregation watched him with such unwavering attention it was like they were watching an oil tanker burn and would not dare look away in case they missed something extraordinary.

She watched Brenden. He was being inspired. Brenden needed to be here tonight! The irony was that even an angel like Alea would not have seen this coming. Only a short while earlier, Alea would have believed fully that Brenden and Shawna were to be meeting with Matt and Marci this Sunday night. The enemy had prevented that meeting at the cost of many dark angels. The enemy would have left the area confident that they had foiled the will of God.

Yet, here sat Brenden. Exactly where the Almighty wanted him! At the expense of a delay to the meeting with the Hollingsworths, God had allowed the enemy to believe they had won the primary battle of the day when in fact it was Brenden being at this meeting that was paramount. Alea was as sure of this deduction as was angelically possible.

So what was it that Brenden was here for? Was it inspiration? What specifically did Brenden need to be inspired to do? At this point, neither Alea nor Zopheniel who had joined her, knew the answer to that question. The answer came in a way Alea did not expect.

The speaker Diego walked off the front of the stage and down the steps directly in front of the first row of onlookers. It was obvious to Brenden that Diego had spoken in public before and was a skilled presenter. Not only had he changed physical location around the stage, he varied the speed, tone and volume of his voice, and he continued to intermix stories with questions and applicable lessons. Brenden had read numerous books about public speaking and felt it was an area he needed to improve in now that he was the spokesperson for the UP. The little Guatemalan was putting it all together like a master teaching his students.

A part of Brenden wanted to analyze the techniques and effectiveness of Diego. This part of him, however, was overruled by the larger portion of his brain which was enthralled by the actual message.

"It was on that day, eighteen months ago, that my life changed," continued Diego. "My life turned, it flipped, it tumbled and it twisted! To that point in my life, I had lived for me. I had shut God out!" Diego slammed an imaginary door. "But lying there, on the bed of a stranger, in a small home in the heart of Guatemala City, I made the choice to put my life in God's hands." The man paused and looked out across the room.

"I said I put my life in God's hands!" Diego shouted from the floor. A few people in the church cheered. Diego looked out again. He tapped the lapel microphone he was wearing three times and spoke again. "I said I put my life in God's hands! Can you hear me people? Satan lost control and God took over!" The church was cheering in a controlled frenzy. People were clapping, others were shouting "amen" or "hallelujah". A few people stood up and the rest of the congregation followed.

As Brenden clapped, Diego Tuarez turned on the jets. "God won my life! The devil lost another! The angels in heaven rejoiced that day! *My* name was written in the Book of Life! I asked the Lord to take *my* heart! I vowed to live the life He had in store for me, instead of treading down my own selfish path! I decided that day to be an ambassador of Life not death!"

Diego stopped. He motioned for the people to sit down again. He waited for the clamor to cease. Then he spoke in the softest, yet clearest voice. "I was saved because someone was true to God's call. That stranger whose bed I slept in became my friend. That stranger picked me up off the ground and saved me from a physical death as I lay on the street bleeding helplessly. Yes, he saved me physically. But then he saved me spiritually. He shared the message of Jesus Christ with me that day. He introduced me to the only true God."

Again Diego paused to emphasize the next statement. You could hear the traffic on the street outside as people sat unmoving, mesmerized. "That man's name was David del Cantro. You wouldn't know him. He's not famous in the eyes of the world, but he is a faithful child of the Almighty God. The Lord worked through David to save me." There was more cheering; the crowd didn't have to be prompted anymore.

"That day, I chose to devote my life to saving others. I chose the path that God had for me even though I wasn't sure where it would lead me. I certainly never dreamed I would be speaking in front of a bunch of great people in the Alderwood Evangelical Church."

"When Phil asked me to speak here today, I asked who the audience would be. He told me it would be a group of people that had accepted Jesus, but that like so many in the Americas, it was people that wanted to do the will of God, people that wanted to do the work of God, but people that were often so busy with their own lives that they were difficult to mobilize into action. Does that apply to some of you?" A few heads nodded. A few hands even went up.

"I know your dollars don't seem to go as far as they used to. I know budgets are tight. I know most of you don't go to bed at night trying to figure out where to spend all the extra money that keeps piling up in your bank accounts!"

"But I know poverty, and you are not poor! I know hardships, and this life," Diego pointed out to the city around the church, "this life, is not so bad. What this world needs, what our God asks, is that we take what we have, big or small, and decide today to devote it to saving lives. God is asking you, the person sitting on your seat, to devote yourself to saving lives!"

"For some of you, that may be saving lives physically. People die each day that would not need to die. Take care of the poor. Take care of the orphans. Take good care of the widows."

"Some of you may be called to save lives spiritually! People around this globe need to know Jesus! They need to know the whole story! They need to know what the Bible actually says!"

"God saved me through the life of one faithful man." Again, Diego paused so no one would miss his last words. "Who will be saved because of the work God does through you?"

"Thank you for letting me share with you tonight. May God bless you and may He bless the lives of the many your work will touch."

The angels who had been assigned to Diego glided to the back of the stage as the congregation applauded and Diego took a seat on the front pew. The worship band took to the stage and led the inspired people in a contemporary version of *How Great Thou Art.* The singing was vibrant. Alea enjoyed the worship of believers. It wasn't the same as in the temple in Center Realm, but the sincerity of it was still undeniable.

The difficulty Alea was having was focusing on the worship. One thing had changed Alea's perspective during the course of the evening. It had come near the end of Diego's talk, and it had once again proven the far-reaching and awesome ways of the Almighty God. It was a name that would have meant little to anyone else listening except Alea. It was the name David del Cantro.

CHAPTER FORTY-FOUR

That power is the same as the mighty strength [20] he exerted when he raised Christ from the dead and seated him at his right hand in the heavenly realms, [21] far above all rule and authority, power and dominion, and every name that is invoked, not only in the present age but also in the one to come.

Ephesians 1:19-21

The angel Zopheniel faced the pastor a short distance to Alea's left. She voiced his name with some vigor, "Zopheniel".

Zopheniel's head spun faster than a human could have perceived. He said nothing, but his golden eyes stared, waiting, anticipating. Alea instinctively glanced at Brenden to assess any possibility of danger or action from the enemy. Nothing caught her attention. The church building remained flooded with the white garments of the many angels sent to protect the people in it. She flew over to her ally who continued to stare back at her.

"I learned something new today," Alea began. Zopheniel's expression remained curious, but unchanging.

"I informed you that this was my second mission since being trained to be a Virtue. That's not correct. I realized here tonight that my involvement with Brenden and Shawna Tavis and the Unification Project is not my second mission. It's my first."

With a slightly raised eyebrow, Zopheniel began to convey his response. "And how is this possi …"

As was happening all too often in recent days, Alea never heard the end of the sentence. The chiseled form of the Archangel Michael appeared in the center of the sanctuary, his deep voice booming three simple words. "Prepare for attack!"

Before seeing the enemy, it was evident that this was going to be serious. The gleaming garment of the Archangel who had spoken the warning continued to rise in intensity until the entire room was flooded in light. Being temporarily mesmerized by the scene, Alea reacted more slowly than she knew she should have. She drew her blue sword even though her true skills were not in swordplay.

Assessing the situation, deducing the enemies target and promoting courage in the people involved to aid in overcoming the enemy; those were her strengths. They were the reasons she had been made a Virtue. Instinctively, she had been doing these things the entire time she had been in the church in the event that the enemy would attack. Now that the service had ended, many of the imminent threats like interrupting the service, flattening the emotion of the speaker, or distracting key members of the audience like Brenden were over. An attack during the service would have made sense, but an attack at the conclusion of the service?

A clanging ring of metal on metal was followed by a deep dousing of darkness in the sanctuary. Alea flashed to a point of protection directly below the Archangel

Michael. She deflected one sword from a huge demon that had plowed through the front line of defense, but before she could counter, the platinum sword of Michael was driven deeply into the demon's form. The dank demon vapor swirled beneath the pews and was gone. Alea looked up to thank Michael, but the Archangel had already refocused on two more of the enemy and had begun his attack.

Shamus was not a part of this battle, but it was comforting to have an Archangel fighting close by. Alea took the available seconds to survey the room. What was the target? Who was the enemy after?

Diego had inspired the congregation, but attacking Diego in a situation like this made little sense. The enemy would attempt to derail the Diego Tuarez train, that was unquestionable, but they would be foolish to try to do that in a building surrounded by the army of the Almighty!

Pastor Phil had demonstrated his faithfulness to God by following his "hunch" to ask some little known Central American speaker to come to Alderwood church. Phil was a crucial member of the UP team and warranted an attack, but why now?

The enemy had, to this point, attempted to discourage the Tavis' at the UP office. They had delayed the meeting of Matt and Marci with Brenden and Shawna. They had sent demons south, most likely to Portland to snuff out any positive effects that Conner and Alana Harris might have on the development of the UP. Presumably, Jerry Moore would have been a target tonight, but Alea did not see anything directed at the traveler who stood visiting with Alyssa.

One thought kept rising to the surface of Alea's reasoning. She would know shortly if it was accurate. Seeing a break in the wall of demon forces, Alea fled the sanctuary and moved unharmed to a position outside where she could survey the makeup of the enemy force. Dark angels covered the sky like a blanket of death. Legion upon legion of destruction fell upon the white light of the angels protecting the people within the church.

It wasn't the number of demons Alea was interested in, however. It was the ranks, the choirs of demons fighting that would speak volumes. It was easy to spot the Dominion Ygal. He directed the attack with practiced success.

Diving in and out of the church building, Alea spotted Garnel, a traitorous Archangel piercing far too many of Alea's allies. She would have loved to see his form turn to vapor at the hand of an angel!

After further scanning, only two dark Powers and one Dark Virtue were definable within the multitudes of demons.

Satanael was not here. The second in command Kilael was not here.

Distraction. The attack had to be a distraction! And if this size of a demonic force was the distraction, the real attack, the real target would be met with an equal or greater force. If Michael had returned here from the Harris', the real attack would not be in Portland where he had followed the enemy to, either. In fact, it was unlikely the real attack was anywhere in the Northwest.

Then it came to her. Against everything inside her that ached to remain near Brenden Tavis, Alea flew away from the battle as fast as her wings could carry her.

It took only seconds to provide reassurance that she had made the right choice. As the war-filled Washington State sky faded out of sight, the equally tumultuous Washington, D.C., focused into view. Angels and demons maneuvered for supremacy at an astonishing rate. Even from the outskirts of the Eastern seaboard city, the dark night sky shone as brightly as a clear summer day. The angels did not light up a world like the Almighty could, but it was nonetheless impressive.

The Dominion Doroniel caught sight of Alea as her form slowed. He veered beside her without taking his gaze from the battle before them. A Power named Ilium approached, took orders from his commander Doroniel, and returned to carry out the directions.

There was no need to confirm the Virtue's suspicions about this battle. Alea allowed her vision to look high above the center of the city. The red piercing eyes of the enemy leader met hers even from this great distance. The connection was short, but it was enough to suck hope from Alea's spirit.

It was Satanael.

Doroniel sparked her back to the urgent present. "You have left Brenden?" The question was succinct, but not condescending.

"I didn't believe the battle in Alderwood was targeted at him, or anything for that matter. This is the battle of importance, is it not?"

"We're greatly outnumbered here, Alea. We need every angel possible or Satanael will gain the advantage he needs. Go! They're coming, but they will not follow you!" The tapered emerald green sword of the Dominion swung into action as Alea flashed back across the continent. She flew directly into the church in Alderwood, a dark blade clipping her left wing as she did so. Her blue sword deflected two other attempts to pierce her before the Archangel Michael noticed her reappearance.

"The White House, Michael. This is a distraction!" It was only seven words, but the power of the sentence she had just spoken cleared the building. Michael sounded a massive note on the pondril horn that hung from a golden chain around his neck. Every angel of light within miles fell into formation behind the Archangel as he disappeared over the eastern horizon.

As if expecting the sudden retreat, the dark Dominion Ygal led his army away in a similar direction seconds later. Alea fluttered lightly to the church floor as she perused who was left in the spiritual world around her. The answer, simply enough, was Zopheniel. The angel assigned to the pastor was still tense with energy and his seamless garment revealed various nicks and slices from the fight. Zopheniel looked at Alea and smiled, relief flooding out of him.

"So, did we win?" he asked expectantly.

"As for the pastor and the realtor, we have, for the moment, won. As for the war, it's just getting started."

"The President?"

"Yes."

"What now?"

"I think we stay." Alea had not considered any other possibilities. There were not many believers left in the sanctuary. Brenden was about to leave the back doors. Pastor Phil was concluding a conversation with Diego who was now slipping on his jacket presumably to leave as well.

"How'd you know?" Zopheniel asked, his grin fading.

"It was the only logical answer."

"You were barely gone, Alea! I was watching when I could. You left the sanctuary, surveyed the situation, visited D.C., and returned to entirely change the battle in the same time span that I pierced a handful of demons."

"You look as though a handful of demons nearly pierced you," Alea commented adding a glimmer of a smile herself.

Zopheniel assessed the damage to his clothing and nodded in agreement. "I guess it's good the Almighty has filled you with this gift. It does appear that I wouldn't have been around to see your return had you moved any slower."

"I couldn't let that happen, of course."

Zopheniel glanced to the back of the church. Alea's golden eyes followed. Brenden Tavis was no longer in the building. She looked back at Zopheniel, spoke a formal "Immanuel" and took her post at the left shoulder of the realtor as he made his way to his vehicle.

The air was still thick with the trailing vapor of the departed angels and demons, but the spiritual world was silent above the Northwest.

Across the continent, the future of the Unification lay in the balance of power above the White House. Hours later, as Alea stood guard in the tall windows of the Tavis house, the evil-ridden eyes of the Deceiver remained embedded in her memory.

CHAPTER FORTY-FIVE

And if I go and prepare a place for you, I will come back and take you to be with me that you also may be where I am.
John 14:3

As the dawn turned the night sky into a pale gray, the outside world looked distorted to Brenden through the raindrops on the high windows of his living room. The usually crisp form of the cedars outside blurred into an abstract semblance of reality. The future, Brenden pondered, was much like the cedars outside. He thought he knew what he was looking at as he looked to the future, but everything ahead lay uncertain, blurred by the unknown in front of him.

The Unification Project had successfully begun. Four different people had approached him after the service to commit themselves to a mission project in the near future! Brenden's own sense of purpose had been renewed in a way beyond anything he had felt since that night the angel had met him. Excitement flowed through him in such a way that he became keenly aware of the lack of urgency he had been living with in the past months.

He had lead meetings. He had spoken to groups. He had taken care of things. The difference now was the belief in the end result! After Diego's story, Brenden's faith in what the Almighty could do through just one excited person was stretched.

Brenden knew he was capable of doing what Diego had done. He exceled at public speaking! He believed in the power of God! He believed in the Unification Project. He had just never put all those things together in one talk on the same night! Not really.

The possibilities of what lay ahead sent a rush through him and explained why he hadn't been able to fall asleep. He had explained, at least in part, what had happened at the church to Shawna when he had got home and that had brought rushing back all the emotions of the evening. She had gone to bed. He had tried, but here he sat watching the beginning of a new morning, and quite possibly a new era in his life.

"God," he prayed. "Thank you for your faithfulness. Thank you for believing in me even when I fall short, even when I fail. Thank you for saving Diego Taurez, and thank you for sending him to us last night. I know the enemy will continue to try to knock me down and discourage me. I know the enemy will distract and discourage, but I ask you to protect me, protect my family, protect the UP from losing faith."

"You are great, God! The world needs to know you! The hungry need food. The children need hope. The church in North America needs to wake up! I need to stay awake. My awesome God, send your spirit, send your angels, send your power to us now. Set the Unification of Your church across this world into full motion! I pray this in the precious name of Jesus Christ. Amen!"

The words echoed off the glass across the room and Brenden realized he had spoken the prayer aloud. A sense of calm and peace filled the room.

Alea watched as Brenden fell asleep. She had watched him and waited for news of the battle in D.C. People continued to amaze her after all these years! Emotions played such an important role in their decision making. Angels weren't like that. The angels pushed emotion back, and carried out their work based on what needed to be done. The Almighty would send out commands, missions were to be accomplished, and the angels set out to successfully complete them. Joys and sorrows would come, but they didn't affect action like they did with people.

The emotion of the meeting, matched with the obvious leading of God, and the right timing all combined to create an atmosphere of commitment in the believers that were at the church. Brenden had recommitted to the UP with a greater understanding of what it was he had committed to. Brenden's original commitment to the UP came with the aid of an angelic visit and the unquestionable will of the Almighty. At the time, Brenden wasn't entirely sure what he was agreeing to help lead. This time, he not only understood, he was beginning to see how *many* lives could be changed through it.

The nagging question for Alea now was whether the enemy angels had been successful in their attacks against the UP.

Three angels dropped into the room. They did not deliver news of the outcome of the Battle in D.C, only directions that Alea was to return to Center Realm. She, along with one of the angels, vaulted into cosmic travel while the other two took up post at the Tavis' house.

She prodded the angel with her for any information about the battle, but he had been in Center Realm at the time of the battle and had only been sent to retrieve Alea. He knew less of what had gone on than Alea herself.

The two angels dove through the gate into the divinely lit realm where they parted ways. Alea was to report directly to the Chamber of Thrones; her partner moved to worship in the temple.

The Virtue flew quickly to the platform that allowed access to the Chamber and proceeded through the immense doors. It was likely that the success or failure of the UP would be recognizable on the faces of the angels inside the Chamber of Thrones she was about to enter.

With faith in the Almighty God, Alea the Virtue stepped into the room.

Her expectation had been to see a group of angels sitting at the table at the far end of the cavernous room. The table was empty. A goblet sat at one end, but otherwise no sign of angels existed.

Alea glanced around. The shelves of scrolls were as impressive as ever. The couches and chairs looked as though they had been recently used. They were not in perfect symmetry, but instead gave the impression that many angels had moved about sitting and standing and moving them slightly. At the moment, however, the couches, like the enormous table, were empty.

The celestial ceiling appeared even brighter then she remembered. Each planet glimmered as if life itself seeped out of it into the chamber. The void in the center of the ceiling remained a total contrast to the dazzling universe around it; it was complete darkness. But something told Alea that through that hole was something important, something substantial.

She looked away and decided to peruse the books and scrolls while she waited for whomever it was that had called her here. The first shelf she looked on contained a series of scrolls entitled "The Creation". She opened the first scroll gently and with extreme care. She had heard of these scrolls, but had never actually seen them. It was said amongst the angels that they contained the Almighty's actual recounting of the creation of the universe along with His reasoning behind the creation.

The angels obviously understood more than the people on the planets because the description of creation in the Holy books, like the Earth's Bible, was basic. The Almighty had provided enough to get the point across, but not so much that early civilizations would be confounded and confused by an act so far beyond their comprehension. Still, the act of creation and how it happened was different then the reasoning behind each creation. No one, angel or person, fully understood the mind of the Lord, but these scrolls would be a fantastic mirror into the reasoning of God!

Alea started to read, but immediately sensed someone was with her in the great chamber. She turned, her eyes rising from the scroll that she held out in front of her. She expected the Dominion Doroniel, or possibly the Throne Aziel, but when she saw the form of the Almighty God, she quickly rolled the scroll and placed it on the shelf as though she were a young child being caught sneaking a cookie from the cookie jar.

"You would find that interesting," spoke the voice of God. A scattering of sparkling lights were floating down from the void in the middle of the celestial dome above the chamber. Alea was nearly certain that the Almighty had come through the black hole.

God knew her mind and responded to her unasked question. "Yes, I came from there. I have promised a new heaven, have I not? Soon it will be ready." He approached Alea and the warmth of His being filled her.

"I would love to read the scrolls, Almighty. I have always longed to understand you more clearly."

"When your current mission is complete, you may read the scrolls, Alea."

"Thank you!" Alea bowed in respectful admiration. The Throne Aziel entered the chamber through a door leading up from the Thrones' quarters.

"You have pleased me, Virtue Alea," continued the Almighty God. "There is still work to do in this mission, but know that you have pleased me." God then turned to Aziel who bowed before Him.

"Please convey my instructions and tell Alea what she would like to know, Aziel."

The lion face of the Throne angel responded simply, "I will." With that, the Almighty God slipped out the very doors Alea had entered into the Chamber of Thrones. The sound of the singing rose in intensity and Alea knew He had just returned to the temple. She wished deeply to follow Him, but that wasn't an option.

"Well," boomed Aziel, "what is it you'd like to know?"

"What happened in the battle in Washington?" Alea asked although she was certain the Throne knew the question she would ask before she had even asked it.

"Sit," said Aziel as he motioned to the deep brown couch to the right of Alea with one of his six wings. Alea sat.

Aziel, being much larger, pulled up a single chair made to accommodate his size, folded in his wings, and sat down across from the Virtue. The Throne named Danethiel entered through the front doors of the chamber, greeted Alea and Aziel with "Immanuel" and disappeared into the door leading down to the Thrones' living quarters.

Aziel turned his human face to Alea before he began to speak. "The enemy targeted a meeting the President was supposed to have with Senator Reese and Conner Harris regarding the connection between Conner's book *The Able Earth* and the Unification Project. The Senator and his son-in-law were hoping to finalize some ways that the government could officially support the UP by giving it press and using it as an example of how the people of America could do their part to eliminate poverty."

"The President knew he would feel pressure from many angles if he openly supported a Christ-centered organization. The Senator and Conner were there to help him see past the small stuff and to see the possibilities of real world change. If the focus of the Presidential support centered on feeding the poor, housing orphans and providing for widows, it would be hard for any opposition to discredit."

"Satanael's plan was to allow the meeting to continue, but to expose the evangelical Christian component to the media through a leak of information before the President had even said a word publically about the Unification. The enemy attempted to interfere in at least three different paths, all with the final outcome being a preemptive attack on the idea of the UP as a Christian, right-wing effort to influence others." Aziel looked to his side and extended a wing to his right. "I find my right wing no different from my left wing, but I guess people have their own way of looking at it." The Throne angel filled the chamber with a deep laugh.

Alea couldn't help but laugh as well, although she found her own voice completed drowned out by the laugh of Aziel. "You said at least three ways?" she asked.

"Our angels successfully blocked three different paths that would have led to the enemy's success. It's possible that we missed one, Alea. If that's true, we will know soon enough and I don't like to think upon those ramifications for the UP and your mission with Brenden and Shawna Tavis."

"So victory is hoped for, but uncertain," concluded Alea.

"That's correct."

Alea thought for a moment before asking for more clarification. "In Alderwood, it appeared to me that Michael and the angels followed a great host of dark angels on a path that would have led to Portland and the home of Senator Reese and Conner Harris. Why would this have transpired if the Senator and the author were in D.C.? Certainly the Archangel Michael would have known that they weren't in Portland."

"You've been observant, Virtue." Aziel nodded in admiration before continuing. "The enemy faked an attack against Conner Harris' wife in an effort to delay Michael and his legions from getting to the White House. When that illusion was clearly exposed, the enemy returned again to Alderwood attempting to keep our angels from the real battle in D.C."

"But Michael knew they were diversions?"

"Yes."

"Then why didn't he lead our angel army to the White House?"

"Michael didn't lead them to the White House because the Almighty already knew Satanael's plan in Washington. It was important for our success that Satanael didn't become aware of that fact. If we had attacked with a full force and clearly stopped Satanael's plans, he would have altered his attack early on in the battle. We understand the Evil One well enough to know he would have had an alternate attack plan ready for just that occasion; an alternate attack plan of which we did not know the details."

"So, Alea, the Almighty allowed Satanael to think he had surprised us with his attack so that he would continue on with his plan at the White House. Michael followed the diversions long enough for that to happen. By the time Satanael and his demons caught on that we knew where their attack was going to be centered, it was too late for him to change his course of action. We successfully blocked all three attacks and, as you already pointed out, hope we didn't miss one."

Alea sat, processing the information. The many eyes of the Throne angel watched her intently. Aziel spoke before Alea could ask her question. "You're wondering why Michael left for the White House when you returned with the news from D.C. and talked to him in the church in Alderwood?"

Alea just nodded.

"You were a perfect part of the Almighty's plan, of course. The Almighty God knew you would figure it out, return to Michael in front of all those demons, and send our angels off to the White House as though we had just found out where the real battle was. Your sincerity and action was a large part of why the enemy believed we had been surprised. The dark Dominion Ygal was watching you closely for any sign that we might have been trying to trick them. You did your part brilliantly, Virtue Alea."

"I did do a great job, didn't I?"

Aziel laughed again. "Yes, you did."

As if on cue, the doors facing the temple in Center Realm swung open and in flew the Dominion Doroniel, the Dominion Kana and the Archangel Michael. The three angels approached Alea and Aziel, greeted them formally and sat down to join them in their conversation.

"As usual, we heard your laughter from outside, Aziel!" said Michael with a lightness in his voice Alea hadn't heard before.

"I was just complimenting Alea on her part in the battle," spoke Aziel, some eyes now diverted to each of the angels in the room.

"Agreed," replied Doroniel. "Alea fulfilled her role successfully."

"I don't think you've ever complimented me like that, Doroniel," chimed in Michael. "What must I do?" He laughed this time, along with the others in the room. When the laughter subsided, Throne Aziel looked again to Alea.

"Do you have any more questions before we give you the Almighty's directions?"

"One more. When will we know if the President's support of the UP is going to be helpful or hurtful?"

"President Mullen is to be addressing the Unification and Conner's book in an interview tomorrow," spoke Doroniel who liked to get to the point. "It's time to prepare the UP for huge growth, Alea. Is Brenden ready?"

"The meeting in Alderwood brought emotions of commitment for Brenden. He's excited about the future of the UP and his faith in the Almighty is strong. He's ready."

"Then we'll get to work making connections between churches and causes around the world. Jerry the traveler is ready to get off the couch and start moving again. Brenden is ready to lead with a solid supporting staff, and the pastor is faithful as always. Lives will be changed! Praise the Lord!" Doroniel yelled the final words so they echoed around the chamber.

From deep below them, the same words shook the building as at least two Throne angels repeated the call, "Praise the Lord!"

CHAPTER FORTY-SIX

Acknowledge and take to heart this day that the Lord is God in ***heaven*** *above and on the earth below. There is no other.*
Deuteronomy 4:39

The temple was as full as Alea had seen it in a long while. Tens of thousands of voices filled the entire realm. In the middle of the temple sat the Almighty God. At his right hand was the Son. The Seraphim encircled the Father and the Son and led the huge choir in true worship. Alea sang, listened and spoke words of praise.

Her directions had been simple; remain with Brenden and Shawna Tavis until the Almighty changed her mission. Alea was joined by an angel named Otheniel who had just finished his training in the North Realm to become a Power. It was his first mission, but his prowess with a sword was well known. His presence reminded Alea of Shamus. She expected that she and Otheniel would grow to understand each other closely as they worked together, but she did miss the familiarity she had achieved with Shamus.

Otheniel and Alea returned to Earth and the familiar Tavis house in the Pacific Northwest. They replaced the angel guardians at the house after receiving any pertinent information about what had transpired while Alea was gone. They had just taken up their posts at the large windows in the great room when Zopheniel, Maspial and Ramuel appeared from above.

"It's good to have you back, Virtue!" spoke Zopheniel as the angels formed a perfect ring around the loveseat. The entire Tavis family was watching TV in the same room.

"I could be here for a while," she replied. "This is Power Otheniel."

"Otheniel," Ramuel chimed in. "We fought the enemy together in Jericho. Your skill with a blade was remarkable then. I am sure it's truly something to behold now that your sword has turned red."

Otheniel nodded in appreciation of the comment. "I expect you may judge for yourself soon enough if we are all to remain connected to the Unification. The enemy will never stop fighting this."

"Then I look forward to piercing some demons with you!" spoke the Principality Ramuel. "Zopheniel is assigned to the pastor, Maspial is guiding the traveler, and I am quite entrenched in my efforts concerning the President. We could all be here for a while."

"Not bad for your second mission, Alea," added Maspial.

"It would be," responded Alea, "but this is actually my first mission as a Virtue."

The other angels, noticeably confused, looked at each other and then back at the feminine angel.

"That leaves only two options," replied Ramuel who was quick to make conclusions. "The first option is that you lied to us about having had a mission before this one.

Considering your character and obedience to the Almighty, I would not think this option to be true. The second option is that you *thought* you had done another mission, but have recently been privy to information that changed that impression."

Although Alea was impressed with the Principality's deductions, she looked at the others with a slightly devious look leaving them unsure about her innocence. "You don't think I could lie to you?" she directed her question right at Ramuel, her face still serious.

Without missing a beat, Ramuel looked deeply into her golden eyes and spoke with a commanding voice. "I didn't say you *could* not lie. I said that I don't believe that you *did* lie. It's not your capability in question, Virtue." He moved even closer to Alea, still staring into her eyes. "I still don't believe you lied, nor do I believe you can pretend to be devious any longer than it would take for me to turn you into vapor."

Alea felt the final words as much as she heard them because Ramuel had moved so close to her face. She remained motionless, staring at him as she replied. "You're actually correct, Principality. True, I didn't lie about my first mission. Also true, I couldn't fake being devious for as long as it would take for you to turn me into vapor because the Almighty would have to bring you back countless times over countless ages before you could actually beat me with your sword!"

The two angels continued to stare at each other for a few moments before they simultaneously burst into laughter.

"Well spoken, Alea," said Zopheniel as he himself laughed a full, joyful laugh.

"So then," Maspial addressed Alea again, "what is it that you've learned?"

"What I thought had been my first mission was actually just the beginning of this one. My first action as a Virtue was in Central America. I was sent to a young man in Guatemala City who was struggling with his faith. He had prayed to the Almighty for a sign, for something that would prove God still cared about him in his little home. The man had asked the Almighty that if He was there and still cared about what was going on in his life in a dark part of a poor city, that God would send an unmistakable message."

"It was I who orchestrated that message on behalf of the Almighty. The man's daughter had been missing for three days! He had feared that something terrible had happened to his beautiful girl. He was questioning everything in his life. The daughter had been taken on the street to be sold into a life of prostitution."

"When I found her, she had not yet been injured or sold, but was locked up awaiting her dismal future. I unlocked her door that night. I closed the eyes of those guarding the room in which she had been kept. The girl walked out and kept walking until she reached her home."

"Her dad cried many tears of joy that night, and he fell to his knees and praised the Almighty God for hours after his daughter's return. That man's name was David del Cantro."

"The other night at the Alderwood church, a man full of the Spirit of God spoke to the people. He inspired many. Brenden made a further commitment to the UP and many others want to join missions through the Unification. It was exactly what the church needed. It was exactly what Brenden needed, and it was exactly what the Unification Project needed."

"The man who spoke was from Guatemala City. It was not David del Cantro. It was a man named Diego Taurez. The night after the Almighty returned David's daughter to him, David del Cantro found Diego Taurez on the street. David took him in. David led him to the Lord. The Almighty God used the faithful David del Cantro to change Diego Taurez's life." The other angels began to nod as they connected all the dots.

"So, our awesome God sent me to prepare David del Cantro to save Diego Taurez who, a couple years later, would come to Alderwood at just the right time to further the Unification Project. The Almighty was in control all along."

"Praise God!" trumpeted the angels enjoying the story.

The sound of the doorbell ended the conversation and sent Amanda, suddenly full of life, running to the door. The rest of the Tavis family seated around the TV rose and followed the speedy toddler.

"Do we know who this is?" asked Alea.

Zopheniel smiled. "This should be the Hollingsworths. They are here to discuss that Bible sitting on the coffee table."

"Are they ready?" spoke Alea with a hint of excitement in her voice.

"They are."

"Does that mean I should get my sword ready?" spoke Otheniel with his own enthusiastic smile.

"That would be a proactive idea," replied Zopheniel.

6 months later

The sunlight was still visible on the mountain peaks to the east, but the air had instantly cooled down in the town of Corison Springs when the warmth of the rays had begun to creep up the slopes. The lake sprawling out to the right of the promenade lay still in the absence of wind. A few families remained on the sandy beach, and two young boys and their chocolate lab still splashed in the shallow waters of the shoreline.

"It's beautiful!" spoke Marci who carried her sandals and was walking barefoot along the path. "We will have to come back here with kids some time," she continued as she patted her clearly pregnant tummy.

"I guess that would be fun, too," replied Brenden, "but we sure love coming here as a getaway from the kids. It would be a different experience having them here."

"I agree!" added Matt. "Something about a stroller, diapers, toys and screaming children still scares me!"

"Get used to it, Hubby!" said Marci as she slugged him in the shoulder.

Matt put up his fists in a mock boxing position and turned toward his wife. He took a couple swings into the air. "You don't think I would hit a pregnant lady, but if you push me too far woman!" He took a few more swings into the air in the general direction of Marci's face.

"One more comment like that, and you may find yourself sleeping on the couch and I'll keep the baby with me in the bed for the next two years."

"If that means you will change all the diapers, I might consider it!" responded Matt looking skyward as though in deep thought.

This time Matt got slugged from the other side. Shawna put up her fists ready for battle. "Pick on someone your own size!" she challenged the unsuspecting Matt.

He turned slowly to meet his new opponent and then raised one finger slowly into the air. "I could crush you both with this one powerful finger!" The words were spoken with a clear Arnold Schwarzenegger accent.

"I am starting to think kids might be calmer to have around then a pregnant lady, a psycho woman and Arnold!" spoke Brenden shaking his head.

"Who are you calling psycho?" Shawna turned and began swinging wildly at Brenden who grabbed her arm, spun her around, and picked her up from behind.

"Hey, Arnold!" said Brenden. "Do psychos float or sink when you throw them in a lake?"

"I don't know, but I would sure like to find out!"

Brenden looked at the water, looked back at his captive, and put her back down. "You're lucky you're cute and I'm hungry." His eyes then focused across the street. "Look where we are."

The expression on Shawna's face tightened as she came to the same realization Brenden just had. "Let's not eat there."

"Bavarian food. It would be excellent!" said Matt continuing perfectly with his Austrian Schwarzenegger accent.

"Nope," was the reply from Brenden. "Let me show you something." He walked ahead down the path until he reached a streetlight pole. Brenden put his hands on it and began trying to shake it. "This one seems pretty solid," he said.

"What're you talking about?" said a confused Marci.

"This is the exact spot where that drunk driver smashed into the pole that used to be here and nearly killed us both," spoke Shawna. She automatically looked down the street half expecting the swerving silver car to reappear.

"That's kind of creepy," replied Marci. "I don't even want to stand here now. Let's go back to the hotel for dinner. I'm getting hungry, too."

"What's new?" replied Matt as he put up his arms to block an expected attack.

Marci just smiled, but offered no reply. The tone of the conversation had definitely become more serious.

"You know, it was right after that accident that we were first asked about the Unification Project."

Brenden nodded at his wife. "You're right. Our lives have sure changed since then."

"I guess you never know what God has in store for us," Shawna continued. The four friends walked toward the hotel. No one spoke until they had crossed the road and entered the hotel lobby. It was Matt who asked the next question.

"I bet you didn't expect that we would become believers and be with you the next time you came here?"

"No. I can't say I did," replied Brenden.

"I guess you never know what God has in store for us!" Matt's words echoed those of Brenden earlier.

"Well," added Marci, "I hope He has a massive plate of seafood pasta and some ginormous chocolate dessert in store for us next!"

"Agreed!" responded the other three in unison.

Even the unseen angels joined in the laughter as they turned to walk toward the delightful smells of the hotel restaurant.

5505604R00196

Made in the USA
San Bernardino, CA
09 November 2013